Look what people are saying about these incredibly talented authors...

About Janelle Denison...

"Janelle Denison treats readers to a wonderful romance full of vivid, sensual imagery, dynamic characters and an emotionally intense story."
—*Romantic Times BOOKclub* on *Christmas Fantasy*

"Oh my, this one was hot, and as usual, I devoured it in one sitting."
—*The Best Reviews* on *A Shameless Seduction*

About Jacquie D'Alessandro...

"Jacquie D'Alessandro delights with *Naked in New England,* a funny yet strongly emotional tale graced by unforgettable characters, sizzling sensuality, and witty banter. A keeper all the way."
—*Romantic Times BOOKclub*

"The tension between the two [characters] is crackling with fiery heat, and the sex is hotter than a bonfire. *Why Not Tonight?* is a fast-paced romance that shows you what can happen if you let a good chance slip by."
—*Coffee Time Romance*

About Kate Hoffmann...

"Kate Hoffmann pens an amazing story!"
—*Romantic Times BOOKclub*

"You will love it! Absolutely love it."
—*Writers Unlimited*

USA TODAY bestselling author **Janelle Denison** is known for her sinfully sexy heroes and provocative stories packed with sexual tension and emotional conflicts that keep readers turning the pages. She is the recipient of the prestigious National Reader's Choice Award, has been a RITA® Award finalist and has garnered many other awards and accolades in the romance-writing industry. For information on upcoming releases, visit Janelle's Web site at www.janelledenison.com.

USA TODAY bestselling author **Jacquie D'Alessandro** has written sixteen contemporary and historical romances. She grew up on Long Island, New York, where she fell in love with romance at an early age and dreamed of being swept away by a dashing rogue riding a spirited stallion. When her hero showed up, he was dressed in jeans and drove a Volkswagen, but she recognized him anyway. They now live out their happily-ever-afters in Atlanta, Georgia, along with their very bright and active son, who is a dashing rogue in the making. Jacquie loves to hear from readers! You can contact her through her Web site at www.JacquieD.com.

Kate Hoffmann began reading romance in 1979 and was immediately hooked. Years later, after a history of interesting jobs in teaching, retail, nonprofit work and advertising, Kate decided to write a romance of her own. Her first book was published in 1993 by Harlequin Temptation. Since then, Kate has written more than thirty books for Harlequin, including Temptation, Duets, continuity series and anthologies. Kate lives in a picturesque village in southeastern Wisconsin in a cozy little house with three cats and a computer.

SINFULLY SWEET

Janelle Denison
Jacquie D'Alessandro
Kate Hoffmann

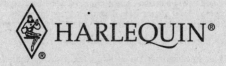

HARLEQUIN®

TORONTO • NEW YORK • LONDON
AMSTERDAM • PARIS • SYDNEY • HAMBURG
STOCKHOLM • ATHENS • TOKYO • MILAN • MADRID
PRAGUE • WARSAW • BUDAPEST • AUCKLAND

ISBN 0-373-79238-7

SINFULLY SWEET
Copyright © 2006 by Harlequin Books S.A.

The publisher acknowledges the copyright holders of the individual works as follows:

WICKEDLY DELICIOUS
Copyright © 2006 by Janelle Denison

CONSTANT CRAVING
Copyright © 2006 by Jacquie D'Alessandro

SIMPLY SCRUMPTIOUS
Copyright © 2006 by Peggy A. Hoffmann

This edition published by arrangement with Harlequin Books S.A.

® and TM are trademarks of the publisher. Trademarks indicated with ® are registered in the United States Patent and Trademark Office, the Canadian Trade Marks Office and in other countries.

www.eHarlequin.com

Printed in U.S.A.

TABLE OF CONTENTS

WICKEDLY DELICIOUS

Janelle Denison

1

REBECCA MOORE FOLLOWED her younger sister, Celeste, through the spacious lobby of The Delaford Resort and Spa, feeling much like a plain sparrow in an elegant, gilded cage— out of her element and surrounded by an opulence that was completely foreign to her. Certain she'd never set foot in such an exclusive hotel again in her lifetime, she took it all in, from the lush, green plants and tastefully neutral decor, to the large, elaborate fountain dominating the middle of the lobby.

While Celeste was marrying into money and had become accustomed to spending it, Rebecca had learned at a very young age to be frugal and economical when it came to parting with cash. Years of scrimping and saving, and being practical with her purchases, had become a way of life for her. Now, even at the age of thirty-two, she just couldn't imagine splurging hundreds of dollars at a luxury resort when a room at the Holiday Inn would do just as well.

But the next three days weren't about what she would have preferred. This weekend was all about her sister, Celeste, and her much anticipated marriage to Greg Markham the Third. And both the wedding and reception would be taking place at The Delaford, thanks to the Markhams' unending generosity and bottomless financial resources.

Since Greg was their only child, they'd insisted on a large, luxurious wedding, not to mention paying for everything, including what the bride's family should have been responsible for. With both of their parents gone, and no close relatives to speak of, the bride's family—specifically, Rebecca—just didn't have the kind of money to pay for such a grand and lavish ceremony and reception, and she was grateful that Celeste was getting the kind of no-expense-spared fairy-tale wedding every girl dreamed about.

"Would you stop thinking about the cost of everything and just enjoy yourself this weekend?" Celeste said as she pushed the button for the elevator.

Her sister's tone was laced with amusement, but the knowing look in Celeste's gaze dared Rebecca to refute her claim. Of course, Rebecca couldn't argue where her thoughts had strayed. The habit of being penny-wise was just too damned ingrained for her to deny.

"Don't worry, I have every intention of having a *great* time while we're here," Rebecca assured her sister with an indulgent grin. "I have a bunch of wedding-related festivities to go to, not to mention a swanky ceremony to attend."

Celeste laughed, her pretty cornflower-blue eyes sparkling happily. "Yes, you do. And if you play your cards right, you might even get lucky this weekend."

Rebecca didn't care for the sly note she detected in her sister's voice, but before she could ask what Celeste meant the elevator doors slid open and they stepped inside. The interior was just as elegant as the rest of the hotel, with flooring gleaming in marble and the walls mirrored and edged in gold trim.

Catching sight of their reflection together, Rebecca was once again reminded of all the extreme differences between herself and her sister that went beyond the six years that separated them. While they both possessed blonde hair and blue eyes, Celeste's hair was long and flowing with no definitive style, and Rebecca's cut was sleek, smooth, and a manageable chin-length. Her sister wore cute, trendy outfits that matched her bubbly attitude, and Rebecca preferred a more tailored, practical look that was a direct reflection of her own sensible personality.

Then again, with Rebecca taking on a parental role to Celeste at the young age of sixteen while their father was working, she'd done her best to make sure that her ten-year-old sister was spared the kind of adult pressures, responsibilities and worries that Rebecca had taken on after their mother had passed away. In a lot of ways, Rebecca had treated Celeste more as a daughter than a sister, in an attempt to make sure that her younger sibling enjoyed a carefree childhood as much as their unconventional lifestyle had allowed. Judging by the radiant, vivacious woman Celeste had become, Rebecca knew she'd done her job well.

As the elevator started its upward climb, Rebecca turned to Celeste, unwilling to let her sister's earlier comment slide without finding out what was behind the cryptic remark. "So, what do you mean by 'get lucky'?"

An oh-so-innocent smile curved the corners of Celeste's pink, glossy lips. "Well, it's Valentine's weekend, and a certain someone is going to be here," she replied meaningfully. "And since you're my maid of honor and he's Greg's best man, you'll be spending an awful lot of time together. It's a perfect scenario for Cupid to strike two people who need love and passion in their lives." Celeste sighed dreamily, obviously thinking of her own passionate love-life with her soon-to-be husband.

Rebecca knew exactly who her sister was referring to and she highly doubted that Connor Bassett, one of San Francisco's most eligible and wealthy bachelors, had any problems finding love or passion. Most likely, with his sexy bad-boy looks and the allure of his fat bank account, both were thrown at his feet on a regular basis by very willing women.

Rebecca shook her head at her sister's whimsical hopes. "You're way too much of a romantic, Celeste." And Rebecca was much too practical to believe in a mythical character such as Cupid.

"One of us has to be," Celeste said with a wave of her hand. The huge, three-karat diamond on her left hand ring finger caught the light in the elevator, nearly blinding Rebecca with its brilliant sparkle. "You've spent all these years raising me and giving up your own personal life in the process. I managed to find my Prince Charming. Is it so bad of me to want you to find yours?"

Her sister had a heart of gold, but if Celeste believed that

Connor Bassett was Rebecca's white knight, her sister was sorely mistaken. The man might have the ability to send her hormones into a frenzy whenever he was near, but he just wasn't her image of an ideal mate. The man was six years younger than she was and spent his days playing video games. Sure, he'd made millions as a gaming expert, but he squandered his money on the most frivolous, self-indulgent things. His devil-may-care way of life went against her much more modest, pragmatic outlook. Other than her intense physical attraction to Connor, the two of them just didn't mesh. The last thing she wanted was for Celeste to hold out any hope that the two of them would hook up in any way.

"I'm sorry to disappoint you, Cece," Rebecca said, using the nickname she'd given her sister as a baby. "But my Prince Charming is definitely *not* Connor."

The elevator came to a smooth stop. When the doors glided open quietly, they stepped out together, making a left toward the north wing of the hotel where Celeste's room was located. "You have to admit that he's a dream to look at," Celeste said of her own fiancé's best friend, apparently not done trying to sway Rebecca. "And he certainly couldn't be more obvious about his interest in you."

Rebecca laughed at that, because over the three years that her sister had dated Greg, she'd quickly learned that Connor had flirting down to an art form. There was no denying that he tempted and teased her with sexy innuendos whenever their paths crossed, but she was smart enough to know that his interest in her wasn't exclusive. If anything, he enjoyed the thrill of the chase and she undoubtedly proved to be a challenge for him. The man was a consummate playboy, and his short-lived track record with other women proved he was more interested in a good time than establishing a substantial or lasting relationship.

"Connor is fascinated by anything wearing a skirt and high heels," Rebecca said lightly. "I don't think I've ever seen him with the same woman twice."

That observation didn't seem to concern Celeste as they continued down the corridor. "Well, he's coming solo this weekend."

So, he was experiencing a slump at the moment. The man was entitled, but Rebecca wasn't looking to be his weekend replacement. "The only arm candy I'll be for Connor is during your wedding," she told her sister. "That's it."

"You're getting too stuffy in your old age," Celeste said, the concern in her tone overriding the insult behind her words, which Rebecca knew her sister hadn't intended. "You need to live a little, Becca. Break out of that parental mode you've been living in since Mom died."

Becoming a maternal figure to her then ten-year-old sister had been a necessary transition for Rebecca, then eventually a habit she couldn't break. Their father, Curtis, had worked for a plumbing parts company that required him to travel often, which had left Rebecca in charge of things at home— not only raising Celeste, but cooking and cleaning, and even handling the finances. And it hadn't taken Rebecca long to discover that her father spent more money than he earned and charged thousands of dollars on his credit cards on big ticket items and never paid off the revolving balance. Mainly because he couldn't.

"I'm getting married and moving out of our apartment as soon as I get back from my honeymoon with Greg," Celeste went on with her sisterly lecture. "You're going to be all alone for the first time *ever,* and you don't even have a boyfriend to keep you company. Heck, for that matter, you've barely dated in the past few years."

"I haven't found anyone worth dating," she said with a nonchalant shrug. "There is a guy in the accounting department at the hospital who's asked me out a couple of times. Maybe after this weekend I'll go to dinner with him and see how it goes from there."

"Ooooh, that sounds *so* exciting and adventurous," her sister said with an exaggerated roll of her eyes. "The two of you can discuss hospital billing codes while eating your meal."

"Stuart is a nice guy," Rebecca said in automatic defense.

They came to a stop at a set of double doors and Celeste retrieved a plastic key card from her purse. "I'm sure he's very nice, but if he's a pencil pusher, my guess is that he's boooorrrring—just like every other guy you've dated," she added beneath her breath.

Stuart was stable, responsible and dependable. Not that she expected her sister to understand Rebecca's need to find a man with the kind of qualities and traits their own father had lacked. Rebecca had done her best to protect Celeste from the harsh realities of their lives after their mother's death so she'd never been truly aware of their father's erratic spending sprees, which had eventually put their house into foreclosure and had forced him to file for bankruptcy.

Celeste had lived a carefree life, never needing to worry about money as a child because Rebecca made sure her sister always had whatever she needed. But for Rebecca, the loss of the only home she'd ever known had been absolutely devastating. Even though her father had died of a heart attack over ten years ago, that event in her life had cemented a deep determination to make sure she never found herself in that kind of dire financial situation again. And that meant finding a man who knew how to manage money much better than her own father had.

Celeste opened the door to her room, and Rebecca followed her inside, once again stunned by what awaited them. She stared in silent wonder at the extravagance of the suite—from the elegant furniture, to the richly textured draperies, to the opulent-looking decor. Everywhere there were fresh flowers arranged in expensive crystal vases, their intoxicating scent filling the air around her.

"Wow," Rebecca breathed, admiring the elaborate crown molding framing the ceiling of the living room, which gave way to cream-and-gold patterned wallpaper. "Greg's family certainly didn't spare any expense on the bridal suite, did they?"

"Will you stop already?" Celeste said in exasperation as she set her designer straw handbag on a glass-topped table.

Rebecca grinned. "Hey, you've had three years to get used to living this kind of life. I'm just getting my first glimpse of 'Lifestyles of the Rich and Famous.'"

Winking at her sister, Rebecca looped her arm through Celeste's and guided them toward the open French doors that led to a terrace. Once they reached the wrought-iron railing, they had a perfect view of the landscaped courtyard below, as well as the rolling fairways of the resort's golf course. Beyond that they could see the faint outline of the shops and boutiques that lined one of the main streets in town.

"So, what's on your agenda for the afternoon?" Rebecca asked, hoping that they'd have some alone time to spend together before everything turned crazy for the wedding.

"I'm meeting with Greg's mom to go over some of the last-minute wedding and reception details with the planner," Celeste said, her expression apologetic. "I have no idea how long everything is going to take."

Rebecca experienced a familiar stab of regret, along with a small pang of jealousy she valiantly tried to shake off. The past few months had been difficult for her, especially having to watch her sister bond with Greg's mother, Carole, over the wedding preparations, when Rebecca wished it were her instead.

When Celeste had first announced her engagement, Rebecca had wanted to be a part of the planning, but with her work schedule and the Markhams footing the bill, it had been easier for Carole to accompany Celeste during those outings. Not that Carole ever made Rebecca feel unwelcome when she had gotten the chance to join them, but it was always a painful reminder that she was losing her sister to another family, and soon Celeste would no longer be a part of Rebecca's life on a daily basis.

"That's fine," Rebecca said, and swallowed the tight knot of emotion gathering in her throat. "I understand."

"Thank you." Celeste appeared relieved. "While I'm gone, I need you to do me a favor, if you can."

Rebecca squeezed her sister's hand. "Anything, you know that." And she meant every word. There wasn't a thing she wouldn't do for her sister.

"There's a brand new candy shop a few blocks from here on Larchmont Street that makes the most incredible chocolates and confections," Celeste said, her expression turning to one of heavenly bliss, since chocolate was one of her greatest weaknesses. "When I was here last week I placed a special order for some petits fours for tonight's cocktail get-together with the bridal party and family. I was hoping you could pick them up for me so that would be one less thing I have to worry about today."

Rebecca figured running the errand for her sister was better than sitting alone in her hotel room for the next few hours thumbing through a magazine. "Consider it done."

"You're the best!" Celeste wrapped her arms around Rebecca in a warm, exuberant hug. "The shop is right down the street and close enough to walk to, or you can take a cab instead, if you like."

"I think I'll walk." Rebecca wasn't about to miss the chance to enjoy such a gorgeous, sunny day by taking a cab ride. "What's the place called?"

"Sinfully Sweet. And I can personally guarantee that the shop lives up to its name."

Rebecca was definitely intrigued by her sister's comment. While chocolate wasn't one of her basic food groups as it was for Celeste, she did enjoy the occasional sweet treat.

Together, they took the elevator back down to the lobby, then Rebecca waved good-bye to her sister, heading out of the hotel and down the resort's entry road that led to the main streets. In no particular hurry to reach the candy shop, she strolled along casually, taking in the sights while enjoying the warmth of the sun on her skin and the slight breeze tousling her hair.

When she reached Larchmont Street she made a right as her sister had instructed, and sauntered past specialty boutiques, a quaint outdoor café, and other unique stores. She window shopped along the way, admiring clothes and jewelry and other one-of-a-kind novelties and antiques until a designer handbag boutique gave way to an adjoining shop displaying in their window the most delectable-looking candies and chocolates. The glossy black and gilt name on the window, Sinfully Sweet, confirmed that she'd reached her destination.

She entered the store and was instantly enveloped by the rich, sweet scent of expensive chocolate. All around her she was surrounded by an array of tempting, tantalizing candies, including different-sized heart-shaped boxes for Valentine's Day and dozens of colorful foil-wrapped chocolates displayed on a table in the center of the shop.

Everything in the place definitely looked *sinfully sweet* and smelled just as wickedly delicious.

Other than a quick "I'll be right there" from the back room, Rebecca was completely alone, and she took advantage of that fact. Closing her eyes, she breathed in slow and deep, inhaling the drugging scent of the chocolate. The fragrance alone was like an aphrodisiac to every one of her senses.

Amazing.

She inhaled again, mainly because she just couldn't help it. There was something about this place that made her feel sensually charged, and she found herself wondering if it was possible for a woman to have an orgasm just from the rich, decadent smell of chocolate.

If so, she was a prime candidate.

"Welcome to Sinfully Sweet."

A woman's voice from behind Rebecca snapped her back to the present. She opened her eyes and turned around, her composure back in place—on the outside, at least. Inside, however, she was still feeling a little bit unbalanced by her reaction to all the chocolate around her.

"Thank you." Smiling, Rebecca stepped up to the counter and peered into the glass case displaying more chocolate treats, from caramel squares, to macaroons, to almond clusters. "Your shop is lovely, and it smells absolutely wonderful in here."

The pretty older woman beamed as she smoothed a hand down the white apron she was wearing. "Well, I can personally guarantee that the candies taste even more fabulous than they smell. We use the finest ingredients available, and it's taken us years to perfect each type of candy that we offer."

And there were dozens to choose from, Rebecca noted. "So, are these candies made from secret recipes?" she asked curiously.

"Well…"

"Yes, they are," an older man replied before the woman could finish her sentence. He appeared from a door leading to the back room, carrying a tray of freshly dipped, chocolate-covered strawberries, which he placed on the counter in front of Rebecca. "All our recipes are top secret. Classified and for our eyes only. Isn't that right, Ellie?"

The woman named Ellie smiled at the other man. "That's right, Marcus."

Marcus kissed her affectionately on the cheek, then glanced at Rebecca. "My wife loves to brag about our exclusive chocolates, but once you try them I'm sure you'll agree that they are the best you've ever tasted. The hard part is deciding which ones to try."

Rebecca was beginning to think that those dipped strawberries were looking pretty good at the moment. They were all plump and juicy looking, with a thick layer of chocolate coating each piece of fruit. The thought of eating one made her stomach flutter with anticipation.

"So, are you here to find something for your special Valentine this weekend?" Ellie asked.

"No," Rebecca said, shaking her head. "There's no one special."

"Ahhh, too bad," the other woman replied before Rebecca could state her reasons for being in the candy shop. "But being single and unattached does make you eligible for the Valentine's Day contest we're having. See that table over there with all those foil-wrapped chocolates?"

Remembering the display she'd seen when first entering the store, Rebecca nodded. "Yes."

"Well, each foil-wrapped candy is one half of a chocolate heart, and each one has a message inside," Ellie explained, her face reflecting excitement over such a clever contest. "The pink half is given to a single woman, such as yourself, and the blue half is for some lucky man. If the two of you manage to find the other person with the matching message before Valentine's Day, you'll receive a romantic prize package from Sinfully Sweet, which includes dinner for two at The Winery and one hundred chocolate hearts."

The concept of meeting someone new via a "match game"

was definitely intriguing, but the timing was all wrong. And, it wasn't as though she lived in the area, but rather ninety miles away in San Francisco. If she met someone here, the distance between them wouldn't be conducive to building a lasting relationship. Why start something she couldn't finish?

"That sounds like fun, but I'm only in town for a few days for a wedding at The Delaford. I'd really hate to disappoint someone who might be diligently searching for their matching heart, when I don't have the time to do the same."

"Don't you believe in fate, my dear?" Marcus asked. "If it's meant to be, you'll find the man who has the matching half to your heart."

In the past, fate hadn't always been so kind to Rebecca and she just couldn't imagine that such a bold tactic as searching for her so-called "match" would work in her favor. But she didn't want to be rude, either.

"I'll think about it," she said, knowing that she'd most likely walk out of the store without ever touching one of those foil-wrapped chocolates. "In the meantime, I'm here to pick up an order for my sister, Celeste Moore."

"Ahh, the petits fours," Ellie said with a nod. "They're ready, but need to be boxed up, which will take about ten minutes."

"That's fine."

Ellie disappeared into the back room, but Marcus remained behind. "Can I get you anything while we're packaging your order?" He motioned to the glass display of assorted candies and confections.

Biting her lower lip, Rebecca eyed those lovely chocolate-covered strawberries again. They were practically calling her name, and she found she couldn't resist their allure. Maybe she did have a weakness for chocolate after all. "I'll take one of those strawberries."

"Excellent choice." With a flourish, Marcus picked out the biggest piece of fruit on the tray, then handed it to her in a paper doilie cup before ringing up the purchase. "Feel free to browse around the shop while you're waiting for your order."

"I will." But first, she was going to enjoy the heck out of her strawberry.

She waited until Marcus had joined Ellie in the back room and she was alone before she focused her full attention on the treat she'd just purchased.

Lifting the decadent strawberry to her mouth, she nibbled on the tip. Rich, smooth chocolate immediately melted on her tongue, and a shimmering warmth suffused her body. The taste was intoxicating. Arousing. Drugging. She felt light-headed and sensual, as if the chocolate had started a hunger in her that had little to do with the confection she was eating and everything to do with unquenched desire.

The sensation rushing through her was extremely pleasant, prompting her to take a big bite of the strawberry. She closed her eyes and moaned as the most luscious flavors filled her mouth. Craving more of that exquisite taste, she let her lips slide further over the chocolate coating and sucked the sweet juices from the fruit.

"Man, you make me wish *I* was that strawberry," a male voice said, shattering her euphoric moment.

Rebecca nearly choked on the nectar that was trickling down her throat and managed, just barely, to swallow it down. The hairs on the back of her neck tingled in acute awareness. Oh, God, she recognized that low, sexy voice and knew exactly who was standing behind her.

It was none other than Connor Basset.

She'd been so enthralled with her treat that she hadn't heard him enter the shop. And as mortified as she was to be caught intimately enjoying her chocolate-covered strawberry, she knew there was no avoiding the man behind her.

Despite the flush on her face, and the way her nipples had drawn tight at the sound of his seductive voice, she turned around and faced Connor, who looked drop-dead gorgeous in a T-shirt, faded jeans, and a black leather jacket. His dark blond hair was tousled haphazardly around his head in a way that told her it had been wind-blown during his ride to the shop. He must have driven one of his convertible sports cars to the resort for the weekend. His eyes, which were the exact color of the rich, decadent chocolate she'd just eaten, were dark and hot and filled with lust—as if he'd truly envisioned being her straw-berry, and her lips had been wrapped around *him.*

Another burst of heat settled low in her belly as she wondered just how long he'd been watching her lick and suck at the plump, luscious fruit while imagining such a provocative scenario.

He shifted closer as his gaze slowly lowered to her mouth. "Mmm. Looks juicy. And very sweet."

Was he referring to the strawberry, or her lips? The man was a master at innuendo, and she self-consciously licked her sticky bottom lip. "It's *very* juicy and sweet." When had her voice turned so husky?

A rakish smile tipped up the corner of his mouth, causing a charming dimple to appear in his left cheek. "Maybe I ought to try it for myself."

Her pulse quickened, and between the chocolate she'd just consumed and Connor's flirtatious comments, she struggled to maintain her poise. "Help yourself," she said, and waved toward the tray Marcus had left on the counter. "There's plenty to choose from."

He lifted his hand, surprising her with the warm, bold caress of his thumb along her lower lip. "I wasn't talking about the strawberries, sweetheart."

Her stomach tightened with desire and need. He wanted to taste—no, *devour*—her lips, which felt electrified from his touch. She was oh-so-tempted to finally give in to the attrac-tion simmering between them and let him kiss her as she'd secretly fantasized about for the past few years. So much so that she let her lips part and leaned toward him ever-so-slightly.

"Welcome to Sinfully Sweet," Ellie greeted Connor cheer-fully. "Can I help you find something?"

Shocked by her brazen behavior, Rebecca immediately jumped back from Connor to put a respectable amount of distance between them. She was grateful that the shop's owner had appeared when she had, or else Rebecca was certain she would have let Connor have his way with her right then and there.

Good Lord, what in the world was wrong with her? It had to be the shop and the chocolate wreaking havoc on her libido because she never acted this recklessly.

Connor's gaze shifted from hers to Ellie, and he graced the older woman with a boyish grin that was the complete opposite of the smoldering look he'd just given Rebecca. "I'm just looking around right now to see what you have."

Ellie tipped her head curiously as she studied them with too much speculation. "Do the two of you know one another?"

Connor nodded. "My best friend is marrying her sister."

"Ahh, the wedding," the older woman said in understanding. "And the two of you are…?"

"We're just friends," Rebecca replied quickly, wanting to set the record straight on that right up front.

Ellie looked to Connor for confirmation, as if she didn't quite believe Rebecca's hasty response. The woman seemed beyond intuitive.

Connor shrugged those broad shoulders of his, that adorable dimple deepening along with his smile. "Whatever she says."

Ellie didn't look convinced, but let the subject go. "Well, you two keep browsing. We're just about done with your order, so I'll be back out in a few minutes."

"Great." The sooner, the better, Rebecca thought.

Much to Rebecca's relief, Connor strolled over to the table that held the foil-wrapped candies, putting much needed distance between them. He read the sign announcing the Valentine's Day contest, then moved on to another section of the store displaying boxes of candies.

Refusing to eat any more of her chocolate-covered strawberry in front of Connor, she put the half-eaten piece of fruit into the doilie cup for later. "So, what brings you in here?" she asked casually, trying not to stare at the way his soft denim jeans molded to his perfectly toned butt. "You don't strike me as a chocolate kind of guy."

He glanced over his shoulder at her, his expression much too direct for her peace of mind. "Chocolate definitely has its time and its place. The moment I saw you eating that strawberry I developed a hankering for something sweet and delicious."

He was referring to more than just chocolate, and they both knew it, too. Even from across the room, Rebecca could see the shameless glint in his eyes that held both humor and heat.

"But, seeing as I was denied that particular treat, I'll have to stick to my original reason for coming in here."

"And that was?"

He reached for one of the red velvet heart-shaped boxes on the shelf in front of him and read the content label. "I'm here to pick up a few Valentine's gifts."

Not *one*, but a *few*. It figured. Even though he'd arrived for the weekend solo, he'd obviously left his female companions behind and wanted to make sure he took care of them for Valentine's Day. "So, do each of these girlfriends know about the other?"

He turned back around with three of the heart-shaped boxes in his hands. "Girlfriends?" he asked, momentarily puzzled by her comment. Then, as understanding dawned, amusement danced in his eyes. "Oh, these aren't for girlfriends. They're for my mother, sister and grandmother. I always send them chocolates on Valentine's Day."

The gesture seemed incredibly sweet, and she didn't know whether to believe him or not.

He set his purchases on the counter. "It's true," he said, somehow reading her mind—or maybe her skepticism showed on her face. "And for the record, I don't have a girlfriend, so, if you're interested—"

"I can apply for the position?" she asked, brow raised.

"No application necessary. The attraction between us is undeniable, and I already know you'd make the perfect girlfriend. In every way." Reaching out, he brushed back a strand of hair that had fallen over her cheek and gently tucked it behind her ear, before letting his fingers trail lightly down the side of her neck. "So, what do you say, Becca? Wanna be my girlfriend?"

His tone was teasing, but his eyes were very serious as they stared into hers. She felt mesmerized, the urge to say *yes* a powerful, overwhelming temptation. What a rush it would be to experience the full effect of all that dazzling, masculine sex appeal of his. Even if it was just a temporary fling.

"Here are your petits fours," Ellie said as she breezed back into the room. She came to an abrupt stop when she caught sight of the intimate way that Connor was still touching her. "Oh, excuse me! I didn't mean to interrupt you two."

Rebecca stepped away from Connor and tried to shake off the sensual spell he'd so effortlessly spun around her. "You weren't interrupting anything," she reassured Ellie. *In fact, you just saved me from making a colossal mistake.*

Rebecca had no doubt that Connor's interest was a transitory thing. And once she succumbed to his charms he'd most likely quickly grow tired of her, as he seemed to do with every other woman he'd ever dated. The man wasn't known for longevity in his relationships.

Succumbing to a twenty-six-year-old millionaire playboy wasn't an option, not for practical, responsible thirty-two-year-old Rebecca Moore. The situation had heartache written all over it.

Since her sister had prepaid her order, there was no reason for Rebecca to hang around any longer. Her job here was done.

"Thank you, Ellie." Rebecca took the handled bag from the other woman. "I'm sure the petits fours will be a huge hit at the cocktail party tonight."

And then she headed for the door.

"Wait!" Ellie exclaimed before she could make her clean escape. "You forgot your pink chocolate heart half!"

Despite the urge to run, Rebecca stopped, turned back around, and forced a smile as Ellie selected one and then pressed it into her hand. She really didn't want to have anything to do with the Sinfully Sweet contest, but took the candy from Ellie out of sheer politeness.

Then she high-tailed it out of the shop—away from Connor and away from the influence of all the heady chocolate affecting her better judgment.

2

CONNOR STARED AFTER Rebecca, wondering why in the world he continued to pursue such a stubborn woman when she managed to cut down every advance he made toward her.

The answer came easily, as it always did when he asked himself this question. Which was much too often.

An intense attraction and sexual tension swirled between them, though he couldn't blame his lasting interest in her on those things. She was classically pretty, with nothing flashy or artificial about her, which he liked. What you saw with Rebecca was exactly what you got. Yet that wasn't what reeled him in and kept him hooked either.

It was other traits and qualities he'd seen throughout the years—her honesty, inner strength, and loyalty—that made him a glutton for punishment, in hopes that one day she'd give him a chance.

Today was not going to be that day, he thought with a resigned sigh.

"You're smitten with her, aren't you?"

Connor returned his attention to the woman behind the counter and grinned wryly. "Am I that obvious?" Or was he just incredibly pathetic?

"To someone who knows what to look for, yes," Ellie said, as if she had knowledge of such things. "She's attracted to you, too, but she's not willing to admit it, is she?"

"She's definitely been a tough one to crack." But that, too, made Rebecca very appealing to him, despite her reasons for keeping him at arm's length. She wasn't like the other women who took one look at his millionaire status, along with his title as San Francisco's most eligible bachelor, and decided that they were going to become a permanent fixture in his life. Instead, she was the first female who *wasn't* influenced by his money. Her lack of interest was a refreshing change and only added to his reasons for being so attracted to her.

"And why is that, do you think?" Ellie asked as she rang up his boxes of Valentine candies.

"Well, I'm fortunate enough, or *unfortunate* enough depending on how you look at things, to get first-hand information through my best friend from Rebecca's sister. It seems that she thinks I'm irresponsible and have a spending problem." Not to mention the issue she had with the six-year age difference between them, and the fact that he played computer games for a living, which didn't fit into her image of a professional occupation.

Ellie took his credit card for his purchases, but hesitated before running it through the register. "Do you have a spending problem?"

Connor laughed at the woman's straight-forward question, feeling as though he was talking to his level-headed grandmother instead of a stranger he'd just met. "No. I have a lot of nice things because I can afford them." However, he'd come to realize over the past year that he tended to buy expensive items and toys to make up for what was really lacking in his life: a strong, solid relationship with a woman. And no fancy imported sports car or pricey electronic gadget could make up for that kind of companionship.

It also didn't help that he was holding out for the one woman who didn't want to have anything to do with him. Yeah, he really *was* pathetic.

"It sounds as though she needs to get to know the *real* you."

He signed the sales receipt and slipped the credit card back into his wallet. "Great advice, but I'm afraid that's easier said than done." Getting Rebecca to go out on a date with him had proved fruitless and frustrating.

"Well, I'm a firm believer that one way to a woman's soul

is through chocolate, and she did seem to favor the chocolate-dipped strawberries."

Ellie's eyes twinkled conspiratorially, giving Connor the distinct impression that he had an ally in the older woman. "You're absolutely right." It was, after all, Valentine's weekend, so why not take advantage of that fact? "I'll take half a dozen, wrapped up with a nice ribbon and a note card to go with it."

Obviously pleased with her match-making attempts, Ellie set about selecting the best and biggest chocolate-covered strawberries on the tray. While she arranged them in a white box and tied it off with a big elaborate red bow, Connor filled out mailing labels so Ellie could deliver the Valentine candies.

"Here you go." Ellie presented him with the beautifully decorated box. "I'm certain she won't be able to resist them."

Of course Connor wanted Rebecca to enjoy the strawberries, but most importantly would she be able to resist the note he attached to the sweets? Only time would tell and he'd have his answer tonight.

Ellie rounded the counter and walked to the display of pink and blue foil-wrapped chocolates, the ones he'd noticed were part of some kind of Valentine contest. Carefully, she selected one of the blue-wrapped candies, then came back to where he was still standing by the register.

"And if those strawberries don't do the trick for you, then maybe this will." Grabbing his hand, she pressed the half chocolate heart into his palm, then winked at him. "I picked this one especially for you."

The woman was as sweet as she was cunning. Connor felt as though he'd stepped into the Willy Wonka chocolate factory and he'd just been given a golden ticket. One that might just help him finally get the girl.

REBECCA EXITED the elevator and headed toward her hotel room, glad that the cocktail party was over and she was able to slip out relatively unnoticed. She'd had a nice time mingling with the bridal party and Greg's family and had managed to avoid running into Connor. However, her attempts at putting distance between them hadn't stopped the rogue from watching her from afar.

Every time she'd happened to casually glance his way their eyes would meet, and with a lazy sweep of his gaze he'd make her feel as though she was wearing provocative, revealing lingerie, instead of the button-up silk blouse, straight A-line skirt, and no-nonsense pumps. Then, as if that hadn't been enough to make her melt, he'd followed up that smoldering glance with a private, breath-stealing smile that had kept her body in a constant state of awareness.

Even now, a pleasant buzz of desire seemed to hum through her veins, and she knew it had nothing to do with the one glass of champagne she'd consumed. No, this intimate longing had been her constant companion since Connor had caught her eating that chocolate-covered strawberry in a very seductive manner. What had begun as a slow burn at the candy shop had gradually increased over the course of the evening into a full-blown craving. For Connor.

Digging her key card from her purse, she shook that notion from her head, only to be replaced by the image of how well he'd cleaned up from his T-shirt and jeans. For the evening's festivities, he'd changed into a pair of brown slacks and a tan knit shirt that did incredible things for his bedroom eyes. His disheveled hair had been combed away from his face, making his gorgeous, chiseled features even more pronounced. And she wasn't the only one who'd noticed how hot he'd looked, either, considering the way a few of Celeste's bridesmaids had tried to capture Connor's attention. She'd expected him to flirt with those other younger women as he did with her, but much to her surprise he remained polite and sociable, expressing no interest in any of the females other than to make cordial conversation—much to the girls' disappointment.

So why did Connor's lack of interest in other women give her such a perverse sense of satisfaction? The question, she decided, didn't bear close scrutiny.

She entered her room and turned on the light in the sitting area, all too aware of how quiet the place was since her sister was staying the night in the bridal suite. Setting her purse and key card down on a small table, she kicked off her pumps and curled her toes into the plush carpeting.

Pink foil in the shape of half a heart caught the overhead light and winked at her. When she'd arrived back from Sinfully Sweet earlier that afternoon she'd left the candy that Ellie had given her on the table, unopened, just to prove to herself that she had the willpower to resist its seductive pull. But now, it seemed to tempt and tease her with its presence, beckoning her to eat the luscious, creamy bit of ambrosia.

"Oh, what the hell," she murmured to herself. She had no desire to take part in the Valentine contest Sinfully Sweet was sponsoring, but there was absolutely no reason why she should waste such a generous piece of the richest, most amazing chocolate she'd ever tasted.

She unwrapped the candy and ate it leisurely, and with as much enjoyment as she had her strawberry that afternoon. Her moans of pleasure were for her ears only as her taste buds savored each bite of pure ecstasy.

Much to her disappointment, her moment of heavenly bliss was over much too soon, leaving her feeling unfulfilled, restless, and aching for a whole lot more. Thank goodness she hadn't purchased a whole box of chocolates for herself or she would have lain in bed tonight with a good book and eaten each and every one.

She scooped up the wrappings to throw them away in the trash, but the strip of paper with a typed message on it caught her attention. No way was she going to gallivant all over town trying to match up her note with someone else's, but she was more than a tad curious to see what her hidden message might reveal.

Unfolding the piece of paper, she read the contents:

> Opposites do attract.
> Be bold. Be spontaneous.
> Go for it!

A burst of amused laughter escaped her. Oh, now that *was* funny, she mused as she made her way back to the bedroom to change, because she was so *not* daring or adventurous.

A white box topped with an elaborate red bow sat on her pillow, stopping Rebecca in her tracks. Once her initial surprise faded, she moved closer. Obviously, The Delaford didn't do little mint chocolates at night. They gave their guests something more memorable. She couldn't argue with that.

Making herself comfortable on the bed, she lifted the pretty box onto her lap. Dying to know what was inside, she slipped off the ribbon and opened the lid to reveal six of the most perfect chocolate-dipped strawberries, all individually wrapped in clear cellophane and sealed with a gold Sinfully Sweet sticker. There was a small envelope with her name on the front, and she pulled out the note card tucked inside. Written in a bold masculine print were the words "Be Mine," followed by Connor's name. Beneath that was his room number.

Her stomach fluttered with a strange inner excitement and delight, and she couldn't stop the grin that tipped up the corners of her lips. The man was definitely creative, she had to give him that. And he certainly wasn't a quitter, even in the face of another possible rejection from her.

Opposites do attract.

The words she'd found inside her chocolate heart half whispered in her mind as she fingered one of the treats. That much was true about herself and Connor. The two of them were as opposite as a couple could get, what with his carefree, laid-back attitude, and her more structured lifestyle. He was impetuous and she was cautious—especially when it came to men.

Unable to resist the strawberries, she tore open the cellophane sealing one of them and took a big bite, certain that she was going to return to work on Monday ten pounds heavier from all the desserts she'd consumed this weekend. At the moment, with the sweetest piece of fruit and chocolate melting in her mouth, she didn't care.

Be bold. Be spontaneous, a little voice repeated, taking advantage of her deepest yearnings and fantasies when she was weak and susceptible from both the arousing chocolate and the loneliness of losing her sister this weekend. But the more those words chanted in her head, the more empowered and daring they made her feel. She took another bite of her strawberry, the sweet juice she swallowed like a liquid boost of courage.

Go for it.

Three little words that were incredibly effective and persuasive, especially when she was under the influence of such seductive chocolate.

All the reasons why she'd resisted Connor for so long fell to the wayside when she thought about their attraction in basic, elemental, physical terms. He wanted her, and Lord knew she wanted him. He was virile, and hotter than any guy she'd ever dated. And sex with him would no doubt be amazing. She shivered as she imagined that strong body of his moving over her, and inside her, in slow, deep strokes...

The sinful thought caused her to press her knees together, the surge of warmth between her thighs a direct reminder of just how long it had been since she'd been with a man. At the moment, it seemed like forever.

Maybe, just maybe, if she accepted the invitation to *be his*, they could both fulfill this craving they had and finally get one another out of their respective systems. Then she could move on and continue her quest for the kind of man she could settle down with. Someone driven, steadfast, and who had the same goals that she did.

Just once in her life she wanted to do something wild and impulsive and wicked. Let her hair down, so to speak, embrace her hidden sensuality, and allow her fantasies to run free. What better guy to do that with than Connor Bassett, a man who'd made it perfectly clear that he was more than willing?

She was going to go for it.

The thought made her grin.

Before she could change her mind or talk herself out of such a rash and reckless decision, she headed for the armoire where her clothes were hanging, hoping to find something more enticing to wear to Connor's room than the too conservative outfit she'd worn to the cocktail party.

Her wardrobe was woefully lacking in the seduction department. She was not a femme fatale, or the kind of fashionably dressed, label-conscious woman Connor was no doubt used to dating. The best she could find at a moment's notice was a coral-colored, flowing tiered skirt, and a satin-and-lace cream camisole under a button-up blouse.

Once she'd changed, a quick glance in the dresser mirror told Rebecca that the blouse made her look much too uptight and maidenly. Many times she'd seen her sister wear just a camisole with a skirt, and while Celeste could carry off such a fresh, youthful look with flair, Rebecca wasn't as confident.

Despite her own personal insecurities, she forced herself to shuck the prim blouse and was pleasantly surprised by the results. Okay, she didn't look like a hussy, and that was her main concern. The lace-edged camisole, worn by itself, was actually kind of sexy, in a subtle and pretty way. Her breasts were full and firm, and the camisole's built-in bra gave her a nice bit of cleavage while keeping excess flaunting to a minimum.

Satisfied with the look she'd achieved, she slipped on the only pair of strappy sandals she'd brought with her, and with a deep breath for fortitude she grabbed the box of chocolate-covered strawberries and headed for Connor's room.

CONNOR WAS BEGINNING to think he'd bit the dust once again with Rebecca when a tentative knock sounded at his hotel room door. Shocked, he jumped up from the couch where he was watching a movie on TV and made it to the entryway in a few brisk strides. A quick check out the peephole confirmed that it was Rebecca standing in the corridor, and she was holding the box of chocolate-covered strawberries he'd asked the hotel staff to deliver to her room while they were at the cocktail party.

A knot of nerves clenched in his stomach, taking him by surprise, and he quickly rubbed his damp palms down the front of his jeans. Jeezus, he was as anxiety-ridden as a teenager going out on his first date!

His reaction was comical and ridiculous, but after three years of pursuing Rebecca and finally getting a positive response from her, he didn't want to blow any chance he might have right off the bat. Didn't want to scare her off before he could show her that there was so much more between them than just a physical attraction.

However, if he had to exploit that sexual tension to get to the emotional depth, then so be it. It was a small sacrifice for a bigger cause.

Inhaling a deep breath, and feeling more in control of his reactions, he opened the door, took one look at what she was wearing, and experienced a rush of pure male appreciation that left him reeling. He had the sudden urge to put his hands all over her, but instead shoved the tips of his fingers into the front pocket of his jeans.

"Wow, you look amazing."

"Thanks." A blush suffused her cheeks, and she shifted on her feet, seemingly a nervous bundle of energy herself. "Can I come in?"

"Sure." He stepped back so she could enter his room, then closed the door and followed her into the sitting area.

Abruptly, she turned around to face him, clutching the small box to her chest in a way that emphasized the provocative curves of her breasts in that oh-so-fascinating top she was wearing. "I've never done this kind of thing before," she blurted out.

Her show of insecurity endeared her even more to him, because it was a side he'd never seen to Rebecca until tonight. "You've never done what kind of thing before?" he asked with a lop-sided grin. "Visit a guy in his hotel room?"

"Well, yes, that too," she said, her eyes a bright shade of blue. "Along with what we're about to do."

She made it all sound so clinical, and while he was pretty certain where this conversation was headed, he wanted to hear what was on her mind. "And what are we about to do?" he asked curiously.

She shrugged her smooth, bare shoulders, making his fingers itch all over again to touch that soft, creamy-looking skin. "Have a...I don't know...a fling."

"A fling," he repeated dully, hating how sordid that sounded.

She waved a hand in the air between them. "A tryst, an affair, whatever you want to call it."

He wanted to call it the start of a relationship, but kept his remark to himself for the time being.

So much for his worry of scaring her off tonight, he thought wryly. She was forging full steam ahead, but not without taking obvious protective measures so that her emotions stayed out of the equation.

He realized she had deep-rooted fears. He just didn't know the cause of them, and he was determined to discover those reasons over the course of the next few days.

She set the box of strawberries on the coffee table, but didn't sit down. "Before we go any further, I think it would be smart of us to lay out some ground rules."

He nearly laughed at the fact that she felt it necessary to issue stipulations, but caught himself just in time. "I don't have any rules."

Her stubborn chin lifted a fraction. "Well, you're used to this kind of thing, and I'm not."

A grin quirked the corner of his mouth. He didn't bother to correct her belief that he indulged in affairs on a whim, because he wasn't certain she'd trust him at this point. But her assumption was far from the truth. Sure, he'd dated a lot of women over the years, but that didn't mean he slept with every single one of them.

She obviously needed these boundaries between them, and he supposed if he knew what they were right up front, he'd at least have the advantage of knowing what he was dealing with. Besides, if the restrictions made her feel better and more comfortable with him, then he wasn't going to argue.

He settled himself in the middle of the sofa and rested his arms across the top cushions. "Okay, let's hear what you have to say."

She paced the carpeted floor in front of the coffee table, as if moving helped to ease her anxiety. "I'm sure this first request isn't going to be a difficult one for you, but I need to say it anyway. This affair goes no further than this weekend here at The Delaford. Whatever happens here, stays here. Once Celeste and Greg's wedding is over, then so are we."

Hell, no, he wanted to say, but instead clenched his jaw tight and continued to listen to her idiotic guidelines. He was too afraid that if he refuted her first rule she'd back out of the deal completely, and that wasn't an option for him. He didn't want a relationship with Rebecca to end before it even had a chance to begin.

"Secondly, I want to be sure that after this weekend is over and we go our separate ways, that we'll still be friends," she went on, meeting his gaze. "My sister is going to be married to your best friend, and I'm sure we'll run into one another socially quite a bit."

God, she was killing the mood, and they hadn't even had a chance to enjoy an evening together. "Being friends isn't a problem for me." Because if he had his way, they'd be friends and much more than that before the weekend was finished.

"Good," she said, nodding succinctly. "And finally, I need to be assured that no one is going to find out about us. I don't want Celeste to know about our affair, and I want you to promise me that you won't say anything to Greg, who would then tell my sister. Oh, and when we're in public together, there will be no open displays of affection, or anything else that will draw attention to the fact that we're...lovers."

She was making his head spin with all her too rational rules. If he did anything this weekend, he was going to make sure he ruffled that sensible, pragmatic personality of hers, but good. Show her how to loosen up and have fun.

He also wanted to show that "opposites do attract," as the message in his chocolate heart half had said. He'd opened it when he'd returned to his room and been pleased at how perfectly suited the words were to the situation.

Starting right now.

"Rebecca?" he said in a soft, low tone that was meant to calm and soothe.

She stopped her brisk pacing, her expression still reflecting a bit of uncertainty he was determined to chase away. "Yes?"

"Come here and sit down." He sat up and patted the spot right next to him. "You're *way* over-thinking this."

She hesitated a moment, then rounded the table and perched herself on the farthest edge of the sofa cushion. She folded her hands in her lap, her spine way too stiff and proper.

"I just don't want either one of us to have any false expectations of what this is about."

Connor assumed she was talking more about herself than
him, considering she'd already pegged him as the playboy type.

God, he so wanted to tumble her back on the couch and mess
up her too perfect hair with his fingers, and kiss her glossy lips
until every inch of her softened and she moaned just for him.
Instead, he settled for reaching over to brush the back of his
knuckles along her cheek.

"Sweetheart, I know what this is about," he said, watching
the way her breathing slowed and deepened as he continued to
caress the side of her neck with his fingers. "It's about you, and
me, and acting on an attraction that's been simmering a long
time. And now, here's *my* rule."

A slow, sweet smile curved the corner of her mouth as she
cast him a side-long glance. "I thought you said you didn't have
any rules."

"This one is absolutely necessary." Because without it, she'd
remain too aloof and uptight. "I want you to relax and enjoy
yourself this weekend with me. Do whatever feels good without
rationalizing every little thing. Do you think you can do that?"

She eyed the Sinfully Sweet box she'd brought with her, and
her teeth sank into her bottom lip as she returned her sheepish
gaze back to his. "Feed me one of those chocolate-covered
strawberries, and I think I can do just about anything."

If that wasn't an invitation, he didn't know what was. And there
was no way he was going to refuse such a prime opportunity to
turn this all too serious conversation into something far more fun
and seductive. "Now that would be my absolute pleasure."

He unwrapped one of the treats, but instead of giving it to
her as she was anticipating, he took a bite off the tip for himself.

"Hey," she said with a throaty laugh that lit up her eyes.
"That's the best part."

"Ummm. Not quite, but it's definitely very good." He lifted
the strawberry to her lips and fed her a piece.

She sighed and moaned her enjoyment as she nibbled and
ate the fruit slowly and thoroughly, seemingly more and more

aroused with each bite she took. Her eyes glazed over and her expression took on a dreamy, rapturous look that made him hard. Juice from the strawberry trickled down his hand, and to his shock and pleasure, she closed her eyes and licked away the sticky sweetness with long, silky laps of her tongue, then closed her mouth over the tip of his finger and sucked.

He nearly came undone right then and there. Somewhere along the way she'd gone from demure and cautious to an outright temptress. Not that he was complaining about the thrilling transformation. Hell, this was how he'd always dreamed she'd be with him.

There was nothing left to the strawberry but the stem, and he pulled away just long enough to set it aside and turn down the lamp next to the couch, which left the light in the far bedroom as their only source of illumination. Then he framed Rebecca's beautifully flushed face in his hands, reveling in the fact that she didn't appear the least bit resistant to what he was obviously about to do.

"Now this is the best part," he said huskily, and brought his mouth to hers.

He kissed her softly, tentatively, at first, despite the instinctive male urge to take and possess and claim. He nibbled on her bottom lip, then stroked the fullness with his tongue, gently feasting on her as though she were a rare delicacy and he couldn't get enough of her—which he suddenly couldn't. After years of wanting Rebecca Moore, he was ravenous for her, and keeping a tight rein on his control took every ounce of willpower in him.

She sighed, returning his heated kisses with a slow building urgency that finally gave way to hunger and need. Amazingly, she was the one who took things to the next level. Her lips parted, opening against his, and her tongue dipped into his mouth, dragging him deeper into the kiss.

Desire and lust coiled low in his belly, making his blood run hot in his veins. Sliding his hand around to cup the nape of her neck, he sifted his fingers into her silky hair, slanted her head to the side, and gave her exactly what she wanted: a hot, tongue-tangling kiss she returned with equal fervor.

She tasted like strawberries and chocolate and feminine temptation, and he lost himself in the sweetness of her mouth, her uninhibited response, and the eagerness now apparent beneath that formal, practical facade of hers.

With a soft mewling sound rumbling up from the back of her throat, she fisted her hands in his T-shirt and pulled him down onto the couch with her. He followed her lead, willing to go anywhere she took him. The couch was nice and wide, and he settled himself to the side of her, so that half his body covered hers and one of his legs was nestled between her parted thighs.

Their greedy, insatiable kisses continued. Rebecca's hands impatiently tugged the T-shirt from his jeans, and he groaned when she flattened her palms against his stomach and began pushing the hem upward in a hasty attempt to remove the article of clothing. The material caught beneath his arms, and when she made a sound of frustration he moved away slightly, giving himself enough room to tug the shirt over his head, then toss it aside.

She gazed at his bare chest in awe and feminine delight. "Oh, wow," she breathed as she reverently skimmed her hands up over his pecs and across his shoulders. "You're absolutely gorgeous."

Her hands were cool against his fevered skin, and the need to touch her was driving him crazy. He glanced down, saw the press of her tightened nipples against the silky fabric of her top, and wanted to see her naked, too.

"Your turn," he murmured, and she didn't say a word to stop him as he slid one of the thin straps of her camisole down her arm, then the other, until both of her lovely breasts were bared to his gaze. She was perfectly shaped and filled his hand as if she'd been created specifically for him.

He grazed his thumb across the velvety tip, and she sucked in a quick breath, her back arching in a silent plea for more. Her hands slid upward and into his hair, and her fingers twisted around the strands as she guided his lips to her breast. He took her in his mouth, grazed her taut nipple with his teeth, and soothed the sting with the soft swirl of his tongue before giving her other breast its fair share of attention.

She shifted restlessly beneath him, and he placed a hand on her knee, gently spreading her legs wider apart. They fell open effortlessly, and he slipped his hand beneath the hem of her skirt and trailed his fingertips up the inside of her smooth thigh. She shivered and moaned, offering no resistance as he continued his slow, lazy quest until he reached the damp fabric of her panties. He pressed his fingers against her, and her entire body jolted.

Abandoning her breast, he crushed his mouth to hers in a kiss that was hard and deep and explicitly carnal at the same time that he slid his fingers beneath the satin material covering her mound. She was so soft and warm and deliciously wet, and as he began to caress and tease her in the same rhythm that matched the stroke of his tongue along hers, she went wild.

Her hands dragged down the slope of his back, until she reached the waistband of his jeans. Her fingers gripped the belt loops and she tugged at his hips, trying desperately to shift their bodies into a more intimate position. Without words, he knew she wanted him inside her. Hell, he wanted to be inside her, but he didn't have a condom with him. Never would have anticipated that things would go so far so quickly tonight.

So, he improvised. Without breaking their kiss, he moved over her and settled the hard, pulsing length of his erection, still confined beneath the zipper of his jeans, right up against the barrier of her panties. He pulled her leg up high over his waist and rolled his hips against hers, deepening the contact. The hard ridge of his cock pressed and rubbed against her sensitive flesh with each successive thrust, taking over where his fingers had left off.

She shuddered and whimpered against his lips, the needy sound and the arching of her body into his telling him that she was so, so close. And then she was there, at the peak and tumbling over the edge, and it was a beautiful sight to see. She tossed her head back, clenched her thighs tight against his, and unraveled.

He'd meant for the pleasure to be all hers, but between her cresting orgasm and her unabashed desire for him, he was too far gone to hold back. So, he didn't even try. He surged against her, hard and deep, one final time, and a ragged growl tore from his chest as the friction launched him into a climax right along with her.

In time, beneath him, Rebecca's muscles relaxed and her breathing slowed. He moved back to the side so the bulk of his weight wasn't on her, then smoothed her skirt back down and adjusted the straps of her camisole.

Her lashes gradually drifted back open, and she stared up at him with a shocked and dazed look on her face.

"Are you okay?" he asked.

She nodded jerkily, slid her quivering legs back down to the couch, and covered her face with her hands with a groan. "I can't believe that you, that I, that we…"

He chuckled in amusement, because she was so damn cute when she was flustered. "Believe it, sweetheart. It's called making out." Gently, he pulled her hands away and traced her chin with his thumb, not wanting her to hide anything from him. "And the last thing you should be is embarrassed."

"I can't say that I've had a whole lot of experience with your kind of making out," she admitted, a slight frown etching her brows, even as her gaze roved over his naked chest. "And I've never had an orgasm with my clothes still on."

"If it makes you feel any better, neither have I," he said wryly. She just had the ability to make him lose control. He could only imagine what it was going to be like when he was inside her for real. Mind-blowing, no doubt.

Her head turned to the side, and she eyed the open box with the strawberries inside. "I swear, there's something about the chocolate…"

He wasn't about to let her blame her enthusiasm and passion for him on the chocolate, no matter how good it had been. "Becca, that chocolate had nothing to do with what just happened between us."

She sighed. "You're probably right."

Connor thought about the next three days he had with Rebecca, and between the wedding activities and ceremony that were planned, he wanted to make sure he got as much quality time with her as possible. And not just for the sex that she assumed this affair was all about. He wanted the chance to get to *really* know her, and vice-versa.

He smiled as he came up with the perfect idea and hoped she didn't balk when she discovered what he was planning, because it was certain to test just how adventurous she was willing to be with him. "Tomorrow night, after the wedding rehearsal and dinner, how about you and I sneak away from this place and do something fun?"

That perked up her interest and made her forget all about the chocolate. "What did you have in mind?

He wanted her to be surprised, but he was beginning to realize that she was a woman who liked to be prepared. So, he only gave her as much information as she needed to be ready for their adventure. "All you need to know is to wear pants and bring a jacket. I'll take care of the rest."

3

"So, how was your girls' day at the spa?" Greg asked Celeste and the bridesmaids sitting at the dinner table around him.

The Friday evening wedding rehearsal for the outdoor ceremony tomorrow had gone smoothly, and now the wedding party and Greg's family were enjoying dinner at The Delaford's five-star restaurant, The Winery. Rebecca had deliberately taken the seat next to her sister and across from Connor to give herself distance. But now she realized her mistake. It put him in her direct line of vision and she found her gaze straying to him much too often. Not a good thing when he met her surreptitious stares with a slow, sexy, bad-boy smile that made her toes curl and reminded her of the wicked things he'd done to her the night before.

Rebecca started in on the salad a waiter put down in front of her and listened as her sister told her fiancé about their day getting manicures, pedicures, facials and massages, while the guys had been out enjoying a game of golf. Celeste was animated and bubbly and filled with excitement, and who could blame her? In less than twenty-four hours she was going to marry the man she loved and become Mrs. Greg Markham the Third.

Rebecca was feeling a tad excited herself, but her anticipation was centered around the man who'd rocked her world the night before—and they hadn't even had sex. He'd been on her mind all day, and she couldn't wait to find out what he had up his sleeve for the two of them tonight. She felt as giddy as a young girl anxiously awaiting her first date, and it had been forever since she'd had that kind of reaction to a man. It was a heady, thrilling sensation she embraced whole-heartedly.

"Those spa treatments must have done wonders," Connor said as he set his fork on his empty salad plate, then shifted his gaze across the table. "Rebecca is positively glowing and she looks more relaxed than I've ever seen her."

Rebecca nearly choked on the drink of water she was swallowing. Oh, his comment sounded innocent enough, but she knew darn well that his "glowing," and "relaxed" remarks had nothing to do with the spa and everything to do with the orgasm he'd given her last night. Heck, he was practically gloating.

Celeste smiled from Rebecca to Connor. "Yeah, she is glowing, isn't she?"

She set her glass back on the table, refusing to let Connor shake her composure out in public. "There's something to be said for a nice, long, pleasurable massage. It has a way of releasing all kinds of tension."

"Ummm, I might have to try one of those massages," Connor said with an incorrigible grin.

Rebecca bit the inside of her cheek to keep from laughing. Only she knew what kind of massage he was really referring to. And, undoubtedly, he'd want it to come from her.

Dinner passed at a leisurely pace, amidst amusing conversation between bridesmaids and groomsmen, a lot of boisterous laughter, and too many flirtatious looks and comments between herself and Connor. If anyone at the table noticed those playfully seductive gestures, specifically her sister, no one called them on it. Or maybe they were all used to the attraction and didn't give it a second thought.

It was after ten by the time the rehearsal dinner ended and everyone went their separate ways. As Rebecca casually made her way out of the restaurant with the rest of the group, Connor came up beside her, lightly touched the base of her spine with his fingers to get her attention, and leaned in close.

"Go and change and meet me downstairs at the side entrance to the hotel," he whispered, and then he was gone.

It took her an extra five minutes to separate from her sister and the other bridesmaids, and ten minutes after that she was walking out the double glass doors to the hotel's side carport area dressed in the only pair of jeans she'd brought with her, a long-sleeved blouse, and a fleece jacket.

Connor wasn't there, but seconds later a big black-and-silver Harley Davidson pulled up in front of her, the rumbling sound of the engine as dramatic as the man sitting on the bike's leather seat.

Connor grinned, those boyish dimples of his beckoning to her. "Hop on," he said, and handed her an extra black helmet that matched the one on his head. "We're going for a ride."

As far as surprises went, this was something she never would have imagined. "You're kidding." She'd never ridden a motorcycle in her life, and the whole idea of doing so intimidated the heck out of her. "Why couldn't you have driven one of your fancy sports cars?"

"Because this is much more fun. You'll see."

She shook her head, not completely swayed. "I think I'm too old for this."

He rolled his eyes at her poor excuse. "You're as young as you feel. Come on, Becca," he cajoled sweetly. "Be a little spontaneous and try something new."

Be spontaneous.

She was certain that his choice of words, which reflected the message she'd found in her chocolate heart half, was nothing more than a coincidence. Still, they were enough of an impetus to give her the courage to be more adventurous than she'd ever been in her life.

Before she came to her practical, rational senses, she took the helmet, slipped it on her head, and let him secure the strap beneath her chin. Then, with Connor's help, she straddled the seat behind him, so that her thighs bracketed his in an incredibly intimate position.

"You need to hold on tight." He grabbed her wrists, pulled her closer against his back, then pushed her hands beneath his leather jacket. "Your fingers might get a little cold on the drive. This will keep them warm."

Warm was an understatement. She splayed her palms over the soft cotton T-shirt covering his taut stomach, the heat emanating from him like a furnace.

He revved the engine, and Rebecca's entire body vibrated right along with the bike. Though they hadn't even started on their way, she could already feel the latent power in the motorcycle, and she felt her heart skip a beat.

"Since this is my first time, go slow and easy on me." She didn't want her first experience to be a wild, fast ride. "I'd rather not be in a body cast for my sister's wedding tomorrow."

He chuckled, the muscles in his belly rippling beneath her palms. "I'll be gentle with you, sweetheart. I promise."

CONNOR WAS A MAN of his word. He'd never been a reckless driver or felt the need for speed, and tonight he was extra careful to keep things low key. He wanted Rebecca's trust. Wanted her to see that he wasn't the kind of guy who was rebellious and wild, or took unnecessary risks, as he knew she believed.

He veered the motorcycle onto the road just outside of where The Delaford Resort was located. It was a gorgeous night, cool but clear, and he took Rebecca on a smooth, leisurely, scenic ride around the perimeter of Crystal Lake.

Initially when they'd started off, she'd been nervous and stiff sitting behind him, but as he navigated the stretch of road ahead she eventually relaxed against his back, and the hands he'd tucked around his waist loosened their death grip.

After a while he found an alcove off the side of the road that had a perfect view of the lake, and he pulled over onto the gravelly area.

"So, what did you think?" he asked once they'd dismounted and removed their helmets, watching as she shook her silky hair, then combed through the strands with her fingers.

Energized after the ride, she turned toward him, a dazzling, exuberant smile on her face. "That was amazing!"

Her vivacious response was exactly what Connor had been hoping for. "Good, I'm glad." He extended his hand to her. "Come on, let's go sit down by the lake."

Without hesitating, she slipped her fingers into his, their cool fingers intertwining intimately. It was a simple, uncomplicated gesture, but it was one of those small things that Connor appreciated and savored, because it felt like an expression of Rebecca's faith in him. Or so he'd like to think.

With only the shimmering moonlight guiding them, Connor led the way down a grassy knoll to a cluster of large boulders near the edge of the lake. He sat down on top of one of the bigger rocks and helped Rebecca up beside him. They were no longer holding hands, and he missed that warmth and connection.

"So, why do I get the impression that you haven't had a whole lot of fun and adventure in your life?" Connor asked.

She tipped her head at him, amusement glimmering in her eyes. "Not all of us can afford the kind of fun you can."

"I'm not necessarily talking about material things," he said, and unzipped his leather jacket so he could enjoy the cool evening temperature. "I've known you for three years now, and you've always come across as so reserved, so completely opposite to your sister's lively, outgoing personality."

She lifted a brow. "So, are you saying I'm a snob?"

Beneath her teasing tone Connor detected a sensitive, guarded emotion he didn't fully understand. "No, you've never come across as a snob," he said, trying to find the right words to get his point across. "You're just so much more serious than your sister."

"Celeste is also six years younger than I am," she replied, as if that alone explained their contrasting dispositions.

Six years also separated him and Rebecca, Connor knew, and refused to let her use that as a defense with her sister, or as a way to distance herself from him. "I don't think the differences in your personalities have anything to do with age."

Her chin jutted out in opposition. "It has *everything* to do with me being older than Celeste."

"Why, because it makes you so much more *mature?*" he asked, rolling out the last word in a humorous attempt to lighten the mood between them.

The corner of her mouth twitched with a smile, giving him what he'd been after, but it didn't completely erase the unease in her gaze. "Let's just say that I had to grow up fast."

Now they were getting somewhere. Beyond the superficial

to the emotional, which was exactly what he wanted. "Why?" he asked, low and soft.

She looked out at the silver cast of moonlight spilling across the lake, and he prayed that she wouldn't shut him out now that he'd finally managed to scale one of those walls of hers. His gut told him that her reasons were key to Rebecca and who she was, and why she was so guarded. And he needed to know exactly what he was up against.

After a silent minute passed, she spoke. "My mother passed away when I was sixteen and Celeste was ten. It was hard enough trying to deal with the adjustment of my mother's death, who was a stay-at-home mom, but my father's job required him to travel often and he was gone more than he was home, even after she passed away."

"That couldn't have been easy for you and your sister."

"No, it wasn't." She drew her knees up and wrapped her arms around her legs, her gaze still focused on the gently rippling water. "Our neighbor at the time, Mrs. Sedgewick, stayed with us while my father was out of town, but I automatically took over the responsibilities at home that my mother used to take care of: cooking, cleaning, shopping, that sort of stuff."

"And taking care of Celeste," he added, already getting a clear view of Rebecca's abnormal childhood. So much responsibility for someone so young.

"Yes." She met his gaze and smiled, and there wasn't the slightest glimmer of regret in her expression for what she'd sacrificed during her teenage years. "In a lot of ways I became a mother figure for her. Our situation was difficult enough with my mother being gone and our father always out of town, and the last thing I wanted was for Celeste to feel insecure, to feel like she didn't have someone in her life she could count on. And because my sister was all I really had, it was easy to focus all my attention on her."

He had a sister, as well, and knew just how strong those sibling bonds could be. "She's very lucky to have you."

"We're lucky to have one another," she corrected emphatically. "Especially since my father didn't provide much in the way of emotional support or even financial security."

He frowned, surprised by that comment. He knew their father had passed away of a heart attack years ago, but Rebecca's remark seemed to apply to their lives right before he passed away. "How do you mean?" he asked curiously.

Again, she hesitated, as if realizing that she'd said too much. Again, he waited calmly and quietly for her to confide in him.

"I always thought that my father had a decent paying job," she finally said. "I never knew how much he actually made, but we lived in a nice house in a good neighborhood, and my father drove a BMW Coupe. We had the big-screen TV, a pool and spa in the backyard, and a computer with all the bells and whistles on it, which cost a fortune at the time. Any new electronic gadget that came out, he had to have, too, and he didn't think twice about his spending sprees."

A gentle gust of breeze threaded through her hair, and she absently brushed a stray strand off her smooth cheek before continuing. "Anyway, after my mother passed away, whenever my father had to go out of town he gave me some cash to buy groceries and whatever Celeste and I needed for school, such as supplies, clothes and shoes. I learned to be frugal and thrifty with what he gave me, which was often barely enough, because I hated asking for more, and I always wanted to make sure that I took care of Celeste's needs." She shrugged, her shoulders shifting beneath her fleece jacket. "I never needed much myself."

Or she'd just learned to do without, he thought, seeing just how incredibly selfless she'd been. It was just another reason for him to fall hard for this woman.

"What I didn't realize until much later was that my father had a spending problem, and he charged everything on credit cards but never paid off the balance. So, over time he'd accumulated a huge debt that was nearly impossible to pay off. And, eventually, that led to him having to file for bankruptcy. We even lost the house we were living in."

Rebecca swallowed hard, feeling the old flare of resentment and pain swell within her, and she struggled to keep that anger toward her father's irresponsible actions from rising to the surface. "Celeste didn't take the news as hard as I did, but I was absolutely devastated by the loss. It was the only home that Celeste and I had ever known, and suddenly it was gone, along with most everything inside. And it never should have happened."

Compassion etched Connor's masculine features. "I'm sorry you had to go through that, Rebecca."

She was touched by his sincerity, yet a part of her was too aware that he had the potential of being every bit as frivolous with his spending as her own father had been. "It was a very valuable lesson to learn, even at such a young age. Losing everything like that taught me the value of saving money and being financially secure. I don't ever want to be in that kind of situation again."

He nodded in understanding. "You gave up so much to raise your sister, even after your father's death."

She dropped her head back and stared up at the clear sky, and its scattering of a thousand brilliant stars. "I'd do it again in a heartbeat."

"I don't doubt that for one second." The gentle caress of his fingers along her cheek made her turn to look at him again, and then he asked, "But what about you, Rebecca?"

Uncertain about what he meant, she blinked at him in confusion. "What about me?"

"You've done a phenomenal job taking care of your sister, but now that she's getting married and starting a life of her own with Greg, what about *your* life?"

How could the man be so perceptive? It was as if he knew what a difficult time she was having letting her sister go, not that she was going to admit it out loud to him. "My life is good."

"As good as you want it to be?"

His dark brown stare was direct and unwavering, making her feel as though he could see all the way to her soul. It was an unnerving sensation, especially since he was the first man that she'd so openly and honestly shared her past with. "Nobody's life is perfect."

"True," he agreed. "But maybe it's time for you to think about what *you* want for a change, and go for it."

Go for it. There was that phrase again, tempting her to give into her deepest desires, which seemed intrinsically linked to this man. Heart, body, and soul.

That frightening thought shook her up inside, but she refused to let her fears override what she longed for the most. "For this moment, and this weekend, I want you," she said, then gave into the impulse to lean toward Connor, place her hand on the soft cotton T-shirt covering his chest, and kiss him.

His mouth was incredibly warm and soft against hers, and when his lips gradually parted she was the one who initiated the kind of deeper, hotter kiss she craved. Tongues touched and mated, and as each slow kiss melded into another, a knot of pure, sensual need tightened in her belly, and lower.

His clean, male scent filled her senses, and beneath her hand she could feel the rapid beat of his heart, which matched her own. Her breasts swelled, her nipples tightened, and before long her entire body hungered for so much more. Like throwing caution and modesty to the wind and making love to Connor right out here in the open.

It was Connor who eventually ended the kiss, then pressed his forehead against hers. "It's getting late," he said, his voice gruff with arousal. "We should head back to the hotel."

She managed a nod, grateful that at least Connor was able to think straight. A soft bed would be so much more comfortable than the hard ground or maneuvering around on a rock. "Okay."

The ride back to the resort seemed to take twice as long. Once they arrived at the hotel, Connor dropped her off at the side entrance where he'd originally picked her up, then went to park his motorcycle.

She entered the hotel alone, wondering if this was the end of their night together since Connor hadn't mentioned anything about seeing her in a few minutes, or even later. Obviously, he was respecting her request that they keep their relationship discreet and not be seen together in public. Or maybe she'd scared him off by giving him a glimpse of her dysfunctional past.

Uncertain what to do, Rebecca let herself into her room and headed toward the bedroom as she unzipped and shrugged off her fleece jacket. A smile curved her mouth when she caught sight of an unwrapped gift that had been left on her pillow. Last night she'd found chocolate-covered strawberries, and upon closer inspection she realized that this present was equally tempting, and made her come to the quick conclusion that her evening with Connor wasn't over after all. Not if she didn't want it to be.

She picked up the jar of Sinfully Sweet chocolate body paint, her mind already tumbling with wicked, erotic scenarios. Tied around the lid was a big red bow and two small paint brushes, along with a note card that read *Do you dare*? in Connor's handwriting.

For once in her life she didn't think twice, or analyze her answer—just went with feminine instincts and desires.

Yes, she dared.

4

As soon as Connor opened the door to his room, a surge of anticipation rippled through Rebecca, and her fingers tightened around the jar of chocolate sauce in her hand. She'd never been one of those women that had seduction down to an art form, but there was something about this man that made her feel wanton and decidedly naughty.

She fingered the tip of the paint brushes and shivered as she imagined the feathery sensation of those soft bristles gliding across her bare skin. "I'm not much of an artist, but if you don't mind me being an amateur, then I'm more than willing to give it a try."

The grin that pulled up the corners of his mouth was blatantly sexual, and all male. "I don't think that chocolate body paint requires you to be a perfectionist. In fact, in my opinion, the messier the better, because the best part is licking everything clean."

She wasn't about to argue with that. "Sounds like fun to me."

"I was hoping you'd feel that way." Taking her hand, he pulled her inside his room, closed and locked the door, then led the way toward the bedroom.

It appeared that after their conversation earlier at the lake, idle chit-chat wasn't necessary. They both knew what they wanted—one another—and neither of them cared to waste time with small talk. Not when there was a perfectly good jar of Sinfully Sweet chocolate sauce waiting to be used.

Once they were in his bedroom, Connor turned on the light next to the bed, then stripped off his T-shirt and tossed it aside.

Even though he'd been half-naked last night while they'd made out on the couch, Rebecca's mouth went dry once again as she took in his sculpted body and thought about all the different ways she wanted to paint on him. His chest alone made one heck of an inspiring canvas.

"I get to paint first," she said, breathlessly.

"You can go first, but I want both our clothes off because they're just going to get in the way."

He took the jar and brushes from her hand and set them on the nightstand next to a few foil packets he must have put there in preparation for tonight's tryst. Then, he started unbuttoning her blouse.

It took the two of them less than a minute to undress down to their underwear, and for the moment Rebecca was grateful for that teeny bit of coverage—on both of them. Without it, she had a feeling that this first time together would be over before they even had the chance to enjoy the paint. She was already shaking from the heated caresses of Connor's hands skimming along her curves as he'd stripped off her top, bra, and jeans.

Much to her own delight, there was no mistaking how aroused Connor was, either. His solid erection pressed against his snug briefs, long and thick. She licked her lips as she envisioned that part of him covered in delicious chocolate, and heard him groan.

She raised her gaze to his face, stunned by the intensity of his expression. It was a powerful, exhilarating sensation knowing that just one glance and a lick of the lips could inflame him so much. But she understood exactly what he was feeling, because one seductive look from him had the ability to make her melt inside, too.

Anxious to indulge in the shameless fantasies dancing in her head, she pressed her fingertips to his chest and gave him a light push backwards. "Lie down on the bed for me," she said huskily.

He did as she asked, stretching his long, lean body in the middle of the mattress, and she didn't hesitate to crawl up onto the bed after him and straddle his hips. She'd never been so bold and presumptuous with a man before, but the heat and desire darkening Connor's eyes, along with the hard shaft pressing against her bottom, urged her to be as uninhibited as she wanted.

Reaching for the jar of body paint, she opened the lid, and the heady chocolate aroma unfurled a deeper hunger within her. With a provocative smile on her lips she dipped one of the brushes into the sauce and playfully swiped it across his chest, painting squiggly lines here and there before swirling the soft bristled tip around his nipples.

Connor sucked in a deep breath, and his hands clenched her thighs as she continued on, painting along the concave of his belly, and the cute indentation of his navel. When he was sufficiently covered in chocolate sauce, she leaned down and tasted him, using her lips, teeth and long, slow laps of her tongue to savor the sweet, delectable flavor of Connor dipped in rich, smooth chocolate.

"Ummm," she murmured against his hard stomach. "You taste a hundred times better than those strawberries."

The only response he could manage was a deep, throaty grunt.

Smiling, she swirled her tongue into his belly button, and nibbled along his lower abdomen until she reached the waistband of his briefs. Wanting them gone, she easily pulled his underwear down his legs and off, then directed her full attention to his jutting erection.

Mesmerized by the sight of that breathtakingly masculine part of him, she dabbed a finger in the chocolate sauce and circled the head of his penis with a light caress that made his sex jerk in surprise. Enjoying his reaction, she scooped up more of the body paint, took him in her chocolate-coated hand, and stroked the entire length of his shaft—once, twice, before lowering her head and taking him in her mouth to finish the job.

Chocolate had never tasted so good, so erotic and tempting. And she couldn't get enough.

She drew him in deep, reveling in his low, rumbling groan of pleasure and the way he tangled his fingers in her hair. She licked at him leisurely, nibbled gently, and teased him with long, suctioning swirls of her tongue that had his hips rising off the bed and his entire body tensing with the onslaught of a pulsing orgasm.

"Not yet," he rasped before she could send him over the edge. In an amazingly coordinated movement he reared up, pushed her back onto the mattress, and swung a leg over her hips so that he was now straddling her.

She stared up at him, surprise rendering her speechless.

"It's my turn to play," he said with a grin, and picked up the jar of chocolate sauce.

Instead of using one of the brushes, he drenched his fingers with the gooey substance and finger-painted her body. He covered her breasts with his coated hands and rubbed his thumbs over her aching nipples. Continuing downward, he playfully drew a heart on her stomach and added the initials "C" and "R", and when he reached her panties, he quickly and efficiently removed them so she was as naked as he was.

He knelt between her parted legs and looked his fill of her, his expression a combination of adoration and lust. "I can't wait to eat you up," he murmured, and gave her a wolfish smile that made her feel like Little Red Riding Hood.

But first, he painted his wet, sticky fingers up the insides of her thighs, and found a sensitive, ticklish spot along the way that he exploited mercilessly, until she was laughing and writhing and begging him to stop the sensual torment.

Eventually, he did, but then replaced one kind of seduction with another equally provocative pleasure. Starting at her knees, he slowly licked away the chocolate he'd smeared on her skin. He took his own sweet time, making sure that he lapped up every last drop. He grazed her flesh with his teeth and used his warm, soft tongue to clean up the chocolate mess he'd made on the inside of her thighs, until he finally reached that ultra-feminine place he'd yet to taste.

He did so now. Settling more comfortably between her thighs, he draped her legs over his shoulders, lowered his head, and made good on his promise to eat her up. He took his time, building her need to excruciating heights, and she gripped the covers in her hands, her hips arching, her body silently pleading for the release he kept just beyond her reach.

Finally, with a deep, intimate stroke of his tongue, and a deep thrust of his fingers, he gave her the orgasm she was desperate for. She tumbled over the edge, her entire body shuddering from the incredible force of her climax.

It took her a minute to come back to her senses, and when she did she found Connor kneeling between her thighs, sheathing himself with one of the condoms from the nightstand. She fully expected him to thrust into her and take his own release, but instead he lowered his head and began licking away the chocolate on her quivering belly. His tongue traced the outline of the heart he'd drawn, and lapped away the initials until there was nothing left except a smear of chocolate.

He moved upward, where he feasted on her breasts and sucked on her nipples as if she were a dessert for him to devour and enjoy. By the time he was done removing every last bit of chocolate that he could, she was trembling all over again, and more than ready for him to be inside her.

He stretched more fully over her, so that they were chest to breast, and his erection nestled in the vee of her thighs. His eyes blazed with need, and a deeper emotion that made her heart beat hard and fast in her chest.

He didn't give her time to dwell on what she'd seen in his gaze. In the next instant he threaded his fingers through her hair and crushed his mouth to hers in a demanding, rapacious kiss. At the same time he drove deep, deep inside her, making her think of nothing but the way he filled her so completely. Instinctively, she wrapped her legs high around his waist as his hips pumped against hers in a hard, rocking rhythm that sent them both spiraling out of control.

Another stunning orgasm rippled through her, causing her inner muscles to clench around Connor's shaft. Groaning against her lips, he thrust against her, harder, faster, and gave himself over to his own scorching release.

He buried his face in the curve of her neck, his breath hot and damp against her skin. It took him longer than her to recover, and in time he lifted up onto his forearms and stared down at her, his slumberous gaze filled with a warmth and tenderness that made her ache for this kind of intimacy on a regular basis.

A slow, lazy smile curved his lips. "You're amazing, you know that?"

She'd never had such great, mind-numbing sex before, so she knew she couldn't take the credit he was offering. "I appreciate the compliment, but I think that honor is all yours."

He nuzzled his cheek against hers and whispered in her ear, "How about we're both amazing together?"

She liked the way that sounded. Too much. Not only was Connor an outstanding lover, but he definitely brought out the best in her, in ways she'd never thought possible. He was a great listener, as he'd proved earlier that night by the lake, and he made her laugh more than any man ever had before. And yes, they *were* amazing together.

She could easily fall for Connor Bassett, if a part of her hadn't already, and that realization terrified her.

Unable to come up with a snappy reply, she shifted beneath him and winced when she realized that the chocolate sauce had nearly glued their skin together. "We sure did make a mess, didn't we?"

"Ummm, that we did." He lifted his head, a satisfied smile on his lips. "What do you say we take a nice, long, hot shower together? I'll scrub your back if you scrub mine." He waggled his brows lasciviously at her.

She laughed, unable to resist his flirtatious charm, or those boyish dimples. So, for now, she didn't even try. "I'd love to take a shower with you."

THE SOUND OF soft footsteps prompted Connor to glance up from his laptop computer to find Rebecca walking out of the bedroom, looking sleep tousled, well loved, and incredibly sexy in the cotton T-shirt he'd worn earlier. There was something so intimate and seductive about seeing her in his clothes, particularly how the soft material emphasized her full breasts and the way the hem ended mid-thigh. He couldn't tell if she was wearing panties or not, and the thought of her being completely naked beneath his shirt caused a surge of heat to spiral straight to his groin.

He couldn't remember ever wanting a woman as much as he wanted Rebecca—in his bed and in his life. They'd finally succumbed to the physical attraction between them, proving without a doubt just how compatible they were sexually. Emotionally, however, he knew he still had his work cut out for him, and he only had today and tomorrow to make her realize that what was between them was more than just a passing fling.

Stifling a yawn, she approached where he was sitting on the couch. "It's after three in the morning," she said, her voice still husky with sleep. "What are you doing up at this ungodly hour?"

"I couldn't sleep." For the most part, he tended to be a night owl, and that's when he came up with some of his best computer game ideas. Tonight, he'd been working on a glitch in one of the newest games he'd created. "What are *you* doing up at this ungodly hour?"

"I woke up and you were gone." She sat down next to him, tucked her legs beneath her on the couch, then smoothed the T-shirt over her knees. "Since this is your hotel room, I figured you couldn't have gone far."

He leaned toward her, nuzzled his lips against her throat, and felt her shiver from his light, playful kisses. Despite the shower they'd taken together, she still smelled like chocolate and great sex, a delicious combination that made him ravenous for her all over again.

"Miss me?" he murmured against her ear.

A soft sigh escaped her, and she tipped her head to the side to give his mouth better access to her neck. "Yeah, I did miss you."

He pulled back, unable to stop the satisfied grin from making an appearance. "Good." He figured her admission was a small start, and could only hope that when Sunday rolled around she wouldn't want their affair to end.

Her brows furrowed as she stared at him, the slumber gradually clearing from her gaze. Then, an amused smile curved her lips. "I didn't realize you wore glasses."

He raised his hand to touch the wire rims. He'd forgotten that he had them on until she'd mentioned it. "I only wear them when I'm working on the computer. With all the hours I spend looking at a computer screen, it keeps my eyes from straining too much."

She studied him intently for a few seconds. "You look…"

Whatever word Rebecca was searching for seemed to allude her, so he helped her out. "Like a computer geek?"

She laughed. "An exceptionally *sexy* computer geek."

He rolled his eyes. "You're taking me back to my high school days, when I was the epitome of a nerd."

"Really?" Her expression was genuinely incredulous. "That's hard to imagine."

"It's true." Seeing an ideal opportunity to share something personal with her—a part of himself he'd never shared with another woman before because no other woman had ever mattered as much to him as Rebecca did—he set his open laptop on the coffee table, along with his glasses, then turned toward her on the couch.

"Growing up, I wasn't one of those guys who was into sports, much to my father's disappointment," he said, having come to terms long ago with the fact that he'd never meet his dad's expectations of what a son should be. "When I was eight, and my sister was five, my mother caught my father having an affair with a woman he worked with, and my mother immediately filed for a divorce. Being so young, it was a really tough time in my life, and the computer became my escape so I didn't have to cope with the fact that my family was being torn apart by my father's infidelity."

"So, we both had to deal with a loss in the family at a young age," she said quietly, her gaze brimming with understanding. "You turned to computers, and I focused on raising my sister."

"Exactly." He stretched his arm out along the top of the couch and grazed his fingers along her shoulder. "I spent most of my free time in front of the computer. If I wasn't playing some kind of video game, I was pulling the hard drive apart to figure out how it all worked. Eventually, I started creating computer games just to amuse myself, but my friends wanted copies and started playing them, too."

Her pretty blue eyes widened in fascination. "How did you end up selling those games?"

"Actually, it was Greg who encouraged me to send one of my games to a software company that produces all types of computer games, and within a few weeks of receiving the program, they made a very lucrative offer for exclusive rights to the program that is now called Edge of Reason."

He threaded his fingers through her hair, loving the feel of those silky strands sliding over his hand. "I was eighteen at the time, and when I realized that I could make a helluva lot of money creating and selling action-adventure computer games, I went for it."

"Sounds like any teenager's dream job," she said with a slight smile. "But now that you're older, don't you ever think about getting a real job?"

"I *have* a real job." he said, "I love what I do, and I get paid extremely well to do it."

"To play computer games," she said, obviously not able to think of what he did for a living as a career.

So, he tried to set her straight. "I create and program the computer games first, which is a lot of hard work and long hours. And, I like the perks that come with my job. I set my own hours, and I can work any time of the day or night. And the best part is that I'm my own boss. It doesn't get any better than that."

She meet his gaze, while her fingers absently pleated the hem of the shirt she was wearing. "Well, there is that other perk of you being voted one of San Francisco's wealthiest and most eligible bachelors."

He winced, hating the superficial title that had been bestowed upon him. "That's more like a *curse*."

Surprise lit up her eyes. "Dating your choice of women is a curse?"

He shook his head. "No, but discovering that a woman is dating you because she finds your bank account more attractive than your personality *is* a curse."

"Oh," she said quietly. "I suppose that would be frustrating, but not all women are that way."

"I agree." And she was proof. He wanted to point that out to Rebecca, but knew she wasn't ready for that kind of serious conversation about the two of them just yet.

Done talking about his money, and his job, Connor leaned closer to Rebecca and gave her something more pleasant to think about. He slipped his hand beneath her shirt, and he wasn't the only one who shuddered when he discovered that she was completely naked underneath.

"We should get some sleep," she said, though not very convincingly, especially considering how she was letting him ease her back on the couch so he could settle between her soft, silky thighs. "We need to be up in a few hours."

"I'm already *up*." Grinning wickedly, he grabbed her hand, pushed it into his cotton shorts, and wrapped her fingers tight around his erection. "In more ways than one."

She laughed, then moaned when he slid his own fingers through her soft, slick flesh and stroked her oh-so-slowly.

After that, sleep was a long time in coming.

FROM ACROSS the elegantly decorated ballroom at The Delaford Resort, Rebecca watched as the bride and groom said their goodbyes to family and friends. The beautiful outdoor wedding ceremony had gone off without a hitch that afternoon, complete with tears during the emotional service, and whoops of joy and congratulations once Celeste and Greg had been pronounced husband and wife. As for the reception, it had been a fun, lavish celebration Rebecca would never forget.

Now, it was early evening, and the bride and groom were leaving to enjoy their honeymoon suite for the night.

Rebecca had already hugged Celeste and Greg and wished them the best, but as she watched her radiant sister gaze up at her new husband with pure, unadulterated love, a huge lump formed in Rebecca's throat, and an odd mix of happiness and sadness clashed inside of her.

She was so grateful that her sister had found such a wonderful, devoted man to marry. A man who adored her and would undoubtedly take good care of her in every way that mattered.

Yet, Rebecca couldn't stop the flow of loneliness that was already settling like a cold, hard knot in her stomach. The apartment that she'd shared with Celeste for the past ten years wasn't going to be the same without her bubbly, vibrant sister, and she dreaded heading back to the quiet, empty place.

"The band is playing their last song," a deep, masculine voice said from behind her. A familiar voice that had the uncanny ability to soothe and arouse her at the same time. "Since we've already said our goodbyes to the bride and groom, what do you say we enjoy one last dance before the evening comes to an end?"

Grateful for the distraction, she turned and smiled at Connor, who looked dashing and gorgeous in a black tux with a red bow-tie and cummerbund that matched her formal gown. They'd been dance partners most of the night—mainly because of their best man and maid-of-honor roles, but at the moment none of that mattered. The band was playing a slow ballad, a love song to send the bride and groom on their way, and there were other couples on the dance floor enjoying the final song of the night.

Since she wasn't looking forward to going up to her hotel room by herself, she accepted Connor's invitation. "Sure, I'd love to dance."

With a hand pressed lightly to the base of her spine, he led the way to the dance floor. Once they were there, he wrapped an arm around her waist and pulled her into his embrace, aligning their bodies intimately from chest to thighs. They swayed in time to the slow tune, and as Connor stroked his thumb along her waist, she let herself relax and unwind. At the moment, she wanted, *needed*, the closeness he was offering to offset the deep, desolate feeling crowding her chest.

"Are you okay?" he asked, those dark brown eyes of his searching her gaze, as if he was trying to see straight to her soul.

She flashed him a quick smile that felt forced on her lips. "I'm fine."

"Liar." Gentle amusement etched his expression. "I saw the way you were watching your sister when she and Greg were saying goodbye to everyone. You're having a hard time letting her go, aren't you?"

Her first instinct was to deny his too perceptive claim, to be strong and not show the slightest bit of vulnerability. It had been her M.O. for longer than she cared to remember, but she was tired of keeping her emotions bottled up inside her. Tired of pretending to always be strong when she harbored worries and fears just like everyone else.

"Okay, I'll admit I'm suffering from a bit of separation anxiety," she said, and glanced over his shoulder because she couldn't bear to look him straight in the eyes while she confessed such a pathetic weakness. "She's been such a huge part of my life for so long, and it's hard to imagine what it's going to be like not seeing and talking to her on a daily basis."

"It's not as though she's stepped completely out of your life," he said gently.

"No, but she has another family now, and she's like a daughter to Greg's mother and father." Considering that Celeste had spent more than half her life without one parent or the other, Rebecca was certain her sister would readily embrace the normalcy of a *real* family.

Connor swept the back of his fingers along her cheek as they continued to dance to the slow music. "Rebecca, you'll always be her family."

She bit her lower lip, feeling another swell of emotion come over her. "It's just…hard," she said, unable to explain.

"I don't doubt that it is." His voice was infused with more understanding and patience than she knew she deserved. "But you're Celeste's sister by blood, and that's a bond that will never break or falter."

God, I hope so, she thought as the band finished playing. She waited for Connor to loosen his hold on her, but instead he put his mouth near her ear and spoke so only she could hear him. "Will you stay with me tonight?"

Funny, but she could have sworn she heard the slightest bit of uncertainty in his voice, and realized that Connor wasn't taking anything for granted. He was openly stating his desire for her, as well as issuing an invitation to share his bed, and other pleasures, with him tonight, without knowing if she wanted the same.

Her answer came much too easily. Connor was quickly becoming another weakness, like the Sinfully Sweet chocolate they'd indulged in the past two nights. But there was no chocolate clouding her judgment or thoughts now.

She didn't want to be alone tonight. Didn't want to think about the empty, unexciting life waiting for her back at home. What she wanted more than anything was to *feel*, and Connor did that for her in a way no man ever had before.

She met his gaze and smiled. "Yes, I'll stay with you tonight."

5

EVEN THOUGH SHE was completely and utterly sated, Rebecca couldn't sleep. Why was it that tonight Connor didn't seem to have any problem drifting off after the second time they'd made love, yet here she was, wide-eyed and awake?

Closing her eyes, she released a soft sigh, enjoying the way Connor had cuddled up behind her, wrapped a strong arm around her waist, and pulled her close to the heat and strength of his body. His hold on her was possessive yet caring, secure yet loose enough for her to move away if she wanted.

At the moment, she was perfectly content.

She immediately blinked her eyes back open, startled by her thoughts—as well as the frightening realization that she'd fallen hard and fast for Connor Bassett in such a short amount of time. Suddenly, she felt caged in and restless. She needed space, along with air to breathe that didn't include his scent.

Gingerly, she eased away from him and off the bed. Finding one of his T-shirts on the floor, she slipped it over her head and quietly made her way into the living room. Leaving the lights off, she stood by the large plate-glass window that gave her a beautiful view of Crystal Lake. She watched the way the moonlight dappled the rippling water with an ethereal glow, which reminded her of last night when Connor had taken her for a ride on his motorcycle and they'd ended up at the secluded spot by the lake.

A smile curved the corner of her mouth as she remembered just how exhilarating it had been to ride on his bike, and the way he'd listened so intently when she'd talked about her past.

While the sensible, practical side to her personality told her that
their time together was nothing more than a brief affair to slake
their attraction to one another, a newer, whimsical part of her
wondered about the possibility of more.

Shaking her head at that foolish thought, she headed across
the room to the small refrigerator to get herself a drink of water.
Except when she opened the door and peered inside, it wasn't
the chilled bottles of Evian that caught her attention, but a blue-
foil wrapped half-heart she recognized from Sinfully Sweet.

It was obvious by the crinkled´foil that Connor had unwrapped the candy to read his secret message inside, then
covered it back again without eating the chocolate. More than
a little curious to see what his note had said, she picked up the
piece of candy, retrieved the small strip of paper tucked inside,
and read the typed message.

> Opposites do attract.
> Be bold. Be spontaneous.
> Go for it!

Her stomach twisted and turned as she read, then re-read,
the familiar words that had given her the courage to jump into
an affair with Connor, unable to believe that he'd received the
same message that she had. Out of all the hundreds of chocolate hearts Sinfully Sweet had been giving away, what were the
chances that she and Connor would end up with identical
messages and matching hearts?

Very slim, her mind whispered, quickly dousing her flare of
excitement with doubts and suspicions.

She thought back to all the times Connor had subtly used
those same words with her. Like when he'd coaxed her to be a
little *spontaneous* and try something new so she'd take a ride
with him on his motorcycle. Or how he'd told her that maybe
it was time for her to think about what she wanted for a change
and *go for it*.

It could have all been coincidence, but every feminine instinct within her told her that there was more at work than just fate. No, she was beginning to suspect that Connor had taken advantage of an opportunity that had presented itself to him. Not that she could blame him for what had happened between them, considering how quick she'd been to jump into an affair with him.

But discovering the truth of how he'd manipulated her certainly put everything back into its proper perspective. Like the fact that their fling was a temporary thing, that every one of his other relationships had been short lived, and that he'd made her no promises of anything more. He was still six years younger than she was, he still played computer games for a living and he was far too frivolous with how he spent his money.

So, in essence, not much had changed in the past three days, not unless she wanted to count her too involved heart and emotions—which she did not.

"Hey, are you okay?"

The sound of Connor's sleep-husky voice startled Rebecca out of her stupor. She turned around to face him, with the chocolate heart half in one hand and the thin strip of paper with the message on it in the other hand. Her traitorous heart picked up its beat as she took in his half-naked appearance. All he was wearing was a pair of cotton shorts, and that gorgeous body of his threatened her good sense and determination to handle this situation with as much poise as possible.

"I came out here to get a bottle of water, but found this instead," she said, and calmly held up the evidence she'd discovered. "You have the matching message to my chocolate heart half. But you already knew that, didn't you?"

He glanced from her hands, then back to her face, resignation passing across his features. "I suspected it, yes."

While most men would have scrambled for some kind of excuse, Connor was honest and straight with her. And she respected him for that, even if her heart hurt more than she could ever remember.

She put on a brave face and attempted to treat the situation with a kind of casual sophistication that was completely foreign to her. "Well, our weekend affair was fun while it lasted, wasn't it?"

Connor placed his hands on his hips, clearly aware of the fact that Rebecca was withdrawing from him and putting up those walls of hers. And he did whatever he could to keep her from shutting him out completely. "Rebecca…it doesn't have to end."

"Of course it does," she said with a little laugh that sounded way too brittle to his ears. "We're two different people who live two vastly different lives. Sex is one thing, but a real relationship takes time and work with two people who have the same goals."

Ahhh, now he knew where this conversation was headed. Her insecurities were clawing their way to the surface and her self-protective instincts were kicking in. "Our goals are very similar, Rebecca, if you'd just let yourself get past what your father put you through."

She visibly stiffened, but surprisingly she didn't issue any kind of defense, proving she was well aware that her past had scarred her when it came to her own personal relationships. Trusting in a man to take care of her, to provide the kind of security and stability she needed in her life, wasn't easy for her to do.

He sighed, knowing he was up against tremendous odds, but willing to fight them to be with her. "Look, I know this all happened so fast, but I've wanted you for a very long time, Rebecca. For me, this weekend was real, and I want it to last. And there's no reason why it can't. Your sister is grown and married and has a life of her own," he said, deliberately touching on one of her most vulnerable spots, because she needed to face what was in store for her in the future. "You've done a great job with Celeste, but it's time to let her go and have a life of your own. Let someone take care of you for a change."

Let me be that person for you, he transmitted with his gaze.

Her chin lifted, and her fingers curled around the strip of paper in her hand. The note that had brought them together… and was now about to tear them apart. "I can manage on my own just fine," she said defensively.

He had no doubt that she could. "But being on your own doesn't keep you warm at night, does it?"

She didn't respond, and he guessed that was because the answer was obvious and because it was something she wasn't ready to come to terms with yet.

God, what had happened to the vibrant woman he'd been with for the past three days? The woman who'd been bold and had taken risks and enjoyed herself? She was gone, having reverted back to someone who believed she had to be in control of her emotions and actions.

Keeping his frustration tamped was incredibly difficult at the moment, but somehow he managed to remain calm. "We'll leave here as friends, just as you requested, but there's something I want you to know." Figuring he had nothing left to lose, he put everything out in the open. "I'm falling in love with you, Rebecca. And it has nothing to do with sex and lust, and everything to do with who you are. You're genuine and loyal and caring, and those are the qualities that make me want you as much as I do. But none of that matters if you aren't willing to meet me halfway."

She was staring at him in shock, and since she didn't seem inclined to reply to anything he'd just said, he knew this was the end. To them and what could have been.

With a heavy heart, he turned and walked back into the bedroom, leaving her in the living room, alone. Just as she preferred.

As THE BEDROOM door closed behind Connor, Rebecca drew in a deep shuddering breath, reeling over his admission. When her mind finally cleared, her first instinct was to deny what he'd said and the way he felt about her. But she couldn't bring herself to do it—because if she'd learned anything these past three days, it was that Connor was a man of his word. Most importantly, he had more integrity than her own father had ever possessed.

In that distinctive moment, she realized she had two choices. One, was to walk out of his hotel room with her dignity, heart and emotions intact, or two, finally confront the fears that had ruled so many years of her life.

She uncurled her fist and glanced down at the crumpled piece of paper in her hand. The words *bold, spontaneous* and *go for it* stared up at her, making her realize that maybe, possibly, she'd been given the pink heart with the same message for a reason. Not so much because of fate, but because her life, and her courage, needed that boost. That push. That shove.

Bold and spontaneous felt so good with Connor. And she knew that if she took the coward's way out and left now, that she risked the possibility of losing Connor forever.

Was she willing to take that chance?

Surprisingly, the answer was crystal clear, and it reverberated inside her with a firm and resounding *no*.

Squaring her shoulders, and preparing herself to be bolder and more spontaneous than she'd ever been before, she headed toward Connor's bedroom, opened the door, and stepped inside. To her surprise, she found him packing his belongings into his duffel bag.

While there was no reason for him to stay since their wedding duties were done, it was nearly four o'clock in the morning, way too early for him to be on the road.

"You're leaving?" she asked, and heard the panic in her own voice.

He spared her a brief glance before shoving a small stack of T-shirts into his bag. "There's nothing left for me to stay here for."

She winced, stung by his words, because she knew exactly what he was referring to. Her. Them.

She swallowed hard, trying to gulp down her fears at the same time. "What if I told you that you should stay? For us?"

He walked into the bathroom and returned seconds later with his toiletry bag. "I got the impression out there that there is no us."

He was moving so fast that he was making her dizzy. "Stop, Connor. Please."

There must have been something in her voice that reached him, because he finally halted by the bed. His gaze was direct, and his body language all but screamed *stay back*. Which she did. For now.

"When I agreed to our affair this weekend, I never thought that it would be anything more than a physical thing." When he continued to stare at her, she shifted anxiously on her bare feet and pushed herself to go on. "But instead, I came to realize what was missing from my life."

He crossed his arms over his broad chest and lifted a brow. "And what's that?"

"Fun. Laughter. Spontaneity." A smile wavered on her lips. "All because of you."

He shrugged. "Hey, that's what *friends* are for." His tone was laced with sarcasm.

He had every right to be frustrated with her, and she struggled to continue in the face of such opposition. "What I'm about to say isn't easy for me, but I hope you'll hear me out."

He remained quiet, but didn't move from where he was standing, and she took that as a positive sign.

"You already know what my childhood was like, and some fears die a lot harder than others. It's like I've been programmed to be responsible and practical, because my father was never those things. And once he was gone, I had to be even more sensible and dependable to give Celeste the stability and security that he left us without."

"That's understandable," he said, softening a bit.

She dampened her bottom lip with her tongue. "And then there's the fact that you're six years younger than I am."

He uncrossed the arms he'd folded over his chest, and let his arms hang loosely at his sides. "It's just a number, Rebecca."

"You're right," she said, nodding. Never once had she thought of him as immature. If anything, he was much wiser than his years because of what he'd faced as a child. "Then there's the issue of you spending money in ways that I can't understand because of who I am and how I grew up."

"I'm not like your father, Rebecca," he replied adamantly. "I invest my money and have plenty of it. I want more than I have in life, but by that I don't mean material goods. Those tangible things aren't important to me." He walked over to her and rubbed his hands up and down her arms, warming her from the outside in. "I want a relationship, one that isn't based on a woman wanting me for my money or what I can give her. I want *you,* because you're everything I've ever wanted in a woman, and more."

Could she truly be that lucky? It appeared that she was, and she would no longer question Fate, or even Cupid. "Okay," she whispered.

He frowned, looking uncertain. "Okay?"

"You can have me, any way you want me." She liked the sound of that. "But be patient with me, because I've got a lot of hangups and insecurities to deal with."

"I know." He grinned, showing off his boyish dimple. "But it's okay because I love you, Rebecca Moore. Just as you are."

Her heart seemed to beat double-time in her chest, and she let herself go with the warm, incredible feeling surging inside her. "I'm falling in love with you, too."

He kissed her, long and hard and deep, pouring emotion into the embrace, as well as a sense of security that eased her fears. By the time he ended the kiss, she was breathless and aroused.

"Do you realize it's Valentine's Day?" she asked, smiling up at him.

"Ummm," he said as he eased her backwards, until she was tumbling onto the bed and he was sprawled on top of her. "I guess that means I'll need to buy you a couple of pounds of chocolate from Sinfully Sweet, huh?"

She didn't know that it was possible to feel so happy. So content. "I have all the chocolate I need." She lifted her hand, showing him the half-heart wrapped in blue foil that she was still holding. "And I have your heart."

"That you do," he agreed.

As she gazed at the candy, Rebecca realized that they weren't so opposite after all. Just like the chocolate heart that had started it all, Connor was her other half. Her soul mate. The man she was meant to spend her life with.

And she planned to do exactly that.

CONSTANT CRAVING

Jacquie D'Alessandro

Prologue

WITH A SMILE of satisfaction, Ellie Fairbanks turned over the sign hanging on the sparkling clean shop window so that the residents of Austell would know that the town's newest store, Sinfully Sweet, was now open and ready for business.

A combination of nerves and anticipation rippled through her at the prospect of the first customer walking through the door. She ran her fingers lovingly over the glossy black and gilt hand-painted script letters adorning the front picture window, then touched the smaller letters beneath the name that read: *Extraordinary Chocolate Confections*. Would this store prove as successful to their scientific research as the last one she and Marcus had opened?

As if thinking Marcus's name conjured up her husband of twenty-seven years, his strong arms encircled her waist from behind. "Mmm," he murmured, nuzzling his lips to the sensitive skin behind her ear, shooting the same thrilling tingle down her spine he'd elicited from the first time he'd touched her. After all these years, his effect on her, her reaction to him…well, there was nothing in the least bit logical or scientific about it. But neither was there any denying it. "You smell…*délicieux*."

"The *chocolate* smells delicious, silly," she said with a smile at his atrocious French accent, tilting her neck to afford him better access. She inhaled deeply and the luscious aroma of chocolate filled her head. The logical scientist in her knew that further research was required to determine the exact amorous effects of chocolate on the human body, but the intuitive female in her instinctively knew that the delectable scent alone made her feel good.

"True," he agreed, playfully nipping her earlobe. "But you smell even better. Like chocolate-dipped Ellie. My favorite." Straightening, he rested his chin against her temple, and Ellie knew he was surveying the shop. As a scientist, Marcus was brilliant, but as a decorator, he was definitely…challenged. For the past three years, since they'd taken early retirement packages from Winthrop Laboratories and embarked on their own research experiment, he'd happily left the store decorations up to her. So far he'd applauded all her choices. Crossing her arms, she rested her hands on his and leaned back against him, absorbing his quiet strength and masculine warmth.

Relaxed in his embrace, she allowed her gaze to wander around the room. Skeins of bright northern California sunshine poured through the windows and glinted off the long glass counters displaying the delicious, decadent, silky-smooth chocolate candies for sale. The highlight of the display was the enormous crystal bowl filled with red, gold and silver foil-wrapped chocolate hearts—the perfect Valentine's Day display—and the distinctive pink-and-blue-wrapped oversize heart halves that were part of the store's special Valentine's Day prize giveaway.

She then cast her critical eye to the gleaming hardwood floors, shiny brass sconces adorning the rich, cherry-wood paneled walls, the simple yet elegant silver bud vases filled with long-stem red roses. Everything was perfect.

She felt Marcus nod against her temple. "Place looks beautiful, Ellie. Even better than the last store in the last town. Too bad we'll only be here for such a short time. You've outdone yourself."

"*We've* outdone ourselves," she corrected. "But still, I'm worried. This location…we're not on a main street as we usually are. I know our market research showed that Austell fit our target town profile perfectly—within two hours' drive of a major city, growing population and low chocolate sales—but what if the potential consumers don't find us? What if—?"

"Ellie." He cut off her question by turning her until they faced each other. Resting her hands against his chest, she absorbed the comforting beat of his heart against her palms, looked up into his steady, dark eyes, and felt her concerns slowly dissipate.

"They'll find us," he said softly. "Who could resist a store named Sinfully Sweet?"

"A name you weren't originally crazy about, if you'll recall. What had you wanted to call the shop when we first started our research? Oh, yes. Marcus's Candy Store." She made a face and looked toward the ceiling.

"So I'm not creative with store names." He waggled his brows in a very suggestive way and nudged his pelvis against hers. "I make up for it in other ways."

She nudged him back and smiled. "No argument here."

"And the ingenious Valentine's Day contest you thought up is sure to entice and intrigue the fine residents of Austell."

"I certainly hope so."

A frown burrowed between his brows. "I only hope it doesn't end up costing us a mint, which it might if we have multiple winners."

Waving away his concern, she said, "It's a business expense. Besides, even if the contest doesn't end up aiding our research, it promises to bring about very entertaining—and interesting—results." A grin curved her lips at the prospect. Each single, unattached Sinfully Sweet customer would receive one of the oversized chocolate hearts that had been cut in half—a pink-wrapped half for the women, a blue-wrapped half for the men—with each half containing a hidden message. Every man and woman who, before Valentine's Day, found the other person whose message matched theirs would receive a romantic dinner for two at The Winery, the five-star restaurant at the nearby Delaford Resort, and one hundred chocolate hearts.

Marcus touched a single fingertip to her bottom lip, yanking her from her thoughts. "That grin of yours looks positively wicked."

She lightly nibbled his finger then looped her arms around his neck. "I was just thinking about the prize of one hundred chocolate hearts. As I well know—thanks to personal experience as well as our research—an evening that involves chocolate is just so much more exciting."

"I couldn't agree more. Now all we need is more proof for the scientific community. And if all goes as anticipated at Sinfully Sweet and with the contest, another step will be taken in that direction." His gaze dropped to her mouth. "Speaking of chocolate, being surrounded by all this deliciousness is releasing an influx of endorphins—"

"That you'll need to save for later," she said, smothering a laugh and trying her best to look stern. "Besides, you have to actually *eat* the chocolate for the endorphins to be released."

"Not necessarily, and I hope to prove it with my new hypothesis—can the mere *smell* of chocolate trigger the release of endorphins? Our research so far indicates that eating chocolate leads to amorous behavior in a majority of subjects. Adding scent to the mix isn't a far stretch."

"I can't deny that every time I smell chocolate, I think of you."

"That's because it's what brought us together in the first place."

"Right. I probably wouldn't have noticed you at all if it hadn't been for the bag of chocolate kisses you always kept on your desk in the lab," she teased.

"Smartest thing I've ever done. I caught me quite a prize with that bag of chocolate. Finding data to support a scientific correlation between consuming chocolate and amorous behavior is the least I can do to repay the scientific community for bringing you into my life."

"Ditto. Besides, the research aspect is—"

"Delicious." He lowered his head and brushed his lips against hers.

"Mmm. In more ways than one. You know, you're pretty romantic for a scientist."

"Back at ya, darlin'."

"You should see me when I'm not wearing this apron."

"I live for the moment."

With a laugh, Ellie stepped out of his embrace. Her gaze moved to the door and her heart quickened at the sight of a car parking in front of the store. "Looks like we might have our first customer," she said.

Marcus gave her shoulder a squeeze. "Excellent. Let the games begin."

1

DANIEL MONTGOMERY TOSSED the large bag filled with moving supplies he'd just purchased into the back of his SUV, then closed the trunk with a satisfying thump. "That's one more thing I can cross off my to-do list."

"What's next?" asked his brother Kevin, not even attempting to stifle his yawn. "Hopefully something that involves a cup of coffee. If I'd known my offer to help you pack required waking up at the crack of dawn, I wouldn't have volunteered."

"It's almost ten a.m. That's hardly the crack of dawn."

"It is when you didn't go to bed until 5 a.m."

Daniel forced himself not to chuckle at Kevin's grumpy tone. "Maybe you should have gone to bed earlier."

"No can do. This is my last semester of college. It's my *duty* to stay out late."

Recalling that he'd pretty much felt the same way eight years ago during his last college semester, Daniel didn't argue. Instead he resettled his glasses on his nose, leaned against the SUV's bumper and slid his to-do list and pencil from the back pocket of his jeans.

After crossing off packing tape and bubble wrap, he said, "Still need to stop at the grocery store—"

"Yeah, where you need to get coffee—"

"—and beer and hot dogs. While we're there we'll pick up more empty boxes. Another dozen or so should do it. Besides my computer equipment, all that's left to pack are my books, CDs, DVDs, some kitchen stuff and my clothes." He blew out a long breath. "Another two weeks and I'll be leaving Austell behind."

Kevin's brows rose. "And that's good…right?"

Daniel hesitated then said, "Sure. Why do you ask?"

"Because you sounded weird. Like unhappy or unsure or something."

"Nah, it's all good. Taking the new job, moving to a new city, it's the right thing to do."

Wasn't it?

He frowned at the scuffed toes of his well-worn Nikes, his stomach tight with the same odd feeling that gripped him every time he questioned his decision to move. Which was crazy. Of course leaving Austell was the right thing to do.

In recent months it had seemed that his life had fallen into a boring, predictable rut. Something was missing—something he couldn't quite put a name to other than to know it filled him with an unsettling sensation of discontent. His recent thirtieth birthday had proven a turning point, jolting him to reassess his life. Make some changes. Try something new. Surely, it was just the anticipation of moving to Boston and starting a new job that caused the momentary stomach jitters.

Not only would the managerial position with prestigious Allied Computers' information technology department be a feather in his cap, being in a corporate office would get him out more. Give him more opportunities for a social life. Force him out of his well-worn rut.

"I think leaving this small town will be good for you, man." Kevin said as if reading Daniel's thoughts. "How you can have a social life here," he waved his arm to encompass all of Main Street, "is beyond me."

"It's a challenge," Daniel agreed. It didn't help that his current job of designing websites didn't require him to leave his home office. In the last two months especially, ever since he'd broken up with Nina—or rather, she'd broken up with him—it seemed as if he'd turned into an all work, no play recluse. But thanks to his life reassessment, all that was about to change.

He looked up and his gaze wandered over the old-fashioned storefronts cast in golden rays of sunshine. He could understand why at twenty-one Kevin couldn't see Austell's quiet appeal, but then he and Kevin were pretty much opposites when it came to living arrangements. Daniel had always preferred low key while Kevin thrived in his frat house surroundings.

Yeah, it would be hard to leave this quaint, picturesque town with its historic downtown, quiet streets, well-kept park and friendly residents where he'd lived for the past eight years, ever since discovering the town while attending the nearby college. Austell had given him a sense of belonging that he'd missed after leaving home. But hey, bigger and better things awaited him.

"So what's next on the list?" Kevin asked. "Tell me quick. Before I fall asleep standing here."

Daniel's gaze fell back to his list and his jaw tightened as he focused on the next two items. "Sod and some top soil."

"Yippee. What's that for?"

"I guess you didn't see my backyard."

"Nope."

"Consider yourself lucky. Another plus about moving is that I'll have new neighbors. No more dealing with Carlie Pratt, aka The Scatterbrain With the Unruly Dogs That Routinely Dig Up My Yard and Wake Me Up At Ungodly Hours With Their Barking, or Miss Headache and the Crazy Canine Crew, for short."

Kevin grimaced. "Bummer. Maybe you should get earplugs."

"I'm better off with the top soil. I'd need a hell of a lot of earplugs to fill up those holes in my backyard."

Daniel pressed his lips together so as not to burst out laughing at Kevin's blank expression. Humor that wasn't Three Stooges slapstick or didn't involve bodily functions more often than not sailed right over his younger brother's head. "Dude, I meant for your *ears,*" Kevin said slowly, as if explaining it to a first grader, "so the barking wouldn't wake you up."

"Oh," Daniel said, very seriously. "Good idea."

Actually, he'd tried earplugs but they didn't help much as they always seemed to fall out. Not much fun waking up with a wad of wax stuck in your hair. But in two weeks, he wouldn't have to worry about that anymore.

Nope, he sure wouldn't miss the chaos that had lived on the other side of his backyard fence since Carlie and The Hole Diggers had moved in three months ago. He wouldn't mind so much if she'd just keep her chaos on *her* side of the wooden fence that separated their backyards, but her dogs—two rambunctious puppies, both of whom showed promise of growing to be horse-like in size—managed to escape almost on a daily basis. And they somehow always ended up in his yard, much to the detriment of his lawn. His Realtor had taken one look at the crater-like muddy holes marking his grass and then decreed in an ominous tone that reeked of plummeting property value, "That mess *must* be fixed *immediately*."

Well, he'd fixed it, but it wasn't long before Peanut Butter and Jelly, P.B. and J. for short—and sheesh, who named their dogs after *food* anyway?—had returned and wreaked havoc on his yard again. Since when did dogs like to dig holes so much? It was as if those crazy canines thought freakin' pirate booty was buried in his backyard. Yeah, Carlie had profusely apologized each time, and he couldn't deny she looked pretty cute while doing so, but, c'mon, enough was enough. Probably he wouldn't have minded so much if he weren't selling the house. Probably. But according to his Realtor, many potential buyers harbored aversions to backyards that looked as if explosives had detonated in them.

"Can't say I'm turning cartwheels at the prospect of going to the nursery for sod and dirt," Kevin said. "What else ya got?"

Daniel once again consulted his list. "Stamps at the post office."

"That doesn't sound the least bit like 'coffee at Starbucks.' What else?"

"Spackle and caulk at the hardware store."

"You're killing me."

"Birthday gift for Mom."

Kevin's eyes widened. "Whoa, I'd totally forgotten."

"So you owe me big time."

"Oh, boy. That doesn't sound good. I'm going to end up filling doggie-dug holes with dirt, aren't I?"

"'Fraid so."

"But her birthday's on Valentine's Day. That's, like, *two weeks* away."

"I want to buy her present today and get it mailed off before I get buried under with moving."

Kevin's expression turned hopeful. "Since we always get Mom chocolate for her birthday, I foresee something sweet to eat in my immediate future. And where there's chocolate, coffee can't be far away." He rubbed his hands together. "Let's go."

Since he couldn't disagree that buying chocolate sounded a lot better than buying sod and dirt, Daniel pushed off the bumper and slipped his to-do list and pencil back into his jeans' pocket.

"There's a new candy place opening today that I read about in the newspaper." He headed toward the corner and Kevin fell into step beside him. "It's called Sinfully Sweet and it specializes in chocolates." He grinned. "I think Mom has met her match."

His grin widened at the thought of their mom, a teacher at the same high school he and Kevin had graduated from. Those teenagers didn't stand a chance against Norma Montgomery. With thirty years of teaching under her belt, not to mention raising two kids of her own—three if you included Dad as she laughingly insisted you should—she knew every trick in the book. Since her birthday was on Valentine's Day, no one in the family ever had a problem figuring out what to buy her for a gift. Ever since he'd been a kid it was the same thing: chocolate. Over the years it had become something of a joke among them all, with Mom trying to guess what sort of chocolate concoctions she'd receive, and he, Dad and Kevin trying to come up with something unusual she'd never guess. Only she always seemed to guess—had to be that "eyes in the back of her head" mom thing.

Well, Mom might be hard to catch off guard, but this year he had an advantage, or so he hoped, in the form of Sinfully Sweet. According to the ad in the newspaper, the shop promised an amazing array of extraordinary chocolate confections.

While he and Kevin walked the short distance to Larchmont Street where the store was located, Daniel enjoyed the contrast of the warm northern California sun tempered by the cool breeze. They'd no sooner turned the corner, however, when the sight of a familiar figure walking toward them slowed his footsteps. Then he halted abruptly. As if he'd walked into a wall, and stared.

Kevin, who'd fallen a few steps behind him, bumped into his back and grunted at the impact. When Daniel remained frozen in place, Kevin moved to stand beside him and asked, "I thought you said the store was this way. What's the problem, bro?"

His powers of speech freakishly suspended, Daniel continued to stare. At Carlie Pratt, sans P.B. and J.—which meant the devilish duo was probably at this very moment joyfully digging more holes in his yard. Carlie Pratt, who, with the golden sunshine gleaming on her tousled, shoulder-length reddish brown curls, appeared to be surrounded by a gilt halo.

But that was the only angelic looking thing about her.

She moved forward with a slow, wickedly seductive stroll that brought to mind cool satin sheets, and hot, sweaty sex. Damn, what a walk the woman had. Like steamy sin in motion. How was it that he'd never noticed it before? Probably because every time he saw her she was rushing around after her dogs. Or driving her car. Or had her arms filled with grocery bags. Or was carrying the large, portable padded table she brought to her massage therapy clients' homes. Or was sitting on a lawn chair in her backyard, where the grass, to be fair, was marred with even more holes than his.

Well, she wasn't rushing or driving or sitting now, and the sinuous sway of her curvy hips as she leisurely walked, her attention focused on the store windows, rooted him to the spot as if he'd turned into a pillar of cement. Normally she was dressed in either a bulky sweater or loose-fitting clothes that resembled hospital scrubs. But not today. No, today she was dressed in a pair of snug faded jeans that hugged every gorgeous curve—and damn, she had more curves than a roller coaster—and a V-neck sweater the color of a ripe, juicy peach. She all but made his mouth water.

Kevin clapped a hand on Daniel's shoulder then said in an undertone, "Whoa, dude. I see what put you in this trance. She. Is. Fine."

Yes. She. Was. He'd thought her attractive from the day

she'd moved in, but had ignored the observation as he'd been with Nina at the time. Then, even after Nina was out of the picture, with both him and Carlie working, they'd seen little of each other—except for the puppy incidents.

Well, he was seeing plenty of her now.

And liked everything he saw.

For a guy who prided himself on being practical, logical and sensible, he experienced a rush of heated lust that all but incinerated and stupefied him where he stood. A reaction that could be described as neither practical, logical nor sensible.

And apparently he wasn't the only one who liked what he saw.

"If that's what the girls in Austell are like," Kevin said, "I'm thinking you're crazy to move. And the way you're looking at her, man, you're a *goner.*" He tapped Daniel non-too-gently under the chin. "You might want to lose the slack-jawed, bug-eyed look before you introduce yourself."

Daniel swallowed and relocated his voice. "No introduction needed. I already know her."

"Yeah? Know her as in the biblical sense?"

A crystal-clear image of Carlie naked in his bed, materialized in his mind's eye, and with a frown, he blinked it away. But not without the image leaving a trail of heat in its wake.

"No." He lowered his voice further. "She's my pesky neighbor, the one with the hole-digging dogs."

From the corner of his eye he saw Kevin's speculative look. "You're not looking at her as if you think she's a pest. If you want my opinion—"

"I don't—"

"She's enough to make a guy want to cover his yard with dog biscuits."

Daniel turned and looked at his brother. He wasn't sure how his expression appeared, but whatever it was, it had Kevin putting up his hands in mock surrender. "Hey, I was just making an observation. No need to shoot me the 'hands off' glare. I want a yard like I want a bad rash. She's all yours."

A frown yanked down Daniel's brows. "She's not all mine. I don't want her. Hell, I can't wait to move away from her."

"Uh huh. Okay. Whatever you say." He jerked his head. "She's stopped."

Daniel's head whipped around. Carlie had paused to look into a store window, affording him a side view, which was just as curvy and outstanding as the front view. The breeze caught her hair, blowing several shiny curls across her face which she tucked behind her ear with an absent gesture. Then without glancing their way, she entered the store and vanished from his view.

Her disappearance yanked him from the stupor into which he'd fallen, and he blinked and rubbed his hand over his face. That's when he realized that his glasses had slid down his nose and his jaw was once again hanging open. Definitely not his best look. Good thing she hadn't seen him. She'd think him a gawking, slack-jawed, nerdy techno-geek. While he couldn't deny he was a techno-geek, and by association kinda nerdy, no way was he a slack-jawed gawker.

At least he hadn't been until thirty seconds ago.

He started walking, his limbs feeling oddly stiff, as if they really had turned to cement, and he craned his neck to see which store she'd entered. He vaguely noted Kevin walking beside him and pretended he didn't hear his brother's poorly suppressed chuckles. Seconds later he realized she'd gone into Sinfully Sweet.

It suddenly struck him that the words *sinfully sweet* and *Carlie Pratt* seemed to go together very well. Sorta like *hot* and *steamy*. *Hot* and *bothered*. *Hot* and *who the hell had lit his jeans on fire?*

Hmmm…was she making a purchase for herself—or looking for a Valentine's gift for a boyfriend? He frowned. Did she *have* a boyfriend? He hadn't ever seriously considered that question before. When she'd first moved in, he'd assumed she had several boyfriends after he'd observed, through his home office window, a number of men entering and leaving her house. Then, when he'd returned her muddy puppies to her the first time they'd dug under the fence into his yard, she'd told him she was a massage therapist at The Delaford Resort just outside of town near Crystal Lake, but that she freelanced on the side, treating a select few, long-term clients at the house. She'd made no mention of a boyfriend, and he hadn't particularly wanted to know.

But all of a sudden, he very much wanted to know.

Yet with his brain once again firing on all cylinders, he frowned and shook his head at this sudden need for knowledge about her personal life, then decided to call it…simple curiosity. Yeah, that's all it was. It wasn't as if her boyfriend status really mattered—especially as he was moving in two weeks.

Kevin nudged him in the ribs. "Hey, there's a coffee shop. I'm going to go order a caffeine I.V. drip. Once I'm revived, I'll meet you in the candy store. That'll give you some time to chat with your neighbor you don't, um, like."

Man, was there anything more annoying than a smirking younger brother? "I never said I didn't *like* her."

"Oh. Right. You said you didn't *want* her."

"That's correct."

"Oh, yeah, that's totally obvious. Anybody could see that. Really." With a chuckle, Kevin made his way toward the coffee shop.

Daniel stood on the sidewalk for several seconds, reorganizing his thoughts that the sight of Carlie Pratt had scattered, splattered and fried. What the hell was wrong with him? Clearly he, too, suffered from caffeine deprivation for the mere sight of her to knock him sideways like that. And why the hell was he still standing out here? Sinfully Sweet had been his destination. He had every reason to go into that store. And if he just happened to strike up a conversation with her, well, that was only the neighborly thing to do, right?

And as much as he might not like it or want to, he was feeling downright neighborly.

Pulling in a bracing breath, he rolled his shoulders, then walked purposefully toward Sinfully Sweet's glass door.

2

THE INSTANT CARLIE stepped inside Sinfully Sweet, her senses were inundated with chocolate, coaxing a moan of pleasure from her throat. Decadent treats beckoned from behind the counter and tempted from a colorful display of foil-wrapped hearts in the center of the store. She inhaled, filling her head with the luscious, mouth-watering aroma. She could almost hear the delectable sweets chanting, *Taste me, taste me.*

Oh boy, this upscale store was the last place a self-confessed chocoholic on a tight budget should be, but after seeing the newspaper ad announcing the grand opening and the intriguing Valentine's Day promotion, she'd been unable to resist the temptation. She could resist a lot of things, but chocolate wasn't one of them. Nor was the chance to win a fabulous Valentine's dinner date at The Delaford's five-star restaurant. One glimpse inside Sinfully Sweet let her know that her willpower not to overspend would be sorely tested.

Just think about the whopper tuition you still have to pay, her inner voice advised. *And the freakishly expensive text books you need.*

Right. As if she could forget. With another year to go before she earned her bachelor's degree in occupational therapy, and the added burden of having to shoulder the house's entire rent payment after her friend Missy had eloped two days before they were supposed to move in together, money was tight. Certainly tighter than she'd envisioned it being by the time she was twenty-eight, but as she'd discovered, life had a habit of throwing curve balls when you expected a nice, easy slider.

Still, she wouldn't let anything keep her from finishing her degree, then securing the job she'd dreamed of—one where she'd help people who faced challenges helping themselves. Like her grandfather, whose stroke ten years ago had set her on the course she'd chosen for herself. And whose recovery continued to inspire her to this day.

At first she'd considered not moving into the house, but given that she would have lost two month's rent and her security deposit, not to mention the fact that she desperately wanted a place with a yard for P.B. and J., she'd moved in, thinking she'd look for another roommate. But after enjoying a few weeks of just her and the puppies, she'd stopped looking and tightened her financial belt in other places to make up the difference.

Indulging in gourmet chocolates had been one of the luxuries she'd painfully axed. Good for her piggybank, but tragic as far as her taste buds were concerned.

But surely after two months of denying herself, of surviving on supermarket chocolate, she deserved a small treat. Right? Her gaze zeroed in on a display of imported truffles and her mouth watered. Oh, God, something from Belgium would be so fabulous….

Clasping her hands together, she closed her eyes and drew in another delicious breath, vaguely aware of the door opening and closing behind her, then the sound of approaching footsteps.

"Wow, it smells really good in here."

Her eyes popped open as she instantly recognized the deep, husky voice coming from directly behind her, and with a quick intake of startled breath, she whirled around. Less than an arm's length away stood Daniel Montgomery, her very attractive neighbor. Who looked very attractive indeed in a dark blue flannel shirt that did great things for his hazel eyes rimmed by his black rectangular-framed glasses and a pair of faded jeans that did great things for everything else. Her very attractive neighbor who had, since the minute she first saw him, the weirdest effect on her pulse. Who rendered her either tongue-tied or turned her into a blathering dolt. And who, except for the holes P.B. and J. kept digging in his yard, didn't even know she existed. And even if he did, what difference did it make? He had a girlfriend. She'd seen them sharing a kiss on his front porch the day she moved in. Plus, he was moving.

Figures. First time in three years she had a straight guy for a neighbor, one who was actually cute, not to mention intelligent, and patient—as proven by his run-ins with P.B. and J.—and who wasn't a whacko. And he was taken. Although from what she could see, *all* the good ones were taken. It seemed that lately the only sort of men she attracted were jerks who thought that "massage therapist" was another name for Woman Who Wants to be Groped and Leered At.

Daniel Montgomery had certainly never leered at her. Or so much as looked at her with anything other than exasperation and mild annoyance. Not that she could blame him, what with the mess the puppies made in his yard. And not that she was complaining about the lack of a leer. Heck, no. She hated to be leered at.

But still, the guy could have at least *looked*. You know, in an admiring, complimentary sort of way.

Sort of like he was…doing right now?

Her heart performed a jiggly little dance and she blinked. Surely the sunlight streaming through the window had obscured her vision. She blinked again and ridiculous disappointment flooded her. Yup, the sun had indeed played tricks on her because that wasn't an admiring look at all. No, it was more like confusion. Like he'd never seen her before. The sun must have messed with his vision, too.

His befuddled expression prompted her to say, "Hi, Daniel. It's, uh, me. Carlie." *Uh ,oh. Tongue-tied time*.

He seemed to snap out of whatever dazed state he'd fallen into—probably a result of the chocolate sensory overload—and nodded. "I know. Hi, Carlie."

Just the way he said her name, in that soft, raspy way, hiked up her temperature a few degrees. His nod had sent his black-rimmed glasses slipping down his nose and he pushed them back up with a practiced gesture while Carlie pressed her lips together to suppress the feminine sigh that rose to her lips. Darn it, there was absolutely *no* logical explanation why she should be so turned on by those nerdy glasses of his, but for some mystifying reason she found them incredibly erotic. One look at him, and all she could think about was planting a kiss on him that would steam up his lenses but good.

Which was *really* inexplicable as Daniel Montgomery was *soooo* totally not her type. She liked jocks, and while it appeared that Daniel was in good shape, he had "computer geek" written all over him. From what she could tell, he spent most of his time in his house, no doubt sitting in front of his PC since he'd once mentioned some sort of home-based computer business. Probably got his jollies counting gigabytes or pixels or whatever the heck they were. Oddly, none of that hadn't stopped her crazy attraction to him. Maybe she was suffering from some freakish hormone imbalance, 'cause, really, give her an athletic, outdoorsy kind of guy any day.

Not that she'd had much luck lately with athletic, outdoorsy sorts, but hey, she'd find Mr. Right eventually. Someday. Probably. Maybe she'd even meet him by winning Sinfully Sweet's Valentine's Day contest. Which she should really go check out instead of staring at Daniel. Unfortunately, that was easier said than done. And really, he could always stop staring at *her* in that very distracting way and get the conversational ball rolling here.

He cleared his throat. "So…how're P.B. and J.?"

"You mean my dogs?" She swallowed a groan and barely refrained from smacking herself on the forehead. *Oh, brilliant reply.* But damn it, he shouldn't be asking her these complicated questions right after he'd knocked her silly with his unexpected appearance.

His lips quirked. "Well, why don't we start with them and then move on to all the other P.B. and J.'s we know?"

That hint of a smile drew her attention to his mouth. His incredibly tempting, beautiful mouth. She didn't know if there was such a thing as a male mouth model, but if there was, Daniel would reach superstar status. His well-formed lips somehow managed to look soft and firm at the same time. Like something that both angels and the devil himself had fashioned purely to see if a heavenly/wicked ideal could be achieved—and they'd met with spectacular success. Like the chocolate, his mouth seemed to beckon her with the same seductive chant: *Taste me, taste me.*

She jerked her gaze back up to his, then licked her own lips in an effort to get them working since they'd apparently forgotten how to form words. "The puppies…they're, um, fine. Great. Safely secured inside my house."

He wiped his brow with an exaggerated gesture. "Whew. My backyard just breathed a sigh of relief."

Then he smiled, a sort of lopsided grin that in spite of not being perfectly symmetrical was somehow utterly…perfect. A smile that creased a pair of sexy dimples in his cheeks that her fingers—and lips—positively itched to explore.

Everything female in her stood up at attention and quivered.

"What brings you to Sinfully Sweet?" he asked.

She leaned a bit closer—certainly not to get a whiff of him—but to confide in a conspiratorial whisper, "I'm afraid I have a weakness for chocolate." She leaned back and suppressed an *oooooh* of pleasure. He smelled great. Clean. Fresh. Masculine. Delicious.

"A weakness for chocolate, huh? Doesn't everyone?"

She laughed, proud that she managed to sound so cool when she felt like she stood over a barbeque spit. "You, too?"

"'Fraid so." Something that looked decidedly heated and hungry and, well, admiring, flickered in his gaze. "Among other things."

Whoa. If she didn't know better, she'd say her sexy, nerdy neighbor whose smile had damn near stopped her heart was *flirting* with her. She instantly discarded the annoyingly pulse-quickening thought. The last thing she needed was any more useless Daniel-induced fantasies running naked through her mind.

Er, make that just *running* through her mind.

Right. Because naked was not a word she should even be thinking while Daniel was around. Of course not. Why, with the guy sitting in front of a computer screen all day, he probably looked all soft and squishy naked.

Although…

Her eyeballs stole a surreptitious glance down his form. His rolled back shirt sleeves revealed some very nice forearms. And his chest looked strong, his shoulders wide and sturdy. And the way he filled out those jeans, well, there didn't appear to be anything soft or squishy about *that*.

Before she could ponder further on the fascinating fade patterns on his Levi's, she looked up and met his gaze—a gaze filled with an expression that made it clear he knew he'd just been majorly ogled.

Embarrassment erupted hot tingles under her skin, and she pressed her lips together to keep from blurting out something that would cause the medical examiner to list "Died of Acute Mortification" on her death certificate. Something like *I wasn't really ogling you. I was just trying to picture you naked.*

Silence swelled between them for several long seconds, with Carlie cursing the ridiculous effect this man had on her. No one had ever thrown her into this tongue-tied/babbling state before, and damn it, she didn't like it. When a soft feminine voice behind her said, "Good morning," she gratefully jerked her gaze away from Daniel and turned, feeling as if she'd been thrown a lifeline to keep from drowning in the Pool of Humiliation.

A petite, attractive woman who appeared to be in her early fifties, wearing a white apron with Sinfully Sweet embroidered across the top, smiled at them.

"Welcome to Sinfully Sweet," the woman said, her brown-eyed gaze filled with warmth and what appeared to be lively speculation as it bounced between her and Daniel. "I'm Ellie Fairbanks, the owner, and I'm delighted you've come for the grand opening. May I help you?"

Carlie smiled in return, thankful that her mental acuity had returned now that she was no longer looking at Daniel. "I'll have two of everything," she said.

Ellie's melodic laugh combined with the deep rumble of Daniel's chuckle. "Are you shopping for Valentine's Day?" Ellie asked after quick introductions had been exchanged. "A special something for that special someone?" Again her gaze bounced between her and Daniel. "Perhaps a special something for each other?"

Heat suffused Carlie's cheeks. Ack! Clearly her ogling of Daniel had been so obvious that even the store owner had picked up on it. "Not for each other," she said in a rush, throwing out the denial before Daniel could, in an effort to salvage what little bit of her pride still remained. "We're just neighbors."

"Right," Daniel said, moving to stand next to her. From the corner of her eye she saw him push up his glasses. "Just neighbors."

"And we won't even be that for much longer, since Daniel's house is for sale and he's moving in a couple of weeks," Carlie blabbed, her mouth running amok as she suddenly abandoned *tongue-tied* and morphed into *blathering dolt*. She again pressed her lips together to stem the lava-like flow of words as she could easily envision herself saying something to Daniel that would force *her* to move—to another continent. Like *You've had me since the minute I laid eyes on you, and that sexy, dimpled smile just clinched the deal. Wanna come over for a warm massage and hot sex?*

"Well, I'm glad you decided to visit Sinfully Sweet before you moved, Daniel," Ellie said with a smile. "If you enjoy our chocolates—and I'm sure you will—we can ship your favorites to your new home."

"Sounds great," Daniel said. "And the shipping services are just what I need today since I'm looking for a birthday present for my mom. Something out of the ordinary."

"You've definitely come to the right place. I'm certain we can find something you'll like."

"Daniel probably needs something for his girlfriend, too," Carlie said, the words sneaking out before she could clamp her runaway lips. Double *ack*! She took a quick look around, praying she'd discover some other lip-flapping fool in the store she could blame for those words, but sadly her prayer went unanswered. That being the case, she didn't even bother to hope for the floor to open up and swallow her.

"I don't have a girlfriend."

Daniel's softly spoken words had Carlie turning toward him so fast she risked whiplash.

"You don't?" she and Ellie asked in unison. Ellie sounded surprised and curious. Carlie noted *she* also sounded surprised. And positively breathless.

He shook his head. "No."

"But you did," Carlie said.

"Yes."

"So you broke up."

"Yup."

A bolt of heat, along with an odd sensation that felt like her hormones applauding, rippled through her. Still, why were men so frustratingly monosyllabic? Getting information out of them was like trying to drag a sausage through a needle hole. Good grief, didn't men know that women thrived on *details?*

The urge to fire out a barrage of questions along the lines of "Who had broken up with whom and why?" trembled on her lips, but she managed to contain them. What difference did it make?

Yeah, her inner voice agreed. *It doesn't matter. The important thing is that he's no longer taken!*

"What about you, Carlie?" Ellie's voice broke into her reverie. "Do you have a boyfriend?"

Carlie looked at the shop owner but was very much aware of the weight of Daniel's stare as she hesitated. Six months ago she could have said yes. But then Paul had issued an ultimatum, and she'd chosen the "or we're finished" option. She'd never regretted her decision, but she couldn't deny that she missed having a man in her life to share things with. Like movies. And meals. Conversation. Laughter. Sex.

She shook her head. "No. No boyfriend."

Ellie's beaming smile encompassed both her and Daniel. "Well, as you're both unattached, you'll qualify for our special Valentine's Day dinner prize with your first purchase." After explaining the rules, Ellie said, "Who knows? Maybe you'll find your perfect match and win."

"I'd like that," Carlie said. Certainly a date would be nice after the dry spell she'd experienced the past few months. But she had the sinking feeling that with the way her luck had been going lately, if she won, her "perfect match" would be some unemployed loser who hated dogs and had an aversion to bathing.

"Why don't you look around, Carlie," Ellie suggested, "while I show Daniel a few things for his mother?"

"All right."

"Just holler if you see something you like," Ellie said with a wink as she led Daniel toward the counter.

"Will do," Carlie said, sorely tempted to holler as her gaze took in the very fine view of Daniel's jean-clad butt.

Oh, yeah, she'd seen something she liked all right. And it had nothing to do with chocolate.

3

DANIEL USED THE sharp end of his shovel to break open another bag of topsoil. In spite of the cool, early evening breeze, his T-shirt stuck to him like a second skin. Nothing like lugging heavy bags of dirt, then filling in holes and laying sod to work up a sweat. Kevin had stuck with him for the rest of his errands, but once they'd arrived back at the house, his brother had taken one look at the backyard and made a hasty exit.

"Gotta study, man," Kevin had claimed as he'd headed swiftly for the door. "Big test on Monday. Good luck with those holes. And your neighbor," he'd added with a broad wink.

Now, three hours later, with the sun's waning light streaking the sky with fiery reds and smudges of mauve, and casting long shadows across his yard, only two rolls of sod remained. After finishing, he'd shower, grab some dinner, and then…nothing.

With a sigh, Daniel thunked his shovel point into the ground and stacked his hands on the handle. And then another evening alone stretched out before him like a dark, yawning cavern, forcing him to admit what he'd tried so hard to deny.

He was lonely.

So lonely he ached with it. Sure, there were friends he could call, e-mail, or chat with online, but as he well knew, neither the phone nor the computer would relieve the growing emptiness inside him. He supposed he could walk around the block and find a neighbor to talk to, but a brief "hi, how are you?" wouldn't satisfy him either. That would be like settling for a fast-food burger when you craved filet mignon.

The mere thought of the word "neighbor" brought a vivid,

mental image of Carlie into his mind. Carlie, with her shiny, cinnamon curls, sunny smile, and jaw-dropping curves. Carlie, whose golden brown gaze had skimmed over him in Sinfully Sweet in a way that had made him feel as if he'd been dropped into a steaming cauldron.

Carlie, who didn't have boyfriend.

Well, he'd wanted to know and he'd found out. And had very much liked the answer.

Now he just needed to decide what to do about it, a mental debate that had raged in his head all afternoon.

I should ask her out.

It's crazy to ask her out—I'm moving.

Yeah, but I'm not moving to Mars, for cryin' out loud.

A two-thousand-mile distance between two people might as well be a galaxy.

So just have fun with her for the next two weeks. She'd know the time limit right up front. We could enjoy each other, then say sayonara, adios, buh-bye.

He couldn't deny that last option sounded pretty damn appealing. Worst-case scenario? After one evening together they'd realize they couldn't stand each other and, so what, since he'd be gone in two weeks? Best-case scenario is they'd have some no-strings-attached fun, then he'd drive away from her and her zany dogs with a happy wave and head toward his exciting new job and life. Yeah, that sounded like a great idea.

But there was one possible hitch in his great idea. What if Carlie told him to get lost?

Except for that unmistakable ogle this morning, she'd never given him any indication she found him attractive. But there'd definitely been interest in her eyes today.

Hadn't there?

He blew out a frustrated breath and dragged a hand through his hair. Maybe not. Maybe he'd read her all wrong. Maybe she'd just had something in her eye. Who the hell knew? Figuring out women was like navigating a mine field wearing a blindfold. According to Nina, Daniel couldn't have traveled through the mine field with a map, a guide, and a GPS system to show him the way—an assessment he totally didn't agree with, by the way. Like most men, he might suffer from bouts of confusion where women were concerned, but he wasn't as *completely* clueless as his ex-girlfriend claimed. Still, why couldn't women just *look* like women, but be easy to figure out—like men? Which only brought him back to the question of whether Carlie had really ogled him, or if it had just been a case of wishful thinking. Maybe—

A soft, low moaning sound cut off his thoughts.

"Ooooooh."

His brows furrowed into a frown. What the hell was that?

"Aaaaahhhh."

His frown deepened. Whatever it was, it sounded—

"Oooooooh. Yeah. Mmmmmm…"

Human.

"Hmmmmmm…ohhhhhh…myyyyyy…"

And female.

"Yeah, ohhhh…that's incredible…"

And sexually aroused.

"Soooooo good…so, so good…"

But where—? His head whipped around and his gaze zeroed in like a laser beam on the fence separating his and—

"Ohhhh, God…"

Carlie's backyard.

"That is sooooooo…aaaaaah…good…"

Everything inside him stilled. For about two seconds. Then, *whoosh*, heat sizzled through him like he'd been struck by lightning, pulsing fire to every nerve. A series of low, guttural, velvety-rough gasps drifted toward him, luring him like a siren's call. Unable to resist the enticement, he released his shovel and moved toward the sound. That sexy, aroused female sound that had everything male in him on red alert.

His conscience spoke to him, as though in the form of a mini, halo-wearing angel. "Daniel Montgomery, don't you even think about looking over that fence."

Another voice, which obviously belonged to a pitch-fork

toting horned devil, said, "Are you kidding me? Whatever's going on over there is definitely a must-see."

"It's none of our business," the angel voice said primly.

Daniel paused and dragged his hands down his face.

"Hey, if we can hear it in our yard, then we have every right to see it, too," the devil's voice shot back.

"Ohhhh, God. Ohhh, God…"

Unable to stop himself, Daniel moved toward the fence, feeling like one of those rats being led by the Pied Piper's seductive music.

"The girl is entitled to her privacy," the angel whispered.

"Oh, button it, Miss Goody Two-Shoes," the devil sneered.

Daniel frowned and mentally shrugged off the two combatants and continued walking. One quick peek. Just to make sure she was okay.

"Whoaaaaaaaaa, baby…"

Damn. She sure sounded okay. And since her moans were the only ones he heard, it seemed clear she was alone. 'Cause show him a guy who could elicit those incredible sounds from a woman and still remain silent himself, and he'd show you a guy with no vocal chords. Just listening to her had Daniel aroused and pressing his lips together to contain a groan.

The fence loomed before him, cast in the deepening shadows from the oncoming twilight. Drawing a deep breath, he took the final two steps. Then looked over the top.

And saw her.

She lay on a blue-and-white striped lounge chair, her hair fanned out around her shoulders, her arms raised above her head. Dressed in the same clothes she'd worn earlier today, she stretched sinuously on the cushion as another raspy groan passed her lips—full, pouty lips she then slowly licked in a way that seemed to open a valve in Daniel's neck, draining all the blood from his brain and redirecting it to his groin.

She rolled onto her side, a position that highlighted her fabulous curves, and examined the contents of a small silver foil box set on the round resin table beside her. After taking a bite from whatever she selected from the box, she eased onto her back, closed her eyes and the throaty, erotic sounds of pleasure started again.

"Ohhhhhh…so good…sooooo good…"

His gaze flicked back to the silver box and recognition hit him, as he had a similar one himself. The box was from Sinfully Sweet.

A deep sigh of utter delight drifted toward him and he found himself gripping the top of the fence, unable to tear his gaze from her. With her body sinuously shifting and those erotic sounds coming from her glistening lips, she inspired more fantasies than his blood-deprived brain could even process. And all this because of chocolate. She was practically orgasmic over *chocolate*. What the hell would a woman who responded like that to *candy* be like in bed?

Wild. Uninhibited. Passionate. Insatiable.

Delicious.

No doubt about it, she was certainly a woman a guy would want to give chocolate to every damn day.

God help him, just watching her, just listening to her, hardened him to the point of pain. But damn it, he wasn't some perverted Peeping Tom. Usually. Time to make his presence known. And he'd do that. As soon as he unswallowed his tongue. An accomplishment that was only achieved with the greatest of efforts.

"I'll have what you're having," he said, his voice sounding as if he'd swallowed a handful of gravel along with his tongue.

She froze mid-wriggle and her eyes popped open. Their gazes met and held and he wondered if she could see the hunger he knew had to be blazing in his eyes. No way he could hide it. And that hunger had nothing to do with chocolate.

She slowly swung her feet to the ground then rose, moving toward him with a hypnotic sway of her hips that did absolutely nothing to relieve the discomfort occurring in the front of his jeans.

"You want what I'm having?" she asked in a smoky voice as she approached.

"Absolutely."

She paused about three feet from the fence, but in his fantasy-addled mind he still saw her undulating. With the last fading strands of golden sunlight highlighting her hair, her eyes gleaming with mischief, and holding a half-eaten piece of chocolate between her fingers, she looked like the personification of Temptation. "Well, there're a couple of problems."

"How fortunate that I'm an expert problem solver. Lay yourself, uh, them on me."

"Well, first, as you can see, I've already taken a bite."

"I don't mind."

"You're not worried I might have a head cold?"

"Not a bit."

"Then there's the issue that I only bought four of these Belgian truffles from Sinfully Sweet, and this is my *last piece*. And it is exceptionally outstanding."

"Really? I couldn't tell," he teased.

"Oh, it's fabulous. Any sort of chocolate will give me tingles. But it takes a very special type of chocolate to inspire a *chocogasm*."

Daniel's imagination immediately conjured up a series of steamy images involving him and her and chocolate and orgasms and, holy hell, sweat broke out between his shoulder blades.

"Chocogasm," he repeated slowly, savoring the word as one would a decadent treat. "That's very…descriptive. And intriguing. I want to experience one."

"You'd be crazy not to."

He nodded his chin toward her half-eaten piece of chocolate. "So how about it? All the problems solved?"

"Not quite. Unfortunately, when it comes to chocolate, I'm sharing impaired."

"I'll give you a million dollars."

"Do you *have* a million dollars?"

"No. But if I did, I'd give it to you."

Her gaze shifted between him and her chocolate, then she shook her head. "Sorry."

"If you share yours with me, I'll share mine with you."

Interest flared in her eyes. "Share your what?"

Anything you want. "My chocolate."

"Oh? What kind do you have? Stuff left over from last Halloween, I bet."

"Nope." He rested his forearms along the top of the fence and leaned forward. "Belgian truffles. Assorted flavors. A pound box of them from Sinfully Sweet."

Her eyes widened. "You do not."

"Do, too."

"I didn't see you buy them."

"You left the store before I did."

"But they cost *fifty dollars* a pound!"

"I know. But I told you I have a weakness for chocolate. Ellie Fairbanks assured me they're worth every penny. Based on your reaction, she's right."

"Oh, she's definitely right. So let me get this straight. You have in your possession a full pound of Belgian truffles."

"Yup. Haven't even opened the box."

"A *virgin* box? Stop toying with me."

He laid his hand over his heart. "Swear."

Something that looked like awe entered her gaze. "You've had them *all day* and haven't eaten even one?"

"I've been too busy." He jerked his head toward his backyard. "Filling in holes, laying down sod. You know, the usual."

Even in the fading light he could see the color that bloomed on her cheeks, an enticing blush that made his fingers tingle with the need to touch her there.

"Oh," she said in small voice. "So, that being the case, it seems I owe you one."

"You do. And as it is, I'll only be getting half a one."

"What about your offer to share your chocolate? That still stand?"

"Depends."

"On what?"

"Whether you share yours with me."

"You have a lot more than I do."

He smiled. "How advantageous for me. And how lucky for you I'm not as sharing impaired as you are."

She stepped forward, until less than a foot separated them—well, a foot and the damn fence. He decided then and there that if he could possess one superpower, it would be the ability to make fences disappear.

Now that she was closer, he caught a whiff of her scent. Something flowery and musky that made his head spin. Or maybe his head was spinning from the way she was looking at him with those big brown eyes. Jeez, this woman was actually making him feel dizzy, just by looking at him. He wasn't sure if that was good, or if it should scare him spitless.

"Well," she said in a voice he could only describe as a purr, "then I guess you can have what I'm having. Allow me to offer you a taste of heaven."

She held out her hand, offering him the half truffle held delicately between her thumb and index finger. Whew. Talk about an offer he couldn't refuse.

Carlie stood in front of him, her heart beating ridiculously fast at the thought of feeding Daniel her remaining bite of chocolate, at the thought of her chocolate slowly melting in his warm mouth. Heated awareness jolted through her, making it impossible to deny she'd like to share a heck of a lot more than her chocolate with him. And based on the way he was looking at her—with enough heat to actually melt her chocolate—he wouldn't be adverse to the idea. Something that was further proven when instead of simply taking the proffered half truffle from her, he reached out, snagged her wrist, then slowly drew her hand toward his mouth.

He leaned forward and his lips brushed over her fingers, stalling her breath. And, oh wow, was that his tongue? Before she could decide, he straightened. Still holding her wrist, and with his gaze behind his glasses steady on hers, his jaw moved slowly back and forth in a way that let her know he knew exactly how to eat a truffle. No chewing, just a long, slow melt into pleasure. She practically experienced another chocogasm just watching him, imagining his tongue slowly sweeping over her skin rather than her chocolate.

After he swallowed, he said, "Wow. That was incredible."

Yeah, for me, too. She found herself involuntarily licking her lips.

Before she could recover her aplomb—which she normally had buckets of—he looked at her index finger and said, "I missed a tiny bit." And with that he slowly drew her fingertip into his mouth.

Holy cow. His mouth was satiny and warm and, oh boy, there was no missing the wet, velvety sweep of his tongue this time. His teeth lightly grazed her skin, turning her insides to the consistency of chocolate fondue

After another slow swirl of his tongue, he slid her finger from between his lips then released her hand. "Delicious."

She nodded. Probably she nodded. It was her intention to do so, but with all her faculties still engaged in recalling the incredible feel of his mouth on her skin, she couldn't be sure.

"Now that you've shared, I guess it's my turn," he said.

She had to swallow twice to locate her AWOL voice. "Right."

"Are you free this evening? Could I interest you in coming over for a truffle?"

The look in his eyes suggested that he had more than truffle tasting on his mind.

Thank God. Because she sure did.

Obviously a fling was all they could have given his imminent move, but since she wasn't looking for a serious relationship, that worked out fine. Even if their fling only lasted one night— hell, one *hour*—the way this guy had her hormones turning cartwheels, she'd take what she could get.

But his invitation brought reality back with a thump and she regretfully shook her head. "I'd love to, but I have a class and study session tonight. I have to head out in about an hour."

Amusement kindled in his eyes. "Listen, I know you like to savor your truffles, but it won't take you an *hour* to eat one." He jerked his head toward his house. "C'mon over. I'll even make a pot of coffee."

Wow. He sure knew how to tempt a girl. All the warnings in the stacks of books she'd read about how women shouldn't make themselves too available, how they should never accept an invitation for the same evening, flashed into her mind. And right back out again.

But that didn't mean she couldn't play hardball.

Tapping her finger against her chin, she said, "Hmmm. That sounds good—except for one thing."

"What's that?"

"This nonsense about *a* truffle, as in one. That's pretty stingy for a guy who has an entire box."

He smiled, flashing those killer dimples, and she made sure her knees were braced. "Okay, more than one truffle. But that'll present a problem for you, sharing-wise, as it seems you're fresh out."

"Of truffles, yes. But…" She hesitated, her courage suddenly failing her. *C'mon, Carlie. You want him? Go get him. Be bold. Be daring. The worst he can do is say no and if he does, you'll only have to avoid him for the next two weeks until he moves. If he says yes…*

Drawing a deep, bracing breath, she shot him her best suggestive look then murmured in her best seductive purr, "But that doesn't mean I have nothing to share."

Her heart rate quickened at the unmistakable flare of heat in his eyes. "Oh? What did you have in mind?"

You. Me. Chocolate. Naked. And not necessarily in that order. "Well, of course it would have to be in the form of an IOU since there's no time tonight, but I was thinking that you might perhaps enjoy…"

"Enjoy what?"

"A massage."

Which, she hoped, would lead to her. Him. Chocolate. Naked. And not necessarily in that order.

4

"Make yourself at home," Daniel said, pulling out one of the oak stools around the green granite snack bar that separated his kitchen from the small eating area. "I'll be right back. Gotta change my shirt."

"No problem," she said with a smile.

He headed quickly down the hall and into his bedroom. After closing the door behind him, he leaned back against the wood panel and pulled in several slow, calming breaths.

What the hell was wrong with him? His heart was racing, his hands weren't quite steady, and his stomach was jittery. But even as he asked himself the question, he realized the answer.

He was *nervous*. In a way he hadn't experienced since he'd been a teenager asking out his first major crush. Which was totally crazy. But there it was.

Pushing off from the door, he pulled his dirt-streaked T-shirt over his head then entered the adjoining bathroom. After tossing his shirt into the hamper, he washed his hands, frowning at himself in the mirror. Why the hell did he feel so unglued? She was just here for coffee and chocolate. A little conversation.

Well, that could certainly explain part of his nervousness. He found the whole "make small talk with women" thing very intimidating. It was like being lost in the jungle—scary, unfamiliar and you never knew when something might jump out and bite you. All those long, awkward pauses. Trying to think of something clever, or at least not boring, to say to fill the silence.

He knew zilch about the stuff women liked to talk about— shoes, make-up, clothes. Those topics invariably led to some variation of that trick "does this make my ass look fat?" question that has led to more conflicts than nations at war. Truth be told, the only interest he had in women's clothes was what was underneath them.

Bottom line, he sucked at small talk, and when he walked back into his kitchen, he'd be required to make some since he couldn't very well say to Carlie, "You just eat chocolate and do that sexy moaning thing, I'll listen and we'll leave it at that, okay?"

He dried his hands as he walked back into the bedroom, then selected a black polo shirt from his drawer. After pulling the soft cotton over his head, he tunneled his fingers through his hair and forced himself to acknowledge that the thought of making idle chitchat wasn't the only thing that had him unsettled. No, it was her offer of a massage. The thought of her hands on him…he blew out a long, careful breath. Better not think about it now. No, now he had coffee and small talk to manage. If he started thinking about her touching him, he'd swallow his damn tongue again—not conducive to making small talk.

After taking one final deep breath, he opened his bedroom door. As he walked down the hallway, he saw Carlie, in profile, sitting on the oak stool, legs crossed, elbows resting on the snack bar, her chin propped in one hand, and his heart performed another acrobatic stunt. She looked really nice, just sitting there at his snack bar. Kinda like she belonged there. Which was ridiculous—just like the hundred other ridiculous thoughts he'd had about her today. Sheesh. He must be sleep-deprived or something.

When he entered the kitchen, she smiled. "Your kitchen is impressively tidy. I thought bachelors were slobs."

"Can't say I'm a neat freak," he said, snagging the glass coffee pot then heading to the sink, "but I have to keep the place picked up or I risk being flogged by my Realtor. Apparently dirty dishes piled in the sink are bad for resale value."

"How long have you lived here?"

"Eight years. I grew up a few hours away, in Cartersville. It's just outside—

"Sacramento," she said, her voice tinged with surprise. "I'm from Farmington."

He pondered that as he added water to the pot, then snagged a filter. "So we grew up not fifteen miles away from each other."

"So it seems." She grinned. "We probably saw each other at the mall a dozen times."

"Doubtful. I rarely hung out at the mall, and besides, I would have remembered seeing you."

"A very kind—and appreciated—attempt at flattery, but if you'd seen me in high school you would have run the other way."

"Again, I've gotta say doubtful. But why's that?"

She grimaced. "I can describe my look in one word—frightening. Bride of Frankenstein hair, braces, zits—not the sort of girl who attracted much male attention." She batted her eyes in an exaggerated fashion. "I've improved with age."

He smiled. "You can say that again."

Carlie's breath caught at that smile and she offered up a silent prayer of thanks that she was sitting down because those darn dimples of his turned her knees to jelly. Since the urge to reach out and trace those sexy creases in his cheek was all but slapping her in the face, she forced her gaze down to his hands and watched him scoop coffee grounds into the filter.

Hmmm...he had really nice hands. Big, broad, long-fingered. Strong and capable. An image of them running up her bare thighs popped into her mind—

Okay, looking at his hands was not helping.

Better to get the conversational ball rolling again. "So why are you moving?" she asked, focusing her attention on his coffee maker.

"New job."

"I thought you owned your own business. Something with computers, right?"

He nodded. "I build and maintain websites."

Her uncooperative gaze had abandoned the coffee maker and slid back up to his face and she was captivated by his glasses sliding down his nose when he nodded. Since his hands were still busy scooping, and she couldn't seem to stop herself, she reached out and gently slid the frames back into place.

He went perfectly still. Behind the black-edged frames, his gaze held hers. For several long seconds neither spoke. It seemed to her as if some sort of sexually charged steam engulfed them and her heart beat so loud she wondered if he could hear it.

Finally, he cleared his throat and said, "Thanks."

"No problem." Which was a total lie. There was a *big* problem and it had all to do with her battle to keep her hands off him.

"They slide down all the time. I probably should just wear contacts—"

"No!" she said quickly and a tad too loudly. His brows shot up and she coughed to cover her outburst, then added more gently, "I mean, your glasses…they suit you."

"Right. It completes the computer geek look."

"Well, not exactly. For the *complete* look, you'd need high-water pants, a white socks/black shoes combo and a pocket protector."

His lips twitched. "I have that outfit. You want me to go change?"

Her gaze wandered over his broad shoulders and chest, which filled out his black polo shirt very nicely. The width of his chest suggested he must bench press computers as well as build websites with them.

"No need to change on my account," she said, relieved she sounded so breezy. "You look…" *Delicious. Incredible. Sexy as hell. So good I want to jump across this snack bar and freakin' attack you.* "Fine."

"Thanks," he said, then poured all the grinds in the filter back into the coffee can.

"Why'd you do that?" she asked.

"I, uh, lost count when you pushed up my glasses."

"Oh. Sorry."

"I wasn't complaining." His smile flashed, then he returned his attention back to coffee scooping.

She waited until he finished, absolutely *not* admiring his hands the whole time, then asked, "What's the new job?"

"A manager for Allied Computers' I.T. department. In Boston."

"Huge change. What about your website business?"

"I'm not taking on any new clients, but I'll continue to maintain the sites I've already designed. Updates aren't that time consuming—not like designing and constructing a site—and it'll provide a nice side income."

"New job, new city—you must be pretty excited about all that."

A frown furrowed his brow. "Uh, yeah." He flicked the coffee maker's "on" switch.

She studied him for several seconds while he busied himself putting the lid on the coffee can. "Must be difficult to leave this town behind."

His head jerked up from his task and their eyes met, his filled with surprise. "What are you, some sort of mind reader?"

If only. She'd give a lot to know what was on his mind, to know if *she* was on his mind. "No. Just…empathetic. I've only lived in Austell three months and I already love it."

"It's a great place to live," he agreed in a voice Carlie thought sounded decidedly wistful.

"I think so. I'm glad I decided to move in after all."

"You weren't going to?"

She shook her head. "My roommate eloped after I'd signed the lease and I would have lost three months' rent if I'd backed out. Financially, the rent payment's a stretch, especially with the cost of books and tuition, but I love the house and yard so much, I decided to just dip into my savings and suck it up for the next year until I earn my bachelor's degree."

"What are you studying?"

"Occupational therapy."

"I've heard of that, but I can't say I really know what an occupational therapist does."

"We help people whose living skills have been compromised, through accidents or illness or birth defects."

He came around the snack bar and sat on the chair next to her. "How did you come to be interested in that?"

Maybe it was because he sounded genuinely interested, or perhaps an attack of the babbles, but she started talking, and before she knew it, she'd told him all about her grandfather's debilitating stroke and about Marlene, the incredible occupational therapist who had made such a difference in Pop's quality of life.

"Pop and Gran had always been so active together—swimming, golf, tennis," she said softly, an image of her beloved grandparents flashing in her mind. "His stroke devastated both of them. Our entire family. I was just finishing high school at the time, and after I saw the difference Marlene made in Pop's recovery, I knew the career path I wanted to follow." She drew a deep breath, enjoying the redolence of brewing coffee. "Unfortunately the school I dreamed of attending was expensive and money was extremely tight. So instead of starting college right away, I decided to get my license as a massage therapist. That way I could earn money for school and still work once I started classes. Now I go to school part-time, work part-time at The Delaford's spa, and take private clients on the side."

"The Delaford doesn't mind you doing that?"

"No, since the spa is only open to resort guests. Which is one reason why Austell is so perfect for me. It's central to both The Delaford and school. I just need to find a way to attract more private clients. Right now it's all word of mouth. I don't like advertising in the newspaper because no matter how the ad is worded, it still comes across like I'm running a massage parlor."

He nodded slowly, his gaze resting on hers, and she forced herself to pause for breath. After several seconds of silence during which he continued to study her, an embarrassed warmth crept up her neck. Yikes, he probably thought she was a total blabbermouth. With a nervous laugh, she said, "Sorry, I didn't mean to go on and on. I told you more than you ever wanted to know, I'm sure."

He shook his head. "I liked listening to you. You're…easy to talk to. And it's refreshing to hear that someone loves what they're doing, that their goals involve helping other people. You're obviously passionate about what you're doing with your life and I find that very commendable. Very admirable." He reached out and brushed a single fingertip across the back of her hand. "Very attractive."

That gentle stroke ignited a firestorm under her skin, and her gaze riveted on the sight of his hand touching hers.

"In fact," he said, slowly stroking her again, "you didn't tell me nearly enough."

"I…I didn't?"

"No." Another slow caress. Another explosion under her skin.

She licked her suddenly dry lips. "Happy to tell you anything you want to know. Especially if you, um, keep doing that."

He took her hand in his and continued to lightly stroke her with the pad of his thumb. "My pleasure. Your skin is amazingly soft."

"I…thanks. I use a lot of lotion in my line of work." She fought the need to fan herself with her free hand. "Was there something else about me you wanted to know? You'd better ask quick, before I melt into a puddle on your floor. I'm a sucker for a hand massage."

"Good to know. And yeah, I'd like to know how it is that someone like you doesn't have a boyfriend."

"Someone like me?"

"Someone with such soft skin." He lifted her hand, touched his lips to her sensitive inner wrist, then breathed deeply. "Someone who smells so good. Someone who's smart and committed to her work." He lowered her hand, still caressing her, and it was all she could do not to purr.

Forcing herself to concentrate on the conversation, she said, "My last boyfriend and I split about six months ago after two years together. After that, I decided I was better off with puppies than another boyfriend."

"My yard might disagree with you," he said in a dry voice.

Heat flooded her face even though the wink he then gave her made it clear he was kidding. "Have I mentioned what a good sport you've been? How incredibly patient?"

His lips curved upward in a slow smile that curled her toes inside her Keds. "I'm a very nice guy."

"Says who—your mom?" she teased.

"As a matter of fact, she does. So what happened with what's his name, or would you rather not talk about it?"

Carlie shrugged. "He was pressuring me to get married because he was ready to start a family—now. I told him that even if we were to marry, I'd want to wait to start a family. Finish my degree then get a couple years of job experience under my belt before taking on motherhood."

"Sounds reasonable."

"I thought so. But he didn't. After going around and around about it, he issued me an ultimatum—marriage and kids now or never. I picked never."

"That must have hurt."

"It did. It also pissed me off that after all our time together he still had no clue how important my work is to me. That he wanted so badly to change me. That he couldn't accept me as I am."

"No regrets?"

"None. Well, except for the next guy I went out with. He lasted two hours. I was done with him after he told me I'd be really cute if I lost ten pounds. That's when I decided I was done with my unfortunate tendency to find men who wanted to change me or make me into something I'm not, and that puppies were the way to go. They're always happy to see me, they don't care that I'm not built like a pencil, they love to snuggle, and they don't speak English. Perfect qualities in a male—no offense."

He laughed. "None taken. And that guy who said you needed to lose ten pounds? He's an ass."

"Thank you. I thought so, too. Especially since he wasn't exactly a Calvin Klein model himself."

"How'd you hook up with P.B. and J?"

"I adopted them from a shelter. I'd only intended to get one dog, but they were the last two from the litter and I just couldn't choose. I figured they could keep each other company, and besides, two watchdogs are better than one."

"I'm sure. Between the two of them, they'd lick the robbers to death."

She laughed. Then, deciding she'd better quit yakking while she was ahead and hadn't yet stuck her foot in her mouth, she said, "And now that I've bored you with all my chatter, it's your turn. When I moved in, you had a girlfriend…" She left the sentence hanging and shot him a questioning look.

He nodded, looking down at where his hand still held hers, his thumb drawing hypnotic circles on her skin. "Nina. She wanted more than I could give her."

"Emotionally?"

"Financially. She wasn't impressed with my job as a website designer, my less than grand house, this small town, my unspectacular car. She always wanted…more. When she finally realized I didn't aspire to be the next Bill Gates, she gave me the heave-ho."

"Heartbroken?" she asked, hoping he'd say—

"No."

Right answer. Still, she couldn't help but ask, "Does she know about your swanky new job?"

He shook his head. "No. We haven't stayed in touch." He gently released her hand then slid off the stool and rounded the snack bar into the kitchen. "Coffee's done. Are you ready for your truffle?"

"That's one of those rhetorical questions, right?"

He smiled into her eyes and Carlie heated up from the inside out, deciding she needed a hot cup of coffee like she needed a hole in her head. While he poured, she asked, "Did you find a birthday present for your mom at Sinfully Sweet?"

"I did. A mini chocolate fountain. It uses special melting chocolate that flows, sort of like those champagne fountains at weddings, only smaller. It comes with great ideas for stuff to dip—marshmallows, strawberries, cubes of angel food cake. She's going to love it."

"How could she not? It sounds like a fantasy come true. The Valentine's Day promotion is a pretty wild idea, isn't it? Find the chocolate heart half that matches yours and you win dinner for two. Did you get your blue-wrapped chocolate heart half?"

"Yup. Haven't opened it yet, though. Did you get your pink-wrapped half?"

"I did. I hid it way in the corner behind the soup cans on the top shelf in my pantry in an effort to make it last at least through the night."

"Good luck with that."

"Thanks. I'm going to need it."

After adding milk to both ceramic mugs, he set the silver foil-wrapped box on the counter with a flourish. "You may have the honors," he said.

Daniel pressed his lips together to hide his amusement as he watched Carlie open the box with a reverence he'd have thought was only bestowed on royalty. The woman definitely loved her chocolate. After removing the lid, she leaned over the box and breathed deeply. Her eyes slid closed and a smoky "oooooh, my" whispered from between her parted lips. His amusement faded, replaced by a punch of lust that practically knocked him on his ass. Her eyes opened and she looked at the truffles as if she were gazing upon a cache of jewels.

"They all look so delicious," she said in that same smoky voice, elevating his temperature another notch. With her gaze still riveted on his chocolates, she asked, "Which one do you want?"

The sexy, curly-haired one. He pressed his lips together before he actually said the words out loud. After clearing his throat, he glanced down at the truffles and after a brief perusal, pointed to one. "What flavor is that?" he asked.

She consulted the inside of the box top, which provided a pictorial guide. "Milk chocolate hazelnut. Yum."

He pointed to another. "How about that one?"

"Ooooh. White chocolate raspberry."

"And this one?" he asked, pointing to another.

"Hmmm…let's see…cappuccino. Double yum."

With his gaze riveted on her rapt expression, he just chose one at random. "I'll take this one."

After consulting the chart, she nodded her approval. "Double chocolate praline. Good choice. I think I'm going to go with the French vanilla." After she picked up the glossy pale treat, she held it out and said, "To your generosity in sharing. Thank you."

"You're welcome," he said lightly tapping his truffle to hers. She slowly lifted the chocolate to her lips, then took a small bite. He watched, fascinated, as her eyes drifted closed, and erotic, sensual sounds of pleasure started coming from her. Her head fell limply back, exposing the tempting length of her neck, and suddenly chocolate was no longer what he wanted to feast on.

"That. Is. Soooo. Unbelievably. Good."

You're. Making. Me. Soooo. Unbelievably. Hard. He would have shifted to relieve the strangulation in the front of his Levi's, but he simply couldn't move. He actually felt his eyes glaze over, probably from his retinas melting from the heat she generated. He stood perfectly still, transfixed, watching her turn the simple act of eating chocolate into a sexual fantasy. When her moans tapered off and she finally opened her eyes, he managed one husky word. "Wow."

"Mmm. I'll say."

"Was that as good for you as it was for me?" he asked.

Her gaze fell to the forgotten truffle he still held between his fingers and her eyes widened. "But you haven't even tasted it yet."

"I was too busy watching you." Setting his truffle back in the box, he rounded the snack bar, stopping in front of her. He felt as if steam pumped from his pores. "I'd rather taste yours."

She blinked, then held up the remaining piece of her truffle. "Oh. Sure. I'm happy to—"

He cut off her words by covering her mouth with his.

The instant his lips touched hers, every thought drained from his head. He drew her off the stool, then into his arms, and she went willingly, twining her arms around his neck. She made that incredible moaning sound and parted her lips, inviting him to delve deeper, an offer he immediately accepted, his tongue exploring the delectable heat of her mouth while his hands roamed slowly down the curve of her back.

So good… God, she tasted so good. Sweet, warm and delicious. The erotic friction of her tongue tangling with his arrowed needles of fire through him. He shifted, leaning against the snack bar, then spread his legs and drew her into the V of his thighs. She pressed herself against him, incinerating him where he stood.

More...more...more. The word pounded through him, demanding, stripping another layer off his control, a situation that wasn't helped at all by Carlie's ardent response. He'd meant to kiss her slowly, lightly, but nothing about this kiss was slow or light. Instead it was a deep, intimate flash fire of heat and hunger and want. His hands tunneled through her silky hair, holding her head immobile while his mouth devoured hers.

He lost all sense of time, and when he finally raised his head, had no idea how long he'd kissed her, other than to know that it wasn't long enough. He looked down at her and saw...

Fog.

Talk about having your eyes glaze over.

He blinked and realized his glasses had steamed over. Yeah, just like the rest of him. Before he could reach for the glasses, he felt her removing them. As she lifted them from his face, she came into view. With her eyes half closed, her cheeks flushed red, and her full lips moist and parted, she looked utterly gorgeous and completely aroused. After she set his glasses on the snack bar, she leaned back in the circle of his arms and whispered, "Wow."

He was impressed she managed to utter a word. He sure as hell wasn't able to. How was it that what was supposed to have been nothing more than a simple kiss felt so damn...complicated? He had to swallow twice and clear his throat just to locate his voice. "Yeah. Wow." He still sounded as if he'd scraped his vocal chords with sandpaper.

"I fogged up your glasses."

"I forgive you."

She studied him for several seconds. "You look different without them."

"So do you. You're sort of...blurry."

She leaned closer, until they were nearly nose to nose. "How's that?"

"Oh, it's you," he teased. He bent his head and touched his lips to the side of her neck. "You taste delicious."

"That was the chocolate."

He lifted his head and looked into her eyes, and experienced that same rush of sensation he felt when he jumped off the high diving board. "No. It was you."

"I've gotta tell you, that kiss made me forget all about my truffle, and that's a sentence that has never before passed my lips." Again she studied him for several seconds. "Probably I shouldn't admit this, but I've wanted to do that for a while."

"Relieve me of my truffles?"

She smiled. "Well, that, too. But I meant fog up your glasses."

"Why shouldn't you admit that?"

"According to all those rule books, I should act coy and mysterious. Unfortunately, that's just not my style."

"Doesn't sound unfortunate to me. I prefer the brutal truth." He tucked a stray cinnamon curl behind her ear. "And the brutal truth is I'd like to continue our conversation—"

"Conversation?" Mischief glimmered in her eyes and she nudged her pelvis against the hard ridge of his erection.

"Our *evening together*," he corrected with a smile, "when you have more time. Are you free tomorrow night?"

"That depends. Are you offering more truffles?"

"That depends. Will you give me that massage?"

"I will if you will."

"Seven o'clock?"

"Better make it eight. I have a load of studying to do."

"Great. Looking forward to it."

And that, he decided, was a sentence that belonged in the Guinness Book of World Records under the heading of "Hugest Understatement Ever Spoken."

DANIEL THOUGHT ABOUT her the whole damn day.

He hadn't felt this kind of anticipation about seeing a woman in a very long time. And never to this degree. The taste of her kiss, the feel of her pressed up against him…wanting to experience those sensations again made the day drag along at a snail's pace. He found himself looking out his office window every few minutes hoping to catch a glimpse of her, a fact that annoyed him and made concentrating on his work nearly impossible.

But the day finally passed and she was due to arrive in forty-five minutes.

Thank God.

Stepping from the shower, he wrapped a towel around his hips then snagged another to towel-dry his hair. After shaving, he dressed in a blue polo shirt and his most comfortable jeans, then glanced around his bedroom. Bed neatly made, condoms stashed in the nightstand drawer. Perfect. Satisfied, he made his way to the den.

His box of truffles, or as he'd renamed them, "The Best Fifty Bucks He'd Ever Spent," rested on the coffee table. He slipped a blues CD into the stereo, lowered the lights and found a pair of candles, which he set on the coffee table. The only thing missing was Carlie.

His gaze once again strayed to the clock. She was due in seven minutes.

He hoped like hell she wouldn't be late.

Sure, the promise of a massage, and what would hopefully follow, was enough to fill any guy with anticipation, but somehow this felt like…more. Which was crazy since they barely knew each other. And especially since he'd be gone in two weeks. Clearly he was imagining things. No doubt because he hadn't been with anyone since Nina had left. Yeah, that's all this was: a case of extreme horniness. A bout—or two, or maybe three or four—of hot, sweaty sex with his hot, sexy neighbor would set his head back on straight.

The thought of hot, sweaty sex made him feel decidedly warm, so he headed to the fridge for a bottle of water. When he opened the door, his gaze fell on the blue foil-wrapped half of a chocolate heart he'd received with his purchase from Sinfully Sweet. He'd put it the refrigerator because every once in a while he enjoyed a eating piece of chilled chocolate while drinking a cup of hot coffee. Instead of grabbing a water, he slid out the heart half, suddenly curious to know what message was hidden beneath the foil. He undid the shiny blue wrapping and pulled out a slender strip of paper.

Pushing his glasses up his nose, he read, "Passion is best described as unpredictable because it's often found in surprising places. With unexpected people. Leading to unanticipated encounters. All of which can result in unforeseen outcomes."

His brows shot upward. Talk about apt. Well, everything except the last part. There was nothing unforeseen about the outcome of any passion he and Carlie might share. It had a two-week expiration date stamped right on it. And they both knew that going in.

He hadn't wanted to accept the half a heart, telling Ellie there was no point in him doing so because with him moving, he had neither the time nor the inclination to try to discover which single woman might have the matching pink half. But Ellie had insisted, saying that if nothing else, he'd enjoy the delicious chocolate. He'd tried one more time, saying that he felt bad knowing some woman might get his matching half and be a definite loser in the contest because of it, but still she'd insisted. So he'd taken it and offered up a silent apology to whoever might receive the matching half.

Before loosely rewrapping the chocolate, he broke off a small piece and popped it in his mouth. Oh, yeah. That was some damn good chocolate. He grabbed a bottle of water, then leaned his hips against the counter. Another quick look at the clock told him Carlie was due right about now.

Which was perfect because he couldn't wait to feel her hands on him. The mere thought shot a bolt of heat through his body.

He *really* hoped she wouldn't be late.

DAMN IT, she was running late.

Carlie jumped from the shower and hastily wrapped a towel around her, sarong style. Why was it that whenever she was in a rush everything went wrong? Her favorite shirt, the one that made her look like she had more cleavage than she actually did, was in the dirty laundry, and while she'd been busy studying, the puppies had gotten into the bathroom and littered three rooms with toilet paper streamers.

In the middle of gathering up the mess—a process hindered by an enthusiastic P.B. and J. who thought "clean-up" was secret puppy talk for "play-time"—her mother had called twice. The first time just to chat, and the second time to bombard her with questions after she'd deduced—in that unerringly accurate way moms had—that "Can't talk now, Mom, I'm busy" was secret daughter talk for "Gotta go, have a hot date with a hot man." Then she couldn't find her razor and no way was she going to Daniel's house without freshly shaved legs.

So now, here she was, soaking wet, with about six minutes to make herself spectacular. She toweled a spot off the fogged-up bathroom mirror and grimaced at what she saw. No way her mirror would declare her Fairest of Them All. Six minutes? Good grief, she needed more like six hours. She looked like something the puppies dragged in from the backyard.

And speaking of the puppies…Hmmm. Usually they waited for her right outside the shower and pounced on her the minute she emerged, licking the water droplets from her toes. She walked into her bedroom, then whistled and called their names. "Here, P.B. and J. C'mon, boys."

The fact that they didn't appear and she didn't hear any noise could only mean one thing.

Doggie mischief was afoot.

"Great," she muttered heading swiftly toward the kitchen. "Listen, guys. I do *not* have time for this. You better not be turning my new slippers into a chew toy."

She entered the kitchen and skidded to a halt at the sight of the unlatched doggie door. Uh oh. She must have forgotten to secure it before she showered. Probably because, thanks to Daniel, her brain cells were all kerflooey. She yanked open the back door then hit the light switch.

Light flooded her backyard, illuminating her small patio. Her hole-pocked lawn. Her flower beds. The fence separating her yard from Daniel's.

Her puppies digging their way under the fence.

"Stop!" she yelled. Clutching her towel, she dashed outside. They must have heard her coming because it seemed they re-doubled their digging efforts.

"Bad puppies! Stop that!"

The patio flagstones were cold beneath her feet, and she stepped as quickly as she could onto the grass, which was not only cold, but damp as well. Goosebumps rose on her wet flesh and she winced as a rock bit into her instep. Jeez, could this situation get any worse?

She instantly cursed herself for asking because the situation immediately got worse as both dogs disappeared under the fence. Since there wasn't a gate between the two yards, she couldn't just snatch the little bandits. No, now she'd have to go back inside and call Daniel and ask him to grab the culprits— quick—before they could dig any more holes in his newly repaired yard. If she waited until she was dressed, Lord knows what havoc they might wreak. And Lord knows what havoc *that* might wreak with her plans with Daniel. Probably he wouldn't be feeling very amorous if he discovered a fresh batch of holes in his yard.

Grasping her towel, her teeth chattering, she hurried toward her back door. And realized that things could go from worse to worser.

The damn door was locked.

WHEN THE KNOCK sounded on Daniel's front door, his heart performed one of those contortionist-type maneuvers it had recently started executing, and he frowned. Ridiculous. She was just a *woman*. The world was littered with them. Two weeks from now they'd be nothing more than former neighbors with, he hoped, a few hot memories between them. Tiny blips on each other's radar screens.

Yeah. But in the meantime...

He had to force himself not to sprint to the door. "Be cool, be calm, be suave," he muttered as he entered his small foyer. "Yeah, that's the ticket. Just do your best James Bond."

Pausing to draw a deep, soothing breath, he opened the door. And stared.

At Carlie, her skin damp, her hair a riotous tangle of glistening, wet curls. At Carlie, wearing a pale pink towel that—yowza—barely covered the essentials.

Holy crap, he'd swallowed his tongue again. Damn it, James Bond wouldn't do that. Hell, no. But then, James had never faced a nearly naked Carlie.

The dam behind the pent-up hunger he'd fought against all day burst, and with a groan, he stepped forward and pulled her into his arms and kissed her.

That same incredible rush of heated pleasure he'd experienced last night roared through him, erasing any doubt that he'd simply imagined it.

She moaned—or was that him?—and parted her lips, and he deepened the kiss, his tongue dancing with hers. Her hands slid into his hair, and his arms tightened around her, his head swimming from a combination of the feel of her curves and moist skin pressed against him and the incredible, fresh scent of her.

When the need to yank off her towel right there on the porch threatened to overwhelm his better judgment, he lifted his head. His glasses were only partially fogged this time. He was gratified to note that she appeared as dazed and bamboozled as he felt.

Clearing his throat, he said, "I don't know much about

fashion, but I'm *really* liking this Bed, Bath and Beyond look you've got going here."

She blinked several times, then her eyes widened. Splaying her hands on his chest, she leaned back and said, "Daniel, we have a problem—"

"Not from where I'm standing."

"I'm so embarrassed—"

"Believe me, you have absolutely nothing to be embarrassed about." And if he didn't get her in the house pronto, the neighbors were going to get one hell of a show. Stepping away from her, he opened the door. "C'mon in."

"Thanks." She stepped across the threshold and he breathed in the sexy, feminine fragrance she left in her wake. He closed and locked the door, then turned. And was treated to a back view of her in that short, short towel.

Before he could recover, she grabbed his hand and tugged. "Hurry," she said, pulling him toward the back of the house.

"Anything you say." He'd planned a slow, leisurely seduction, but hey, he was flexible. The lady wanted quick? Fine by him. He was more than willing and, after spending an entire night and day fantasizing about her, definitely more than ready.

"Hurry," she repeated, in a breathless, urgent voice, leading him into the kitchen.

Whoa, baby. A little on-the-counter action? This just got better and better. Damn it, he should have stashed a condom in here—

"They're outside. I hope we're not too late." She released his hand then jerked open his back door.

Huh? "*They? Who's they?*"

But she'd already disappeared outside. His question was answered when he heard her calling, "Peanut Butter, Jelly, where are you?" followed immediately by, "Hey, Daniel, can you hit the lights, please?"

Uh oh. This didn't sound good. Neither for that kitchen-counter quickie he'd envisioned nor for his backyard. He quickly flicked on the light switch, then headed outside.

"There you are, you devils," Carlie said, dashing toward the

Play the
Lucky Hearts Game

and get...

2 FREE BOOKS
and a FREE MYSTERY GIFT...
YOURS to KEEP!

yes! I have scratched off the silver card. Please send me my **2 FREE BOOKS** and **FREE mystery GIFT**. I understand that I am under no obligation to purchase any books as explained on the back of this card.

Scratch Here!
then look below to see what your cards get you... 2 Free Books & a Free Mystery Gift!

351 HDL EE29   **151 HDL EEZX**

FIRST NAME   LAST NAME

ADDRESS

APT.#   CITY

STATE/PROV.   ZIP/POSTAL CODE   (H-B-02/06)

Twenty-one gets you
2 FREE BOOKS
and a **FREE MYSTERY GIFT!**

Twenty gets you
2 FREE BOOKS!

Nineteen gets you
1 FREE BOOK!

TRY AGAIN!

▼ DETACH AND MAIL CARD TODAY! ▼

BUSINESS REPLY MAIL

FIRST-CLASS MAIL   PERMIT NO. 717-003   BUFFALO, NY

POSTAGE WILL BE PAID BY ADDRESSEE

HARLEQUIN READER SERVICE
3010 WALDEN AVE
PO BOX 1867
BUFFALO NY 14240-9952

NO POSTAGE
NECESSARY
IF MAILED
IN THE
UNITED STATES

far left corner of his yard where two balls of fur, one pure black, the other brown and white, were digging furiously.

"Stop that this instant!" Carlie yelled, still running.

Jogging after her, Daniel watched P.B. and J. pause and raise their heads. The instant they saw Carlie, they abandoned their digging. After a series of joyful yips, they raced toward her, tongues lolling, tails wagging. He glanced at the hole they'd made and ruefully shook his head. Good thing he had some sod left over.

Probably he should be annoyed or aggravated, at least something other than amused. But one look at Carlie trying to hold her towel in place and not get knocked on her ass by her exuberant, jumping pups—well, he couldn't help but smile. When he joined them seconds later, Carlie was kneeling on the grass, the recipient of a frenzied overabundance of canine happiness as the dogs yipped and licked and wagged.

"I'm so sorry," she said, looking up at him, stretching her neck to avoid P.B. and J.'s attempt to bestow frantic kisses on her lips.

Hmmm. Smart dogs.

"They escaped into my backyard through the doggie door while I was in the shower. Before I could catch them, they'd dug under the fence."

He crouched beside her and was immediately besieged by a frenzy of pure puppy joy. "Not that I'm complaining about your outfit, but you could have called me," he said, trying to evade receiving his own puppy kisses on the lips. "I would have held down the fort until you were dressed."

She picked up Peanut Butter and cuddled the squirming bundle of black fur while he did the same with Jelly. "That was my intention—until I discovered I'd locked myself out."

Their gazes met over doggie heads and he couldn't help but chuckle at her exasperated expression. Her eyes instantly narrowed. "Are you *laughing?*"

He immediately sobered. "Who—me?"

"Yeah, you."

"Heck no."

"Good. Because this is *not* funny."

"Right." Still clasping Jelly to his chest, he reached out and brushed his fingers over her bare shoulder. "Clump of dirt," he said, fighting the urge to laugh.

She looked skyward, then shook her head. "Clump of dirt. Perfect."

"Do you have a spare house key hidden somewhere?"

"If I did, do you think I would have shown up at your house wearing a towel?"

"I don't know, but hope springs eternal."

"Ha, ha. No hidden key. But you better believe I'm going to remedy *that* situation tomorrow. Of course, that doesn't do me much good now. And naturally all my windows are locked." She stretched out her arms and held Peanut Butter in front of her. "What on earth am I going to do with you?"

Peanut Butter wiggled and yipped, trying to lick anything his tongue could come in contact with. "You are *so* lucky you're cute," she muttered to the squirming dog. Heaving a sigh, she pulled the puppy against her then looked at Daniel with big brown eyes filled with dismay. "This is not exactly how I envisioned this evening going."

"Oh? What had you envisioned?"

"Brutal truth?"

"Absolutely."

"You. Me. Chocolate. Naked."

Okay, who lit the blow torch in his jeans? "That sounds good to me." *Good*? When the hell had he become such a master of the understatement?

"Definitely no puppies," she continued. "And definitely me wearing something other than a towel. At least to start with."

His gaze roamed over her. "I like your outfit just fine."

A huff of laughter puffed past her lips. "Thanks."

He stood, then held out his hand. "C'mon. Let's go inside before you catch a chill. We'll get the dogs settled, then call the locksmith. While we wait for him, we can enjoy some truffles."

She looked up at him and he felt the impact of those huge, questioning eyes right down to the soles of his feet. "So we're still on? In spite of the dogs and the new hole in your yard and my towel?"

"Yes, *in spite* of the dogs and the new hole in my yard, but actually *because* of your towel."

With a laugh and still holding Peanut Butter, who, like Jelly, had quieted down, she took his hand and he gently pulled her to her feet. When she was upright, less than a foot separated them. Well, a foot and two suddenly drowsy puppies. He looked into her eyes, and his heart started thumping as if he'd run a race. Maybe he was allergic to dogs.

Or maybe he was just painfully attracted to this woman. Like he'd never been attracted to anyone before.

"Calling the locksmith, helping me with the dogs…seems as if you've solved the immediate crisis."

"I did tell you I'm an expert problem solver."

"In addition to being an expert problem solver, you're also an expert kisser."

"You're not so bad yourself." Another whopper of an understatement.

"Believe it or not, I'm usually not such a Calamity Jane."

"Maybe you call showing up at my house in a towel a calamity, but I sure don't." He smiled, then, with a gentle tug on her hand, started walking toward the house. Her bare shoulder brushed against him as they made their way across the grass, shooting arrows of heat through him. Her palm felt warm and soft and smooth nestled against his, and heated tingles sizzled up his arm from the contact.

Since when did a simple gesture like holding hands feel so…sexually charged? So…intimate? His fingers flexed and she gently squeezed in return, firing pure lust to every nerve ending. How did she get him so worked up just by holding his hand? Cripes, if he got any hotter, he'd start glowing in the dark.

After crossing his small brick patio, he released her hand and held open the door for her. "Follow me," he said, leading the way toward the den. He snagged a quilt from the coat closet on the way. Once in the den, he spread the quilt in the corner, then gently set down his drowsy furry bundle. Jelly let out a huge yawn, then promptly entered doggy dreamland. Carlie laid down P.B., who plopped his head on Jelly's rump and also slept.

He straightened and found himself staring at her, unable to look away. He knew he was supposed to do something involving a locksmith, but looking at her, flushed and disheveled and practically naked, he was damned if he could recall so much as his own name.

Touch her. He simply had to touch her. Reaching out, he brushed his fingertips across her flushed cheek. A small spray of golden freckles decorated her soft skin, filling him with the urge to study each tiny mark, then play connect the dots. With his lips.

Her eyes drooped half closed. The small, breathy sound that came from between her parted lips tensed every muscle in his body.

"You know that you, me, chocolate, naked thing you mentioned?" he asked softly, dragging his fingers slowly down the curve of her neck to run along the skin just above the top of her towel.

Her eyes seemed to darken. "Absolutely."

"You overly fussy about what order that all happens in?"

For an answer, she flicked her fingers at the top of her towel and the terry cloth slithered to the floor.

"Absolutely not."

6

STANDING IN FRONT of Daniel wearing nothing except her best seductive smile, Carlie watched his eyes darken with a smoldering heat and hunger that infused her with a powerful surge of feminine satisfaction. There was no doubt that he liked what he saw.

Now she couldn't wait to see what he intended to do about it. And since it had been six months since she'd had sex, the sooner the better as far as she was concerned.

But instead of simply grabbing her and putting out this damn inferno he'd lit inside her, he made no move to touch her. Instead his gaze tracked slowly down to her feet, then back up, igniting tiny fires on her skin and tightening her nipples. She felt that leisurely perusal as if he'd caressed her, and her skin grew increasingly warm and prickly with want.

When their gazes met again, he said in a husky voice, "You're like an unwrapped present." He reached out and traced his fingertips along her collarbone, halting her breath. "And it's not even my birthday."

Any reply she might have made evaporated into nothingness when his hands wandered lower to palm her breasts. His thumbs brushed over her aroused nipples, a light feathery caress that dragged a moan from her throat and pulsed pure want straight to her womb.

"You're beautiful," he said, his voice a raspy whisper.

She opened her mouth to say something that resembled thank you, but he again stole the words when he lowered his head and drew her nipple into the satiny heat of his mouth. With a gasp, her head fell limply back and she grabbed his shoulders for support.

While his lips and tongue laved her sensitive flesh, his hands skimmed lower, one roaming over her abdomen while the other curved around to cup her bottom. His fingers glided between her thighs, and she spread her legs wider.

Her long *ooooohhhh* of pleasure filled the air as he teased her with a light, circular motion that weakened her knees. Her fingers slid into his thick, silky hair, then slipped beneath the collar of his shirt to stroke his back. His skin was hot and smooth beneath her palms and she desperately wanted, needed, to feel more of him. All of him.

But instead of speeding things up, he continued to torment her with his unhurried pace. His lips moved upward to explore her neck and the sensitive skin behind her ear. He tortured her with slow, deep, drugging kisses, his tongue caressing hers as his fingers glided over her slick feminine folds until she felt ready to implode. Skimming his hand down her thigh, he lifted her leg, and with a groan she hooked her calf around his hip. His talented fingers continued their maddening arousal, slipping deeply inside, slowly stroking. She tried to sustain the pleasure, to not fall over the edge, but his gentle assault on her body was relentless. Her orgasm throbbed through her, dragging a cry from her throat that tapered off into a deep sigh of sated satisfaction.

No sooner had her shudders subsided than he scooped her up in his strong arms. He walked swiftly down the hall, and she buried her face in the warm spot where his neck and shoulder met and grazed his skin with her teeth. He smelled fresh and clean and warm and delicious and he'd made her feel *so damn good*.

His low groan vibrated against her lips. "If you keep that up, we won't make it to the bedroom."

"I already didn't, in case you hadn't noticed."

"Believe me, I noticed. If I'd thought to have a condom in my pocket, you wouldn't have made it out of the den."

"If you weren't carrying me, I wouldn't have made it out anyway. My knees feel like limp, deflated balloons—a condition for which I heartily thank you, by the way."

"The pleasure was all mine."

"Actually it wasn't, but I'm looking forward to returning the favor."

"That makes me all kinds of lucky."

"Oh, honey, trust me, you are definitely going to get all kinds of lucky."

Seconds later he deposited her on his bed with a gentle bounce. Standing next to the edge, looking at her with an expression that all but breathed fire, he was about to pull his shirt over his head when she rose to her knees and stilled his hands. "Not so fast," she said, skating her hands under the soft material. "You undressed me; now it's my turn."

Daniel released the ends of his shirt and settled his hands on her hips and pulled her closer. The soft curve of her belly bumped against his erection and he sucked in a breath. His palms drifted slowly up and down, exploring her exquisite curves.

"Not to put too fine a point on it, but I think *you* actually removed your towel, for which I'd like to heartily thank you, by the way," he said, echoing her earlier words.

"You're welcome." Reaching out, she touched his glasses. "Can you see okay without these? I wouldn't want you to miss anything."

He slid them off then tossed them onto the nightstand. "I'm really nearsighted. I'll have to stay pretty close."

"Consider it done. Now—off with the footwear."

After he toed off his sneakers and kicked aside his discarded socks, she said, "Hands in the air."

He raised his arms. "Am I under arrest?"

"Yes. You have the right to remain…" She lifted his shirt over his head then tossed it aside. He lowered his arms and her gaze and fingers strolled down his chest, igniting bonfires and tensing his abs. "Really, really hot."

"I thought I had the right to remain silent."

"You do, but it's not necessary. Make all the noise you like." She slowly rubbed her breasts against his chest and a wicked grin curved her lips. "You already know I'm a moaner and groaner."

"Yeah. That's a shame. Really."

She smoothed her hands slowly down his torso, then trailed her fingertips around the sensitive skin just above the waist of his jeans, while she leaned forward and gently bit his earlobe. When a growl rumbled in his throat, she whispered in his ear, "That's a promising sound. For starters."

Moving off the bed, she stood in front of him. When he reached for her, she shook her head, her eyes dancing with mischief. "Oh, no. It's my turn. No touching from you."

His gaze roved over her full breasts, their erect nipples a whisper away from his chest. "Okay. But that's asking a lot."

For an answer, she leaned down and slowly brushed her tongue over his nipple. Another growl of pleasure rumbled in his throat and his eyes slid closed. She kissed her way across his chest while her hands lightly kneaded his back. He could only guess that she was an excellent masseuse because her hands were nothing short of magical.

Given her unhurried pace, she obviously planned to have revenge on him. Not that he was complaining—hell, no—but he didn't know how long he'd be able to withstand the exquisite torture.

When he felt her hands at his waistband, he opened his eyes and watched her flick open the button on his jeans then slowly drag down the zipper.

"Is that a few dozen truffles in your pants, or are you just happy to see me?" she asked in a sultry, teasing voice, easing her hands beneath the waistband of his boxer briefs.

"I am extremely—" he sucked in a swift breath as she freed his erection then skimmed his jeans and underwear down his legs in one, smooth motion "—happy." He pushed the discarded clothes aside with his foot.

"So I see." Touching her index to the center of his chest, she walked slowly around him, dragging that single fingertip along his skin. When she stood directly behind him, she said, "View is exceptional from the back as well."

He would have thanked her, but she stole whatever command he still retained over the English language when she stepped closer and slowly rubbed herself against his back. A shudder ran through him at the sensation of her skin brushing against his. Her fingertips drifted over his hips, down his thighs, while she pressed openmouthed kisses across his shoulders.

Her hands continued their gently teasing marauding, roaming up and down his torso and legs, touching him everywhere—except his erection. "You're killing me," he said, his voice gravelly with need.

She walked around until she faced him again. Then ran a single fingertip down his hard length. "Better?"

"Yes. No. I don't know. Better do it again."

Wrapping her fingers around him, she gently squeezed, dulling his vision. "Good?"

Incredible. He tried to say the word, but all that came out was a guttural groan. Tipping his head back, he endured the sweet torture of her stroking him, cupping, teasing and caressing him until the need to come approached overwhelming. Lifting his head, he looked down at the erotic sight of her hands pleasuring him and knew he couldn't take anymore.

He grasped her wrists, tumbled her onto the bed, then followed her down, making quick work of grabbing a condom. After rolling on the protection—a delay that nearly unhinged him—he covered her body with his. The slow, slick glide into her tight, wet heat dragged another growl from his throat. She wrapped her legs around him, urging him deeper, meeting his every thrust. Sweat beaded on his forehead and his every muscle strained with the effort to hold off his release until she came. The instant the first ripple of her orgasm gripped him, he let himself go, and with a feral groan, followed her over the edge.

He wasn't sure how long he lay there, still deep inside her, his face buried in the soft, fragrant curve of her neck, before he found the strength to lift his head. A minute? An hour? Damned if he knew. He propped his weight on his forearms and gazed down into her eyes. She looked drowsy and satisfied and sexy as hell, and for reasons he couldn't explain, he felt as if he'd been sucker punched. Right in the heart. Cripes, he'd thought their simple kiss had felt complicated? The tangle of unexpected, unsettling feelings roiling through him after what should have been nothing more than a breezy bout of no-strings sex had him positively reeling. Several seconds ticked by as they simply stared at each other. Then she licked her lips and whispered, "Holy cow."

If he'd been able to string two words together, those were the two he'd have uttered. Since one was about all he could manage, he said, "Yeah."

"That was…"

"Yeah."

"That couldn't *possibly* have been as incredible as I think, could it?"

More so. "Maybe," he said as if his entire world hadn't just tilted on its axis, "but I'm not positive, so I vote for a re-do, just to make sure."

"Count me in. I, uh, didn't know computer nerds had so much…"

"Stamina?" he provided helpfully. "Willpower?"

One corner of her mouth quirked upward. "I was thinking along the lines of skill and finesse, but hey, if the shoe fits…"

"It's the glasses," he said in a perfectly serious voice. "Men who wear glasses are frequently underestimated."

She ran her fingers down his back and lightly pinched his butt. "Hmmm…I suppose that's true with some guys, but I never doubted you'd be as clever in the bedroom as you are with a computer. Trust me, you could be the poster boy for skill and finesse."

"Thanks." He smiled and tucked a wayward curl behind her ear. She turned and pressed a warm kiss against his palm, and his sucker-punched heart rolled over.

"Guess what I want?" she asked, nudging him with her hip.

He nudged her back. "Same thing I want?"

"I was thinking 'chocolate.'"

"I wasn't. But I'm willing to concede." He dropped a quick kiss on her lips, unsettled by how much he wanted to turn it into something more than a quick kiss. "For now anyway."

Five minutes later, Carlie entered the kitchen, wearing one of Daniel's dress shirts, with Daniel following her. He nuzzled her neck from behind as she opened his refrigerator. "Got milk?" she asked.

"Got anything you want." Probably he should let her go, but damn, he just couldn't keep his hands off her. Still nibbling on her neck, he reached around her with one hand and snagged the carton of milk.

"Is it sour and lumpy?" she asked eyeing the container with clear suspicion. "I know how you bachelors operate."

"No lumps in the milk."

Just as he was about to hip check the door closed, she pointed to the top shelf and said, "Oh—there's your heart half from Sinfully Sweet. Have you read the secret message?"

"I have." With an effort, and just to prove to himself that he could, he released her, then reached for two glasses. "Feel free to take a look."

While he poured the milk, she unwrapped the blue foil and pulled out the slender strip of paper. "Passion is best described as unpredictable because it's often found in surprising places. With unexpected people. Leading to unanticipated encounters. All of which can result in unforeseen outcomes."

"Pretty prophetic, huh?"

When she didn't answer right away, he looked up and their gazes met. Something he couldn't define flashed in her eyes, then she nodded. "Very. And very familiar. It matches mine."

He raised his brows. "You're kidding."

"I'm not. I have the other half of your heart."

"Which means I have the other half of yours."

"Right. Which means—"

"You're my perfect match," they said in unison.

Their eyes met and those four words filled Daniel with a warm sensation he couldn't name. That warmth was immediately followed by something that felt suspiciously like relief that he'd be her Valentine's date and not some other guy. "I guess that means you're stuck sharing the Valentine's Day dinner prize with me," he said.

"I guess so," she agreed, sauntering toward him with a sinful sway of her hips. "I'll try not to complain too much."

"I'll try to not to give you anything to complain about."

"You can start right now." She twined her arms around his neck and pressed herself against him. "By giving me one of those expert kisses."

His hands glided under her shirt to touch her warm, soft skin. "Happy to. But I thought you wanted chocolate."

"You're better than chocolate."

And that, Daniel decided as his mouth settled over hers, was one hell of a compliment coming from the Queen of the Chocogasm.

7

THE NEXT TWO weeks passed so quickly, Carlie felt as she'd merely blinked and they were over. Valentine's Day dawned bright and clear and she spent the morning working her shift at the Delaford spa, then visiting a client on the way home. At two o'clock she stowed her portable massage table in the trunk of her car, then slid into the front seat. Her regular weekly session with Mrs. Fanning had gone very well, especially considering that during the entire hour, Carlie's mind had stubbornly wandered from the task at hand to the one thing she'd spent the last two weeks thinking about.

Daniel Montgomery.

She closed her eyes and a veritable slide show of Daniel-induced memories flickered through her mind. Daniel, smiling, his dimples flashing at her. Pushing his fantasy-inspiring glasses up his nose. Falling asleep on her sofa with her puppies sprawled across his stomach. Lying in all his naked glory on her bed as she gave him a massage. The two of them feeding each other his chocolate truffles. Playing with P.B. and J. Walking hand in hand through downtown Austell. Playing Frisbee in the park with the dogs then enjoying a picnic lunch. Renting a James Bond flick and snuggling in with a bowl of popcorn. Talking, laughing, sharing childhood memories over pizza and late-night cappuccinos. Daniel gazing at her, his eyes dark with want. Whispering her name. Touching her. Over her. Under her. Buried deep inside her. His hands and mouth…everywhere.

And it was all about to end. Moving day was tomorrow.

Skulking beneath her happiness of the past two weeks was

a sensation that had grown each day, until it now sat like a rock in her stomach. She'd tried to put various euphemistic names on the feeling, but the way it squeezed her right now, there was only one word for it: desolation.

Throughout the past two weeks she'd felt as if an egg timer were counting down the minutes of their time together, an incessant internal ticking clock that she'd forced herself to shove to the back of her mind. But there was now no more room to shove because as of tomorrow morning he'd be gone. Another wave of desolation washed over her, this one nearly drowning her.

An image flashed through her mind of how she'd last seen him before departing his house this morning: in the shower— a heart-stopping sight she was now very familiar with—water sluicing down his lean, muscular, aroused body. Just the memory shot tingles down to her toes.

The man occupied every corner of her mind. *Occupied?* Ha. More like he'd pitched a tent, settled himself in a comfy chair, and taken up permanent residence in her brain cells. Which was bad enough. But she greatly feared the situation was far worse than that—that he'd managed to take up permanent residence in her heart as well. Which, given his imminent departure from Austell, was *really* bad. She needed help. A pep talk. Pronto. Since there wasn't a twelve-step "Fight Your Daniel Addiction" program listed in the phone book—and she'd looked—she settled for the next best thing. Digging her cell phone out of her purse, she quickly dialed.

"Hello?" said a familiar voice.

"Hi, Mom."

"What's wrong, sweetie?"

Carlie couldn't help but laugh. "I literally said two words. What makes you think something's wrong?"

"I'm a mother. I know these things. And based on your voice, I'm guessing that whatever's wrong involves a man, most likely your neighbor Daniel you briefly mentioned when we spoke last week."

Briefly? She'd said his *name*. And only because Daniel had been there when her mom had called and she'd heard his voice in the background while he'd played with P.B. and J. "Okay, you've always been good at guessing, but this time you're scaring me. What do you have—a crystal ball?"

"No, just the 'I know when my baby needs me' chromosome that never goes away, no matter how grown-up that baby might be. So tell me what's wrong."

"Maybe I'm just calling to wish you a happy Valentine's Day."

"Thank you. Same to you. Now what's wrong?"

Since there was no point in trying to deny she was troubled, Carlie blew out a long breath, then tried to put into words the unsettling thoughts spinning around in her mind, grateful she and her mother could discuss anything.

"Over the past two weeks, Daniel and I have been, um, seeing quite a lot of each other." Literally. Another image of him naked flashed through her mind. "And things have been… terrific," she continued, although "terrific" didn't even begin to do justice to what they'd shared. "He's very…nice," she grimaced at the lukewarm word, "and I don't mean just between the sheets. Which is really the problem. And I guess that's why I'm feeling so…out of sorts. He's moving tomorrow, and well, I'm just…sorry he's leaving. I…I'm going to miss him." To Carlie's dismay, her bottom lip trembled and moisture pushed behind her eyes. "Which is something I hadn't anticipated. I knew going in that our time together had an end date tattooed on it. We both did. And that was fine with me. Believe me, the last thing I was looking for was a man to clutter up my life. You know that I'd sworn off serious relationships, at least until school is finished."

"I recall you telling me that, yes."

She raked her free hand through her hair. "But Daniel turned out to be so…different. So unexpected. He makes me laugh. He's talented and smart. Kind and generous. Easy-going and patient to a fault with P.B. and J. He's nice to his family. On top of all that, he's spent hours designing and building me this fabulous, professional website, that I'd never be able to afford, to advertise my massage therapy services. Our time together was supposed to be no-strings but instead I find myself tied up in big, huge knots."

"And why do you think that is?"

"I guess because I…like him." She pinched the bridge of her nose and forced herself to admit the frightening truth that she could no longer deny. "Problem is, I think that maybe I like him a little too much. Certainly more than I wanted to."

"Hmmm. And what are you planning to do about that?"

"Planning?" Carlie, frowned then shook her head. "Uh, well, nothing. There's nothing I *can* do. He's leaving for Boston tomorrow. This was nothing more than a fling. For both of us. My life is here. His life is there. I don't have the time or energy to devote to a long-distance relationship. And even if I did, he hasn't given me any indication he'd be interested in doing so."

"Have you talked about it?"

"We agreed we'd 'keep in touch,'" she made air quotes her mom couldn't see, "but you know what that means. We'll exchange a few e-mails or phone calls that will turn painfully awkward once he starts dating someone else. Which I bet won't take long once the women of Boston discover him." An unpleasant sensation that could only be called jealousy slithered through her, making her want to slap the entire female population of Massachusetts.

"And also awkward when *you* start dating someone as well," Mom said.

"Right," Carlie agreed, trying to picture herself in another man's arms and failing completely.

"Does he know how you feel?"

"*I* don't know how I feel. Except that I'm…confused. And irritated at myself for letting my heart get even the smallest bit involved."

"Do you think it's possible that maybe his heart's involved, too?"

Carlie's pulse jumped at the softly spoken question but then she shoved aside the ridiculous flare of hope it ignited. "I hope not because the bottom line is it wouldn't matter. He's leaving, I'm staying and there'll be an entire country between us."

Her mom's sigh came across the phone. "I'm sorry, honey.

I wish there was something I could say to make you feel better. A bandage I could put on your boo-boo."

A sad smile tugged at Carlie's lips. "Me, too. But I appreciate you listening. I'm just being silly. Sentimental 'cause it's Valentine's Day and all. Once he's gone and I'm not seeing him every day, everything will be back to normal. I'll be fine. Perfectly fine."

"I'm sure you will be. But…"

"But what?"

"Is fine good enough?"

Carlie frowned and gripped the phone. She hesitated for a moment, thinking, then said, "Being 'fine' sounds like I'm settling for something, as opposed to, say, being 'deliriously happy.'" Her frown deepened. "And maybe being deliriously happy is something I shouldn't give up so easily."

"Maybe it's not. You're a smart girl, Carlie. You'll know the right thing to do."

Her throat tightened at her mom's assessment. She didn't feel smart. In fact, she felt as if she'd foolishly ventured beyond a *thin ice* warning and was about to crash through and sink below the surface.

"But I can't give up something that was never mine in the first place, Mom. The only thing definite about my time with Daniel was that it was temporary." She heaved a sigh, then glanced at her watch. "I need to go. Daniel and I are having the dinner we won together tonight and I have to get ready."

"At least you won the Valentine's Day contest," Mom said in an overly cheerful voice.

"Sure did." Which was exactly what she'd wanted.

Unfortunately, she feared she'd gotten much more than she'd bargained for.

WITH A BOUQUET of tissue-wrapped flowers clutched in one hand, Daniel stood on Carlie's porch and drew a deep breath. For reasons he refused to examine too closely, he felt unnerved. Tense.

It's just all this moving stuff, he told himself, flexing his shoulders to work out the stiffness. Yeah, all the last-minute tasks. Packing his car for the cross country drive. Settling everything with the Realtor. Getting the phone shut off and the mail forwarded.

Saying goodbye to Carlie.

And that, unfortunately, had somehow turned into an insurmountable task.

Which was ridiculous. He'd known from minute one that their time together would be brief. Hell, part of the beauty of the whole situation was that he'd be able to walk away with no regrets. Fun and games with no strings, no commitments, no problems.

Except he hadn't counted on enjoying her company so thoroughly. He hadn't doubted they'd be good in bed—and he'd definitely been right on that score—but he hadn't expected to enjoy her so much out of bed. Hadn't known she was so compassionate, so deeply committed and loyal to the things that were important to her, so witty. Hadn't anticipated her thoughtful intelligence, her goofy sense of humor, her ability to laugh at herself. Hadn't foreseen liking her so damn much. Hell, he even liked her dogs. And the thought of leaving tomorrow…it made him tense with an unpleasant sensation that felt like an all-over body cramp.

He dragged his free hand through his hair. What the hell was wrong with him? He should be on top of the world. The Realtor reported that someone was very interested in his house. A great job in a great city awaited him.

He was just…nervous. Yeah, that's all it was. Once he was settled in Boston, he'd be fine. Just fine. Perfectly fine.

Feeling better, like the coach had just pumped him up with a pre-game pep talk, he rang Carlie's doorbell. P.B. and J. set up a frantic chorus and he smiled at the commotion. Seconds later the door opened, and Carlie appeared, flustered and laughing, trying unsuccessfully to hold back the puppies. His heart executed the now familiar roll it performed every time he saw her.

She wore a fire-engine red dress that hugged her curves in a five-alarm way. With its high neck and long sleeves, the dress showed no skin at all, yet the way it showcased her form earned it the title of Sexiest Damn Outfit He'd Ever Seen. Strappy silver heels made her toned legs appear endless. A memory of those legs wrapped around his hips, urging him deeper into her body flashed through his mind, leaving a trail of steamy heat in its wake.

Her glossy curls looked soft and had "mess with me" written all over them. A shimmer of gloss that matched her dress made her lips look like a delicious candy apple, filling him with an almost painful anticipation of tasting that luscious mouth.

"P.B. and J. are happy to see you," she said loudly, to be heard above the noise.

"Every guy likes an enthusiastic greeting."

"Oh? Then you're gonna love this." She wrapped her arms around his neck, pressed herself against him and kissed him.

Those candy-apple lips tasted as good as they looked, and with a groan, his arms went around her, pulling her closer, pressing the flowers into her back, deepening the delicious kiss she'd initiated. Her delicate, musky, floral scent filled his head and it flashed through his mind that he'd never again be able to smell flowers and not think of her. When he finally lifted his head, his glasses were—no surprise—fogged over. After pulling them off, he looked into her gorgeous eyes, which she'd outlined with some sort of smoky color that made them appear larger and more luminous than usual.

"You were right," he said, slowly rubbing himself against her. "That was very much enthusiastic. And I loved it."

She waggled her brows. "Wait till you see what I have planned for later."

Later…when they would say good-bye. He dropped a quick kiss on her forehead then forced a smile. "Can't wait." After releasing her, he stepped back and presented the bouquet with a flourish. "For you. Happy Valentine's Day."

She accepted the flowers, then buried her face in the blooms. "They're beautiful. Thank you."

"You're welcome. And speaking of beautiful…" He ran his fingers down her sleeve. "You look incredible."

Her gaze tracked over his charcoal-gray suit, white dress shirt, and red paisley silk tie. "I was about to say the same thing to you. C'mon in. I'll put my flowers in water and then we can leave." She turned and headed across the threshold.

"That sounds…" His voice trailed off. Her dress, which completely covered up the front of her, left her entire back—from her neck to her hips—completely bare.

"Sounds what?" she asked over her shoulder as she headed toward the kitchen.

"Er, great." With his gaze fastened on her gorgeous bare skin, he entered the house, closed the door, then followed her into the kitchen. P.B. and J. scampered ahead of him, racing toward their food bowls, sliding across the hardwood floor. He came up behind her as she reached up to pull a glass vase from an upper cabinet, wrapped his arms around her waist and buried his face in her fragrant hair.

"That's some dress. But I think it's on backwards," he said, gently nibbling on her earlobe.

She laughed, reaching back to encircle his neck, then tilting her head to afford him better access. "Now *that* would cause quite a stir at the restaurant."

"Sweetheart, you're causing such a stir right here, we might not make it to the restaurant." To prove his words, he pressed his erection more firmly against her buttocks, then groaned when she wriggled against him. "Are you wearing anything under this?" he asked, skimming his hands over the silky material.

"Mmmm…you mean besides skin?"

"Yeah."

She turned around and, with her eyes dancing with mischief, slipped her hands beneath his suit jacket to skim her palms up his back. "If I told you, it would ruin your Valentine's Day surprise."

"The only thing that'll surprise me is if you make it out of this kitchen without my finding out."

"I see." She reached behind her, then drew forth a package wrapped in shiny red paper. "Then I guess this won't come as any big shocker."

His brows shot up. "What's that?"

"A present. For you. Happy Valentine's Day."

Surprised pleasure washed through him as he accepted the rectangular-shaped gift. "Are you a magician? Where'd it come from?"

"It was right there on the counter the whole time."

"Ah. That explains it. I was mightily distracted." He moved to stand next to her, leaning his hips against the counter. "Should I open it?"

She looked toward the ceiling and blew out an exaggerated breath. "Clearly you don't know what the heck a 'present' is."

A sheepish grin tugged his lips. "Okay, silly question. I'm officially a dork."

"True. But you're adorable."

"I guess that makes me…adorkable?"

She laughed. "Exactly. Now open your present so we're not late for our dinner reservation."

His gaze tracked down her luscious form. "If you didn't want to be late, you seriously wore the wrong dress."

Her lips twitched. "Would it help if I took it off?"

"That depends on what you're hoping to help. If it's our punctuality, definitely not. But leave it on. I want to be the one who takes it off you. In the meantime, I'll try to focus." Turning his attention to his gift, he removed the wrapping paper and found himself holding a hardcover book with a dark brown glossy cover that looked so much like a chocolate bar, he was tempted to take a bite.

He ran his fingers over the gold embossed letters on the cover and read "*Nothing is Better Than Chocolate.*"

"I bought it at Sinfully Sweet," she said. "It has tons of great pictures and Ellie Fairbanks said it provides an interesting history of candy-making. It's sort of a dual Valentine's Day-going away gift. A little something to remember me by."

Her words brought an odd lump to his throat. As if he stood any chance of forgetting her. "Thanks. It's great."

"Like with anything chocolate, I couldn't resist. Besides," she added, bumping his hip with hers, "I think we actually proved the title wrong. At least a few times."

"At least." He turned to look at her. He wanted to smile, to keep the moment light, but the instant his gaze found hers, all remnants of amusement faded. "Actually, as far as I'm concerned, we proved that title wrong *every* time." He set the book on the counter, then snagged her into his arms and lightly kissed her soft mouth. "Thank you."

"You're welcome." When he moved in to kiss her again, she leaned back and pressed her fingers against his lips. "Oh, no. You have that look in your eye. I know that look."

"I bet you do. And you should. You put it there. You and…" his hands skimmed over her hips, "this dress."

"Good. I'm glad, seeing as how that was the point." She splayed her hands against his chest and shot him a stern look. "But this dress stays *on* until after dinner."

"How long after?" he asked, mentally calculating the number of seconds he'd require to peel the soft, stretchy fabric off her.

She considered for several seconds, then with a wicked grin said, "Until we get home."

He groaned.

"And inside the house."

He groaned again. Damn. There went any plans to get her naked the instant he parked in the driveway. "You're killing me. Seriously. I may be dead by then."

She shot him a saucy wink that revved his pulse into the danger zone. "Don't worry, Mr. Adorkable. I'll revive you."

8

THROUGHOUT THE ELEGANT meal at The Delaford's five-star restaurant, Carlie felt as if she'd been divided in two. Part of her enjoyed the fabulous seven-course meal; the romantic atmosphere, courtesy of the luxurious surroundings, soft music, muted lighting and candle glow; the delicious, chilled champagne; the stimulating conversation with Daniel whose undivided attention and heated, admiring gaze made her feel feminine and desirable, interesting and witty.

Hot and bothered.

But during the entire evening, another part of her was consumed by the ticking of that incessant internal countdown clock, while her brain silently repeated the words, *He's leaving tomorrow. This is your last night together.*

Over and over, the words reverberated through her mind, a haunting mantra that taunted her with the knowledge that each moment of this magical evening was one that wouldn't be repeated. There would be no more romantic dinners, no more flirting over a champagne toast, no more holding hands between courses, no more intimate glances, no more smiles and laughter over a shared joke.

No more Daniel.

By the time they left the restaurant, she felt as if a weight sat on her chest, and a heavy silence swelled between them during the ride home. She remained quiet thanks to the lump that had settled in her throat, but what was his excuse? She peeked at him from the corner of her eye. He was frowning and a muscle ticked in his jaw. Tiny tendrils of something that felt suspiciously like desperation licked at her insides. By the time he pulled into her driveway, the ticking clock and the mantra echoing through her mind had reached epic proportions.

The instant he put the car in Park, she unfastened her seatbelt, then reached over to unclick his and turn off the ignition. The headlights flicked off, leaving them ensconced in intimate darkness. Before he could move, she grabbed his lapels and dragged him toward her.

"You kiss me now," he said, his voice a deep, warning growl, "and I swear we won't get out of his car until—"

"Perfect," she said, shifting her butt over the console and settling herself across his lap. "Can't wait."

"Perfect." His mouth came down on hers in a wild, demanding kiss that stole her breath. In a heartbeat, his hands were everywhere: cupping her breasts, teasing her nipples through the stretch jersey material, gliding up her legs, over her thighs, then beneath her hem. When his palms glided over her bottom and discovered she wore nothing under her dress, his feral-sounding groan vibrated in the air.

He yanked the stretchy material upward, and she rose onto her knees and straddled him. With her two remaining brain cells that still functioned, she grabbed her small satin purse and pulled out the condom she'd stashed there—no easy task with his magical fingers skimming over her bare bottom then slipping between her thighs to caress her slick, swollen folds.

Heart pounding, breathing choppy, she slapped the condom against his chest. "Want you," she whispered. "Inside me. *Now*."

The few seconds it took him to free his erection and roll on the protection nearly sent her over the edge. The instant he finished, she took him into her body with a heart-stopping, breath-stealing downward glide that perfectly matched his upward thrust.

The ride was wild and fast and hard. Her orgasm crashed over her, pulling her under, dragging a ragged cry from her lips that echoed Daniel's harsh groan.

With pleasurable aftershocks still rippling through her, she dragged open her heavy eyelids. At some point one of them must have tossed Daniel's glasses aside. A thrill of feminine satisfaction trilled through her at his glazed expression and flushed skin. His dark hair was rumpled from her frantic hands and a lock fell across his forehead. Reaching out, she gently brushed back the silky strands with fingers that weren't quite steady. When her gaze again found his, she discovered him watching her through very serious eyes.

For several long, intense seconds they simply stared at each other, and to Carlie's horror she felt moisture pushing behind her eyeballs. The urge to say something overwhelmed her, but anything breezy or lighthearted was beyond her. And she had to forcibly press her lips together to contain the completely unacceptable words that trembled there, aching to be said.

Please don't leave.

Something of her distress must have shown on her face because he frowned. "You okay?" he asked, his fingers drifting over her cheek.

No, damn it, she wasn't. She felt...ambushed. Hijacked. And it was all his fault. Him and his gorgeous dimples and sexy smile and the way he made her feel...and all the wonderful stuff that made him Daniel.

"Yes, I'm fine."

One corner of his mouth pulled up. "I'd like it noted in the record that even though it nearly killed me, I had every intention of honoring your request and waiting until we were in the house before pouncing on you. As it was, I did manage not to take off your dress." He ran his hands over her bare butt. "Yet."

She gave a solemn nod. "It shall be duly noted."

He leaned back against the head rest and studied her for several heartbeats, then said softly, "You're beautiful."

Her heart tripped over itself. "Says the nearsighted guy who isn't wearing his glasses."

"That's not what I meant, although you are undeniably gorgeous. Anybody can be beautiful on the outside. You're beautiful on the inside."

Damn it, that moisture was pushing at her eyeballs again. "Thank you. So are you."

"These past two weeks have been…great."

"Really great," she agreed in a rush, relieved to say it out loud. "I'm…I'm going to miss you."

He didn't say anything right away, just looked at her with an indecipherable expression that rushed embarrassed heat right up to her hairline. Why, oh, why had she blurted that out?

"I'm going to miss you, too, Carlie. Very much." He hesitated, then said, "I wish I didn't have to leave so soon."

His words tossed another brick on the heavy weight already pressing against her heart. "Me, too. But you do. Have to. Leave." She'd tried to sound light and breezy, but failed miserably.

"Yes, I do."

She cleared her throat and tried again for light and breezy. "And we both knew that." Another failure.

"Right. It just seems like the two weeks have gone by so fast."

"In a heartbeat," she agreed softly.

He looked troubled, confused, and for a brief instant an insane flicker of something hopeful flared in her. But then his expression cleared. "Why don't we go inside and see what we can come up with for our last night together?" he suggested.

His words extinguished the ridiculous, fragile flame of hope and she forced herself to nod. "What do you have in mind?"

His lips quirked upward and his dimples flashed, but the smile didn't seem to reach his eyes. "I'm thinking you. Me. Chocolate. Naked. And not necessarily in that order. For starters."

"Sounds…great." Except for the fact that when the him, her, chocolate, naked thing was finished, she knew there'd be no more Daniel.

9

AT NOON ON the day after Valentine's Day—five hours after she'd awakened to find herself alone—Carlie sat on her sofa and listlessly clicked the remote, watching talk shows and game shows flash by. Dressed in her rattiest, faded sweatpants, thickest wool socks and a faded green sweatshirt that warned Give Me the Damn Chocolate and No One Gets Hurt, she felt as frumpy and dumpy as she looked. Her normally bright den seemed dismal and dark from the lack of sunlight, the gray, overcast sky outside perfectly matching her mood.

Good grief, had only five hours passed since she'd awakened alone? It felt more like five years. She'd been crushed to find him already gone, but her common sense told it was for the best. He'd saved her the embarrassment of what undoubtedly would have turned into a messy, tearful goodbye on her part.

She'd spent the first two hours clutching the pillow that still bore traces of Daniel's clean scent, re-reading the one-line note he'd left on the pillowcase. *Thanks for a beautiful night.* And it had, indeed, been beautiful. She'd tortured herself reliving the magic while tears had tracked silently down her cheeks. Their frantic mating in the car. Their leisurely lovemaking in the shower with warm water cascading over them. Then Daniel carrying her to bed and making tender, exquisite love to her that said "goodbye" more clearly than any words. Falling asleep nestled in his strong arms.

Then she'd spent the last three hours here on the couch, sipping coffee that had long turned cold, and further tortured herself by replaying in her head the highlights of the entire past two weeks. More tears had soaked her cheeks, and all she had to show for the time was a stuffy nose, a wad of used-up tissues and a nagging headache. Even P.B. and J. had eventually tired of listening to her sniffles and were now sleeping on their favorite blanket in the corner.

With a sigh she turned off the TV and forced herself finally to admit the reason for her abject misery, because there could only be one explanation for why her heart felt as if it had been surgically removed.

She'd fallen in love.

"Argh!" Closing her eyes, she thumped her head against the back of the sofa. *Fabulous, Carlie.* If falling in love at the wrong time with the wrong guy were an Olympic event, she'd win the freakin' gold medal. Her only hope was that this bout of love would fade quickly. Maybe it hadn't had time to really grab hold of her and, like a bad cold, she could shake it loose with some TLC. Like a hot bath and a piece of chocolate.

Oh, yeah—*that* would help her get over him. *Not.* An image of them together in the bathtub materialized in her mind's eye, and she groaned. And probably for the next fifty years or so she'd think of Daniel whenever she ate chocolate. Okay, so maybe her TLC would have to be something more along the lines of a glass of orange juice and a vitamin pill.

Heaving a sigh, she rose and shuffled toward the bathroom, determined to splash some cold water on her face and get her butt in gear. She had a chapter to read before her class tonight. And having class tonight was good. Nothing like a couple of intense hours of organic chemistry to take her mind off Daniel and her battered heart. She'd concentrate on school and forget all about him. Yes, that was an excellent plan.

Walking into the bathroom, she slapped on the light and grimaced when the bright glare hit her in the eye. Then she looked in the mirror. And recoiled in horror.

Gack! She looked like something that the puppies wouldn't even want to bury in the back yard. Her hair was a rat's nest of frizz that stuck up from her head at all angles. Her eyes were swollen and sported half moons of mascara beneath them.

Blotchy skin, pale, tear-stained cheeks, red nose—yikes. She was eyeballing her lipstick on the counter, tempted to write *out of order* across the mirror, when the doorbell rang. The puppies began furiously barking, and she heard the skidding sounds of them hitting the wood floor as they raced toward the front door.

"Easy, guys," she said, entering the small foyer. As was her habit, she looked out one of the slender windows flanking the door. And froze. For about three seconds. Then she yanked open the door and stared at Daniel in stunned amazement.

While the puppies offered their ecstatic tail-wagging, tongue-lolling, yip-yapping greeting, she managed to say, "Hi."

"Hi." He pushed up his glasses then blinked. "Were you watching a scary movie?"

"Scary movie?"

"You sort of have that 'hair standing up on end' look." His gaze flicked over her ratty sweats and he smiled. "You look—"

"Don't say it—"

"—Amazing."

Before she could tell him she was very well aware that she looked like Godzilla's ugly sister, he stepped over the threshold, adroitly maneuvered around the prancing puppies, pulled her into his arms and laid a kiss on her that left her reeling as if she'd been clocked upside the head with a brick.

"Amazing," he repeated, nipping kisses along her jawline.

"Your glasses must be fogged over," she felt compelled to point out, clinging to his shoulders so she didn't slither to the floor.

"No. They must have been before, but not now. Everything's perfectly clear now."

She leaned back in the circle of his arms. "What are you doing here?" She'd been a whole three minutes into her plan to forget all about him. How was she supposed to forget him if he kept coming back?

For an answer, he closed the door, clasped her hand, then led her into the den. The puppies clamored after them, then gamboled off to the kitchen, no doubt to raid their kibble bowl.

He sat on the sofa, tugging her down next to him. Once she was seated, he said, "We have to talk."

Oh, God. *We have to talk*. The four scariest words in the English language. "What about?"

"Us."

That single word echoed through her head and warning tingles prickled along her spine. She searched his eyes and noted with alarm their serious expression. The only way there could be an "us" would be if she gave up everything here: her job, her schooling. Was that why he was here? To ask her to do that? A scary thought. But not nearly as terrifying as the knowledge that she might actually want him to ask.

"Us?" she repeated. "There is no more 'us.'"

"What if I told you I wanted there to be?"

Her heart performed a crazy dance. "How could that happen? Are you thinking in terms of a long-distance relationship?"

He shook his head. "No. That's not what I want."

Not sure if his answer left her more relieved or terrified, she asked, "What *do* you want?"

Reaching out, he clasped her hands. "Lately I've felt…unsettled. I couldn't put my finger on exactly what was wrong, so I put it down to moving-related stress. But over the past two weeks, since we've been together, this unsettled feeling has gotten a lot worse."

That didn't exactly sound promising. Not sure how to respond, she murmured, "Oh."

"I was bombarded with all these feelings I hadn't anticipated and it took me a while to get it all straightened out. But I finally figured it out, finally realized what was wrong. It hit me this morning. Which is why I left. But now I'm back."

"And I'm confused. What was wrong?"

"I wasn't happy. And the reason I wasn't happy was because I was leaving here. Turns out, deep down, I wasn't overjoyed about moving even *before* you entered the picture. Once you came on the scene, I grew even more miserable."

"Uh, thanks."

He shook his head and blew out a breath. "I didn't mean that the way it sounded. *You* didn't make me miserable, but the thought of moving away from you, of losing what we've started here, made me realize that I didn't want to go. I never wanted to go. Not really. I guess I saw my thirtieth birthday as a good time to reassess my life, my choices, and that, combined with pressure from my ex-girlfriend, had me momentarily convinced that I needed to change things, shake things up. So I did that, by finding a corporate job and making plans to get out of this small town."

He looked down at their joined hands, then lifted his head. When their gazes met, he continued, "Problem was, I love having my own business, making my own schedule. And I love this little town. And then came you. And as it turns out, I love you, too."

Everything inside Carlie stilled. "You do?"

"I do. As is. With no desire for you to change a thing or be anything other than the extraordinary woman you already are." A bemused smile flashed across his features and he shook his head. "Falling in love—one of those unforeseen circumstances predicted by our matching messages about passion. Unforeseen…but really great."

"In love with me," she repeated in a stunned whisper. "Since when?"

"Sweetheart, you had me at the chocogasm."

Emotions swamped her, but before she could open her mouth to speak, he rushed on, "You don't have to say anything, Especially if what you'd say isn't something good. I just… wanted you to know. And to tell you that I've spent the entire morning on the phone and at the Realtor's office. My house is off the market, Allied Computers is out a manager, and I'm not going anywhere."

Oh, God. She needed to breathe, but it seemed she'd forgotten how. *In with the good air, out with the bad air.* "Not going anywhere?" she managed to say.

"Nope. Well, except out to the porch. I left something there. I'll be right back."

Utterly dazed, Carlie watched him go. As soon as he was out of sight, she pinched her arm. Ouch! Okay, yes this was real. He returned seconds later, carrying a huge box bearing the Sinfully Sweet logo, which he set on the coffee table in front of her.

Carlie stared at the box, which covered more than half the table, then turned to him. "I can only guess that the contents of that box represent a dietary disaster. A caloric catastrophe. And based on its size, a financial fiasco. What did you buy?"

"What you said you wanted."

"What's that?"

"The day of Sinfully Sweet's grand opening, you told Ellie Fairbanks you wanted two of everything." He nodded toward the box. "That's two of everything."

Her jaw dropped. "Two of *everything in the store*?"

"Yup. It's all for you, but I'm hoping you'll share."

"With you."

"That's the plan."

"It would take us a very long time to eat all that chocolate."

"That's also the plan." With his gaze steady on hers, he said, "The night you showed up at my house wearing that towel, I'd been anxiously waiting for you to arrive. I remember thinking that everything was ready—the only thing missing was Carlie. Turned out those were very prophetic words."

She stared at the huge box and a sense of pure wonder and amazed happiness washed through her. Turning back to him, she asked, "And what if my feelings aren't the same as yours?"

"Then I'd just have to pull out all the stops to convince you that what we have together is really good. And that it will only get better. That we belong together. That you're everything I've ever wanted. And that I could make you very happy."

"I...see. So I guess that means if I were to tell you right now that I'm in love with you, I'd forfeit those 'pulling out all the stops' perks."

"Hell, no. God, no. Are you saying...? Do you mean...?" He looked so worried and so serious and so hopeful, she felt ashamed for teasing him for even a second. Framing his face between her hands, she said, "I love you, Daniel. Very much. And you don't have to convince me that what we have together is really good. Or that it will only get better. Or that we belong together. I already know. You're everything I've ever wanted. And I'm going to make you very happy."

With a groan, he dragged her onto his lap and kissed her until her head spun. Then he abruptly leaned back. "You're not just saying that because I bought you two of everything from Sinfully Sweet, are you?

"No." She waggled her brows. "But that definitely helped seal the deal."

He smiled. "I should have known I didn't need to look any further than my own backyard for happiness. Quite literally in my case."

"You sound like Dorothy from *The Wizard of Oz*."

"Huh. Not a very masculine comparison."

She leaned forward and ran her tongue over his bottom lip. "Oh, honey. I'd be delighted to tell you—and show you—all the fabulous ways you're masculine."

"Oh? What did you have in mind?"

"I was thinking you. Me. Chocolate. Naked." She shot him a wicked grin. "And not necessarily in that order."

SIMPLY SCRUMPTIOUS

Kate Hoffmann

1

DARCY SCOTT FINGERED the delicately stitched hem of the French cotton sheet. The fabric felt like silk and she closed her eyes and imagined those same sheets on her naked skin, the impossibly high thread count turning an ordinary night in bed into a positively sensual experience.

A handsome man suddenly appeared in the vision, a familiar face that had haunted her dreams over the years. His nude body was curled up against hers, his long leg thrown over her hips. He watched her with sleepy blue eyes, his sun-streaked hair mussed and a satisfied grin curling the corners of his mouth. And when he drew her nearer, his lips parted, ready to cover hers.

Darcy sucked in a sharp breath, then cursed silently, snapping herself out of the daydream. Once it had been real, but not for a very long time. She glanced over the restaurant table to find her assistant, Amanda Taylor, staring at her with a bemused smile.

"They're just sheets," Amanda said.

Darcy cleared her throat, trying to banish the image from her head. "According to you, they're the finest sheets in the world. How much?"

"Ah, Madame," Amanda teased in a heavy French accent. "But who can put a price on zee comfort of your guests? Imagine yourself between zeez sheets. Would you have anything else touch your naked body?" Amanda sighed as she tucked the neatly-folded sheet back into her tote. "I mean, besides a man with sensitive hands and deep blue eyes and gorgeous hair and a really big—"

"How much?" Darcy repeated, her voice cracking slightly. From now on, no more daytime fantasies! They were beginning to interfere with business and Darcy had already decided to put her profession ahead of anything else in her life. It made things so much simpler.

She hadn't always been prone to thoughts of a sexual nature. But since she'd broken her engagement over a year ago, Darcy hadn't enjoyed the pleasures of a man's body. In truth, she hadn't been touched by a man in exactly 435 days. She'd never meant to keep a precise count except that last week, she'd become curious and decided to figure it out. Now, with every day that passed, she felt compelled to add to the tally, unable to get the ever-growing figure out of her head.

"Your father has given you carte blanche," Amanda said, drawing Darcy back to their conversation. "My French is a bit rusty, but loosely translated, I believe that means big wallet…or blank check or…well, it means spend a lot of money."

"I just don't want to make any mistakes. Daddy can take this job away from me just as easily as he gave it to me, especially if I don't control the budget."

Darcy had been manager of The Delaford for over two years, the youngest person to hold a manager's position in Sam Scott's string of hotels—and the only woman. The job had been temporary at first, a way for Darcy to gain more experience while her father searched for the right person to take over. But Darcy had been good at the job and her father had delayed finding a replacement.

The Delaford Spa and Resort was small and very exclusive. Set on a stunning piece of property just ninety miles from downtown San Francisco, it was a popular destination for West Coast celebrities. It boasted a luxurious hotel, a championship golf course, tennis courts, stables and a full-service spa and health club. Located on the shores of Crystal Lake, the hotel had 180 guestrooms that averaged 95% occupancy year-round. For the past three years, the gourmet restaurant had earned a five-star rating and regularly drew evening dinner guests from the city.

"I can get the sheets for five hundred a bed as long as we sell them in our gift shop," Amanda said. "That's well below wholesale. And they'll hold up much better than the sheets we use now. The more you wash them, the better they feel." Amanda reached for her water and took a sip. "I've had housekeeping put a set on your bed. Sleep with them for a few nights and you'll think they're a bargain at twice the price."

Oh, that was just what she needed, Darcy mused. Another reminder that the only thing she'd been sleeping with for exactly 435 days was her bed linen. "Thanks," she murmured. "I'll give them a try."

Amanda motioned for the waitress, then asked for the dessert tray. "Since we aren't eating lunch at The Delaford, I want to see what kinds of goodies they serve here. Would you like to join me?"

"I've got a better idea," Darcy said. "We're doing a Valentine's Day promo with the new chocolate shop in town. We're giving away a dinner at The Winery to the winners. In exchange, they're doing a new monogram chocolate for our pillows."

"Nice trade," Amanda said.

Darcy nodded. "Ellie Fairbanks should have some samples ready for us." She dropped cash on top of the bill, then pushed back from the table. "While we're there, I'll buy us both a half-pound of truffles and we'll indulge together."

They walked out of the restaurant into bright afternoon sunshine. The day was warm for early February with just a slight chill in the brisk breeze. Darcy and Amanda strolled down the charming main street of Austell, lingering at the window of a floral shop before heading down Larchmont Street to Sinfully Sweet. Freshly painted gilt letters adorned the front window of the shop and a bell rang as they went through the door.

The interior of the shop was quiet and softly lit. Gleaming glass cases displayed a seductive array of chocolates, from buttery toffees to rich pecan turtles to decadent flavored truffles. Ellie was waiting on a gentleman customer but she waved at Darcy, promising that she'd be with her momentarily.

Amanda perused the chocolates while Darcy passed the time studying the broad shoulders and narrow waist of the customer ahead of her. She couldn't tell his age, but he was dressed fashionably in dark trousers and a fitted sweater, clothes that enhanced his tall, lean form and long limbs.

Her gaze rose to his neck where sun-streaked hair curled around his collar in a tantalizing way. Darcy's fingers twitched as she imagined them slipping through the thick strands. She bit back a soft moan. Now she was lusting after a total stranger! What was wrong with her?

"And are you looking for love?" Ellie asked.

At first Darcy thought the question had been directed at her, but then she realized that Ellie was talking to the man. Darcy peered cautiously around his shoulder and saw Ellie place a huge basket of chocolates on the counter in front of him.

"The candy is for my sister," he explained, his voice deep and rich. "She's addicted to chocolate. She has twin boys and I think she self-medicates with the stuff."

Ellie slipped the chocolates into a pretty shopping bag. "Well, here's a special little treat for you." She pointed to the basket of chocolate heart halves wrapped in blue foil. "There's a message tucked inside. If you find its match before Valentine's Day, then both you and the lady with the matching half will win a romantic prize."

Darcy drew a deep breath, the citrusy scent of the man's cologne teasing at her nose. The guy had to be single. Married men just didn't smell this good. She fought the ridiculous urge to stand on her tiptoes and press her nose into the curve of his neck.

"Well, Ellie," the man said, "I appreciate the sentiment, but I'm not looking for romance."

"Who knows? Romance might be looking for you," Ellie replied. She sent Darcy a sly smile, then picked out a chocolate heart and tucked it into his bag.

He chuckled softly as he gathered his purchases. But Darcy hadn't realized how close she'd been standing. When he turned, she stood squarely in his path. She quickly stepped to the left at the very same moment he stepped to his right. Their little dance continued for a few silent measures, back and forth, before Darcy risked a glance up at him.

The breath froze in her throat as their eyes met—eyes she'd seen in a fantasy no more than ten minutes ago. Not much had changed in ten minutes—or in five years. Kel Martin was still the kind of handsome that left a woman weak in the knees. His hair, usually cropped short for the baseball season, now fell carelessly across his forehead. And his blue eyes were even bluer, if that was possible.

"Now that we've mastered the two-step, would you like to try a tango?" he teased with a boyish grin. The smile sent a shiver skittering down her spine.

"Wh-what?" The word came out as a nervous croak. "Oh, right. Dance. No. I mean, I'm sorry." Darcy quickly stepped aside, but for a long moment, he didn't move. His gaze was still fixed on her face and a tiny frown wrinkled his suntanned brow. For an instant, she saw a flash of recognition in his eyes, but then it was gone.

Her cheeks warmed with embarrassment. Did he remember her? Was he even now scrolling back in his mind, through all the girls he'd slept with, winding back to that wild night they'd spent together in his hotel room?

He'd been a handsome stranger, nursing a beer in the bar of the Penrose, her father's San Francisco hotel. She'd just flown in from San Diego for a board meeting, and after a tense day, was looking for a way to unwind. One glass of champagne had led to another and before she knew it, they were riding the elevator up to his room, unable to keep their hands off each other.

They hadn't bothered with last names or even discussed why they were both alone in a hotel bar. It didn't seem to matter at the time. All that mattered was getting out of their clothes and into each other's arms as quickly as possible.

Once they'd accomplished that, the rest of the night had passed in a haze of desperate commands and electrifying sensations. He'd explored her body so thoroughly at first that she'd felt certain she'd go mad the moment he finally entered her. And when at last he did, Darcy had shattered with an intensity that she'd never felt before—or since.

Even now, after all this time, she could recall every single moment, the weight of his body against her hips, the warmth of his mouth, the sound of his voice, low and ragged as he exploded inside her.

She felt his fingers on her arm and Darcy blinked. "Are you all right?" he asked, bending closer to catch her gaze.

"Yes," she murmured. "Of course." She took another step to the side and a moment later, he was gone, just as he had been that morning when she'd found herself alone in his hotel room.

Darcy waited until she heard the bell on the shop door tinkle, then released a tightly-held breath, the lack of oxygen making her a bit dizzy. Amanda rushed to her side and grabbed her elbow. "Do you know who that was?"

"Yeah, I know," Darcy said numbly. "Kel Martin."

Amanda seemed taken aback. "I didn't think you followed the Giants."

"Everyone knows who Kel Martin is," Darcy replied. He was always in the news, if not for his league-leading ERA, then for his colorful love life. According to the gossips, Kel favored leggy models, rising starlets and the occasional jet-setting heiress. Though Darcy was reluctant to admit it, whenever he appeared in a newspaper or magazine, she made sure to search the article for details and study the photo until she had catalogued every one of his handsome features all over again. He was a stranger to her and yet she felt as if they were still lovers, the memory of their night so vivid in her mind.

"He touched you," Amanda said.

Darcy glanced down at her forearm, then rubbed her palm over the spot. The tingle seemed to have spread down to her fingers and toes. "Did he?"

"He's very handsome," Ellie Fairbanks commented. "Have you two met before?"

Darcy shook her head. "Why would you say that?"

The shopkeeper shrugged. "It seemed as though there was a… connection between you." She smoothed her palms over her apron. "Well, I have your samples all ready. But you must try some of our other chocolates. Whatever tempts you will be my treat."

"I'll take some of that romance you were offering," Amanda said. "What about you, Darcy? Are you in the mood for love?"

"I think I'll stick with the truffles," Darcy insisted.

Ellie wandered over to one of the display cases and Amanda trailed after her. As they discussed the merits of the various flavors, Darcy tried to calm her nerves. What was Kel Martin doing in Austell? Was he vacationing here or just passing through? Oh, God, could he be planning a stay at The Delaford?

Amanda hurried back to her side, a pair of truffles resting on her palm. She offered one to Darcy and, without thinking, Darcy popped it into her mouth. The creamy chocolate melted instantly, a hint of raspberry in the ganache center. A tiny groan slipped from her lips. If anything could make her forget her brush with the past, the truffles were definitely it. But it would take more than just one.

"Get me a half-pound of the raspberry and a half-pound of the mocha," Darcy murmured. "And add five of those dark chocolate turtles and some of the coconut clusters. Then get whatever you want and we'll start an account."

Good chocolate was definitely better than bad sex. But how much chocolate would it take to forget her night with Kel Martin? Two or three tons?

Darcy had always known there was a chance she'd run into

him again and she'd even fantasized about how it might go. But now that it had happened, Darcy cursed the decision to forgo dessert at the restaurant. Her life could have gone on normally had she never seen him again. But even as she thought it, Darcy knew it was a lie. No matter how much time passed, she'd never forget her night with Kel.

Ellie chatted with Darcy as she put their chocolates into a pretty red bag. Her husband, Marcus, appeared from the back room with another box filled with the pillow chocolates, embossed with the "D" of the Delaford logo.

"Before you leave, I have to give you one more thing." Ellie smiled slyly then held out another basket, this one filled with pink hearts. "Choose one," she said. Darcy plucked a heart out of the basket and Amanda took one for herself.

"There's a message inside," Ellie explained. "If either of you finds its match before Valentine's Day, then you and the gentleman will win a romantic dinner at The Winery at The Delaford and one hundred chocolate hearts." She laughed softly. "You have heard of The Delaford, haven't you?"

Darcy turned the heart over in her hand. "What if no one finds their match? What are the chances of finding a complete stranger with the same message?"

"All lovers are strangers in the beginning, aren't they?" Ellie replied.

Darcy tucked the heart into her purse. "I wish I had time for romance," she murmured, turning for the door.

"Hey, I'll give it a shot," Amanda said. She caught up to Darcy and pulled open the door. "I really don't want to spend another Valentine's Day sitting at home in front of the television, trying to convince myself that I'm happier without a man. Here's my Valentine fantasy: flowers and candy and maybe a pricey piece of jewelry. Spending the night in bed, making wild, sweaty love with a man who'll at least pretend he's a romantic for a day."

"But the fantasy is always better than the reality," Darcy murmured. "And sometimes it's a lot easier on the heart."

KEL MARTIN sat in his car across the street from Sinfully Sweet and watched through the windows of the Mercedes convertible as the two women left the store. His gaze fixed on the slender brunette and he pulled his sunglasses down so he could see her more clearly. Once she'd disappeared around the corner, he absently reached for the box of chocolates beside him and popped one in his mouth.

When he'd first looked into Darcy's eyes, he'd been sure it was her. And then, a heartbeat later, he'd thought perhaps his imagination had been playing tricks on him. But once she'd spoken, all doubts had disappeared. That voice, so soft and captivating, was impossible to forget.

His thoughts drifted back to that night, to all the new and exciting experiences they'd shared. He'd had his share of one-night stands, but this had been different. It was as if their anonymity had broken down every wall between them, robbing them of their inhibitions.

They'd both felt completely free to test the limits of their desire. He recalled her words as he moved inside her, murmuring things that no woman had ever said to him before, making him feel as if he were the only man in the world who could pleasure her.

"Darcy," he said softly. He'd never asked her last name, nor had he bothered with a phone number or an address before he'd walked away. At the time, he'd stupidly believed there would be others like her, women who could reach into his soul and take control of his body as she had. It was only later that Kel realized what they'd shared: pure pleasure, an almost mystical connection between their bodies and their minds.

He'd spent the past five years trying to find it again and Kel had come to the conclusion that it had been a moment lost in time. He raked his hand through his hair, groaning softly. They'd barely even spoken that night and yet every minute they'd spent together had been burned indelibly on his brain.

Kel had heard a lot of stories in the locker room, one wilder

Simply Scrumptious

than the next. And he'd contributed his share of experiences to the discussion. But he'd never once talked about Darcy, never tried to put what they had shared into words. With her, it had been more than just a one-night stand.

All those years ago… At first glance, she'd seemed unapproachable. The bar had been nearly empty and she hadn't noticed him at first. And when he had caught her eye, there hadn't been any recognition.

At that moment, all Kel had wanted was a normal conversation with a woman—no baseball talk, no plastic smiles or casual caresses, no silly giggling over every wry comment he made. He had wanted something simple and easy. He'd never imagined the pleasures he'd been about to experience.

Over the years, Kel had tried to convince himself that Darcy wasn't any different from other women. He'd told himself if he got to know her, she'd turn desperate, grasping, anxious to claim him like some trophy she could show off to her girlfriends. But deep down, he suspected he'd made a mistake in walking way.

"The hell if I'll make the same mistake twice," Kel muttered. If he harbored any hope of putting that night out of his head, then he'd have to prove to himself that Darcy *was* just an ordinary woman and not the ultimate sex goddess.

Kel stepped out of the car and jogged across the street. Austell was a small town. It shouldn't be too difficult to find her. Hell, she was probably married and raising two or three children. That would put a quick end to his fantasies.

He opened the door of the shop and stepped back inside. Ellie Fairbanks smiled at him as he approached, her hands braced on the counter. "I know why you came back," she said.

"You do?"

"You dipped into those chocolates you bought for your sister and now you need a new box."

"Yes, I do. But this time I'd like to have them delivered."

"Where does your sister live?"

"I want to send them to that pretty brunette who was in

here a few minutes ago. You have her name and address, don't you?"

"I do," Ellie said.

Kel nodded. "And what would that address be?"

She hitched her hands on her hips and regarded him suspiciously. "I got the distinct impression you knew her, but now I'm not so sure."

"Darcy and I are old friends. Let's just say, I'd like to renew our acquaintance," Kel replied. "Give me a small box of your most decadent chocolates."

Ellie gathered a selection of chocolates and then returned to the counter. She handed him a gift card, but he pushed it back at her, shaking his head. "On second thought, I should deliver these personally." He cleared his throat. "And where would I do that?"

"Try The Delaford," Ellie said with a soft chuckle. "It's a resort and spa out on Route 18. Just follow the signs."

He pulled his wallet from his pocket and paid for the chocolates, then sent Ellie a grateful smile.

As he exited the store, he let his gaze wander over the quaint street. He'd come to Austell to take a look for a lake home, a quiet place outside the craziness of San Francisco, a place where he could exist in relative anonymity, where he could walk down the street without people staring. He'd intended a quick stop in Austell to look at a few properties before he continued on up the coast to his sister's place. But a chance meeting in a candy store had derailed his plans.

Kel's step was a bit quicker as he walked back to his car. He would see Darcy again; he'd make certain of that. But when he did, he wasn't sure what to say. What was the protocol? Were they supposed to pretend they didn't know each other? How exactly should a gentleman bring up the subject of their previous one-night stand?

Kel got behind the wheel of the Benz and started it. But he left it idling at the curb as a trail of possibilities drifted through his mind. What if she didn't remember him at all? He'd managed to turn that one night into the pinnacle of his sex life. What if she'd forgotten about him years ago?

He thought he'd seen recognition in her eyes, but was it real or was he just fooling himself? Right now, Darcy could be trying to place him, wondering just where she'd met him before. Kel tipped his head back and closed his eyes. Or maybe she had recognized him from the papers. Maybe to her, he wasn't the man she'd spent one incredible night with, he was Kel Martin, pitcher for the San Francisco Giants.

"If I see her again, I'll just pretend I don't remember her," he murmured. "Unless she remembers me, then I'll remember her." It was a plan, though Kel wasn't sure it was the best he could devise. He just needed some time alone with her, just a few minutes to figure out where he stood.

He pulled the car out into traffic and headed west. Just as Ellie Fairbanks had said, the signs directed him to The Delaford. He'd been invited to play a celebrity golf tournament there a few years back. Had he accepted, he might have renewed their acquaintance sooner.

A long brick drive wound through beautifully landscaped grounds. The three-story hotel, a mix of new California and old Spanish architecture, was nestled in the center of the golf course, huge pillars flanking the entrance. Kel drove beneath the columned portico and a parking attendant jogged up to the car. As soon as Kel stepped out, the attendant grinned. "Hello, Mr. Martin. Welcome to The Delaford."

Kel was so used to people recognizing him that it barely registered. He smiled at the attendant and tossed him the keys. "My bags are in the trunk," he said.

The lobby was cool and serene, awash in soft colors and green plants, soothing music drifting through the air. The desk clerk greeted him with a warm smile. "Mr. Martin! We weren't expecting you today. How nice that you chose to visit The Delaford."

"I don't have a reservation. I was just in the area and thought I'd see if you had a room. Anything will do."

The desk clerk glanced over at her computer. "We have two suites and several deluxe rooms available. Which would you prefer?"

"I'll take the suite. For a week if that's possible." Kel pulled out his credit card and handed it to her. "I'm hoping you can help me. I'm looking for…Darcy. Do you know her?"

"Miss Scott?"

"Tall, brunette, very pretty. Really great legs."

The clerk nodded. "That sounds like her."

"Yes, Miss Scott," Kel said. "Darcy Scott." He noticed the name of the hotel behind the desk. The Delaford Resort and Spa. A Scott Hotel Property.

"Of course I know her. Would you like me to get her for you?"

"No," Kel said, deciding to bide his time before their next meeting. "But I would like to know how to get hold of her if I need her."

"Just call the front desk and ask for the manager."

"The manager," Kel repeated. Beautiful, sexy, intriguing Darcy Scott was the manager of The Delaford. He hadn't expected that. Kel pointed to the sign. "And does her husband own the hotel?" It was a clumsy way to gather information, but he had to know the score.

"Oh, no," the clerk said. "Sam Scott is Darcy's father. Darcy isn't married." A few moments later, she handed him the key. "I've put you in the Bennington Suite. It has a lovely terrace that overlooks the lake. Just take the elevator to the third floor and follow the signs. The bellman will bring your luggage, and if you don't mind, I'll send up our manager of guest services and she can arrange for any services you'd like scheduled."

Though a massage would go far to relieving the constant ache in his shoulder and a long soak in the whirlpool sounded like pure heaven, Kel had other priorities. He wasn't here for his health; he had come for peace of mind. And the only person that could provide him with that was Darcy Scott.

"I look forward to my stay," Kel murmured with a smile.

2

DARCY CLICKED ON the Lake Country Real Estate website and navigated to the photos of the four-bedroom, three-bath house on Crystal Lake. She re-read the description as she had so many times over the past few weeks. Wide, wrap-around porch, Victorian gazebo overlooking the water, original boathouse. But even the thoughts of buying her dream home couldn't take her mind off Kel Martin.

She glanced down at her arm, at the spot where he had touched her. In that single, ordinary moment, at that brief contact, she realized that she'd never really gotten over him. He was nothing more than a stranger to her, yet if he took her hand and led her into his bedroom, she'd be hard pressed to refuse him anything.

How could a man have such an incredible hold over her? Was it Kel? Or was it just loneliness? While she'd been engaged, she'd barely thought of him.

She ran a hand through her hair. That wasn't entirely true, she admitted to herself. There had been more than a few times that she'd caught herself reliving that night in her mind.

With a frustrated sigh, Darcy turned her attention back to the website. Kel Martin was part of her past. This house was her future.

The house, a sprawling shingle-style cottage, sat on a lovely piece of lake frontage, almost directly across the water from The Delaford. "West Blueberry Lane," she murmured. In a few months, that address could be hers—if she gathered the courage to make an offer on the place.

Darcy had lived in a suite at the resort since she'd arrived two years before, never quite sure how long she'd be staying. But it was finally time to force her father's hand. Either the job at The Delaford was hers to keep or it wasn't—and if it was, she was going to make some major changes in her life. She was going to buy a house and put down some roots.

No more waiting around for Mr. Right. No more putting her life on hold in the hopes that Prince Charming was waiting just around the corner. Darcy closed her eyes, another image of Kel Martin invading her thoughts.

Yes, he was handsome and, yes, they'd spent an incredible, unforgettable night together. But Darcy was five years older now and much wiser. One night of passion could never guarantee a lifetime of happiness, no matter how alluring that fantasy might be. If she was meant to spend the rest of her life with a man, then he'd have to find her. She was tired of looking for him.

The door to Darcy's office crashed open and Darcy spun around in her chair. Amanda stood in the doorway, breathless. She grabbed the door and slammed it behind her, collapsing back against it. Fanning her face with her hand, she drew a deep breath. "Guess who's at the reception desk?"

Darcy's stomach twisted nervously. "My father?" She wasn't ready for him yet. She hadn't worked out exactly how she would word her demands. Talking to Sam Scott was like playing chess. She had to plan her attacks and anticipate his responses.

"No!" Amanda cried. "Guess again!"

A flood of relief raced through her. "I don't know. Arnold? J.Lo? Madonna? We cater to a celebrity clientele here. Famous people don't impress me much anymore—you know that."

"Kel Martin. You know, the guy we saw today in the chocolate shop. He's here and he's planning to stay for a week."

Darcy gasped and jumped up from her chair. "You didn't give him a room."

"Of course I didn't. Olivia did. She's working the front desk."

"No, no, no," Darcy cried, wringing her hands. "He can't stay here. You have to go back out there and tell him Olivia made a mistake. There are no vacancies; we have a huge group coming in. He'll just have to find another place to stay."

"Why would I do that? We have two very nice suites sitting empty this week. His money is as good as anyone else's. Plus, we have the pleasure of looking at that gorgeous face for seven days and nights. It's a win-win situation, wouldn't you say?"

"It's a disaster waiting to happen," Darcy insisted.

"Why?"

Darcy shifted nervously. Amanda was not going to give up on this without a good reason. But did Darcy really want to tell her the whole story? "I once stuck my tongue on the playground jungle gym in the middle of a Chicago winter," she finally said.

Amanda frowned. "What?"

"And I home permed my hair the night before my senior prom. I majored in paleontology in college. I bought my very first Gucci bag with rent money. I've made some really stupid mistakes in my life." Darcy paused. "And, about five years ago, I had a one-night stand with Kel Martin."

Amanda's eyes went wide. "You *slept* with Kel Martin?"

"We didn't sleep. We spent the whole night…getting busy. The next morning, he left and I never saw him again. Until about a week later, when I saw his photo in the newspaper and found out who he really was."

Amanda's jaw dropped. "Wait, you didn't know who he was when you slept with him?"

"He said he was new in town and I don't follow baseball. I picked him up at the bar at the Penrose. We went to his room, had fantastic sex and that was it. End of story."

A gleeful smile spread across Amanda's face. "End of Chapter One. Beginning of Chapter Two Kel Martin takes a room at The Delaford."

"Now you know why I can't have him staying here. I've never been able to get that night out of my mind."

"Maybe you could rekindle your romance or have a nice tidy little affair. You haven't had a man in your bed for a long time. If you don't get a little practice once in awhile, you're going to forget how to do it."

"We never had a romance. It was just lust, two people scratching an itch."

Amanda crossed the room and put her arm around Darcy's shoulders. "Better stock up on calamine, Darcy, because that itch just booked a room for a week."

"I'll just inform him that we can't possibly accommodate him for that long. Besides, I don't have time for sex right now. Daddy is coming at the end of the week and everything has to be perfect. We're going have a heart-to-heart discussion about my future at The Delaford and my plans to run his company after he retires."

"But you've always been great at multi-tasking."

"You're no help at all," Darcy muttered as she walked through the office door.

She had always wanted a career working for her father. Darcy had spent her childhood trying to please Sam Scott. She got the best grades, participated in all the proper activities in school. She'd even managed to get herself into an Ivy League college. Yet nothing she did could change the way Sam Scott looked at his daughter.

Since she was a child, he had stressed the importance of Darcy making a good marriage, not a good career. Instead, he'd steered his two sons into the family business. But Darcy's two older brothers had been uninterested in working for their demanding father, instead founding successful business ventures of their own.

When Darcy had been invited to step into her father's world, she'd been thrilled with the opportunity to prove her worth. But it was only after she'd taken this job that she'd realized her father had no plans to let her keep it. Sam Scott still insisted that Darcy's primary focus ought to be finding a husband, preferably one interested in stepping into the family business.

Neil Lange had been the perfect choice. He had managed her father's Beverly Hills hotel and, to Sam Scott's delight, had shown an immediate interest upon meeting Darcy. Darcy had allowed herself to be swept her off her feet and, for a time, had thought she was in love. But she'd delayed setting a date for their wedding.

In the end, Darcy had realized that marrying Neil was just one more attempt at pleasing her father. And all Neil really had been interested in was an executive office at corporate head-quarters. The engagement ring had been returned and, at that moment, Darcy had decided that she'd done enough. If Sam Scott couldn't accept her for the talented, driven, creative person she was, then she was prepared to walk away for good.

When Darcy reached the lobby, Kel was nowhere to be seen. She cursed softly as her heart began to pound in her chest. Was she nervous about kicking him out, or was it seeing him again that made her pulse race? Maybe she ought to avoid a confrontation and stay out of his way for the entire week. She had more important things to occupy her energy than worrying about him.

"Scratch, scratch."

Darcy jumped, then turned to find Amanda standing behind her. "So, did you send the man on his merry way?"

"No," Darcy said. "I didn't catch him in time."

"Darcy, what's the big deal? Are you even sure he remembers you?"

"If he doesn't remember me, then why did he show up here?"

Amanda pressed her finger to her chin. "Oh, I don't know. Maybe he's looking for a relaxing vacation. Maybe he wants to play a few rounds of golf or enjoy our spa. Who knows?"

"What if he does remember me?" Darcy challenged. "And what if he wants to start something up again? He probably thinks I'll just dive right into his bed. Which I probably would. But that's beside the point." She shook her head. "If he doesn't remember me that would be even more mortifying, because I certainly remember him. Every single inch of him."

"And how many inches were there?" Amanda asked, eyes wide with curiosity.

"That's not what I meant." She turned and grabbed Amanda's hands. "Will you please tell him he has to leave? I promise, I'll owe you big time."

"Nope. This is your problem. I'm the manager of guest services. I don't tell guests to leave when we have available rooms." She squeezed Darcy's hand and pulled her along to the elevator, then punched the button. "He's in the Bennington Suite."

"It's your job to arrange guest services."

"But I'm not the one who needs an excuse to see him." The elevator doors opened and Amanda gave Darcy a gentle shove. "I'll be waiting in your office for a full report."

The doors closed and Darcy leaned against the wall. She'd kicked her share of guests out of The Delaford and it had never been a pleasant experience. But Kel Martin wasn't trashing his room or partying until dawn or abusing the staff. He had the dubious distinction of starring in her wildest sexual fantasies. Something that could hardly be considered a crime. She'd have to come up with a plausible excuse to get rid of him.

But then again, maybe she ought to stick with the truth. How difficult could it be just to tell him that she felt uncomfortable with his presence? "That would make it clear I still think about our night together," she murmured. "And I'm not about to admit that."

The doors opened onto the third floor lobby and Darcy stepped out. "Just do it, quickly and cleanly. Maintain your professional composure." She walked down the hall to the Bennington Suite, then straightened her jacket and smoothed her hands over her skirt. But just as she was ready to knock, the door swung open.

Kel stood in the doorway, dressed in only a pair of surf shorts that hung low on his hips. The ice bucket was tucked beneath his arm. Darcy stared at his chest, smooth and muscular and gleaming in the soft light from the hallway.

"Hello," he said. "We meet again."

Darcy's eyes darted up to his face. "Again?" Good God, he did remember her!

"Didn't I see you at the candy shop this morning?"

Relief washed over her. "Mr. Martin, I'm afraid I have—"

"You know my name?"

"You just registered downstairs. I'm the manager of The Delaford and I—"

"You're here to ask me what I need." He chuckled softly, then braced his shoulder on the doorjamb and lazily rubbed his chest. He watched her, his gaze skimming over her face. "So, what are you offering…" He leaned closer and fixed his gaze on her nametag. "Darcy Scott?"

He hadn't changed at all. He was still far too charming to trust. She was well aware of his reputation with the ladies and she wasn't about to fall into his arms again. But, oh, what incredible arms he had. Darcy drew a deep breath. "There's a book on the desk that lists all our services. Once you've had a chance to look at it, we'll be happy to make reservations for you. We'll see to your every need."

"Every need?"

He leaned closer and Darcy was suddenly unable to continue. She wanted to step back, out of reach of his undeniable magnetism. But instead, she was drawn closer. She needed to reach out and touch him, to gauge his reaction to the contact. She slowly raised her hand and smoothed her fingers along his jaw line, rough with the stubble of a day-old beard.

"Every need within the law," Darcy murmured.

A soft groan rumbled in his chest and he slipped his arm around her waist and pulled her against him. An instant later, his mouth found hers and she lost herself in his kiss. Memories flooded back and the five years between them evaporated like lake mist on a sunny day.

His tongue teased at her lips and she opened beneath the gentle assault. The taste of him warmed her blood and seeped into her soul. He tasted like…chocolate? She hadn't remembered that, but it was pleasantly addictive, a taste she wanted to savor. Yes, it had been years, but it seemed as if they'd shared this same kiss not so very long ago at all.

He pulled her tighter, drawing her thigh up along his leg until her skirt was bunched at her hip. His palm slid up until he cupped her backside. Wild sensations raced through her, sharp currents that electrified every nerve in her body until she trembled with need. This was how it had happened the first time, impulse had turned to action quickly and without a conscious thought.

"That's good," he murmured, his breath hot against her lips, his fingers furrowed through her hair.

"Good," she replied weakly.

"You satisfying my every need. Me satisfying yours."

A door behind her closed and the sound was like a shock to Darcy's system. She jumped back, out of his embrace, then shoved her skirt down and combed her fingers through her hair. "I should go." Darcy pressed her palms against her flushed cheeks.

"It was nice meeting you, Miss Scott," he said, before stealing another kiss. "I hope we'll see much more of each other."

Darcy slowly backed away, unable to take her eyes off of him. She stood like a fool in the middle of the hall until he stepped back inside his room and closed the door. The moment the lock clicked shut, her knees almost buckled and she pressed her fingers to her lips. They were still damp.

"What am I doing?" she murmured.

She didn't have an answer to the question, but that didn't seem to matter. She wanted Kel Martin, beyond all reason. She wanted him to open the door, drag her back inside and thoroughly seduce her.

"No, no, no," she muttered to herself. "I'm supposed to be older and wiser." Darcy knew precisely what would happen if she knocked on his door and, for a long moment, she contemplated doing just that. But in the end, she gathered her resolve, drew a deep breath and walked back to the elevator.

Kel was exactly like chocolate. She might want †
now, to allow herself just one tiny taste. But Darcy was an
that one little taste might lead to a week-long binge. And after
that, she'd crave a steady diet of Kel Martin.

KEL SLID onto a barstool and ordered a whiskey, then turned
his attention to the basketball game on the television above the
bar. He'd enjoyed a long, leisurely dinner in the hotel restaurant, hoping he'd run into Darcy again, but she hadn't shown.

It was obvious by the kiss they'd shared that she remembered
him. He didn't know much about Darcy Scott, but he knew she
wasn't the type to kiss a complete stranger just a few minutes after
being introduced. He frowned. Or maybe she had kissed her fair
share of strangers and he had been just one more on her list.

He rubbed his palms together, recalling the feel of her silky
hair slipping through his fingers. Everything he'd experienced
today with Darcy seemed more intense, as though vividly
colored with a desire that had been simmering for five years.

"Thanks," Kel said as the bartender set the tumbler in front
of him. The bartender nodded, then walked down to the far end.
Kel's gaze followed and came to rest on Darcy. He hadn't noticed her at first, hiding in the shadows.

Their eyes met and he held his breath, a knot of anticipation
tightening in his stomach. She had been waiting for him,
knowing that he'd be looking for her. Still, Darcy's expression
was far from encouraging. She looked as if she might just bolt
at any moment—or throw up.

Kel took a sip of his whiskey, the liquor warming his blood
and fortifying his courage. Hell, he could understand her
nerves. When they'd encountered each other five years ago, neither one of them had worried about the consequences. It had
been a one-night stand, pure and simple. But now, there seemed
to be so much more at stake.

He stood and strolled to the end of the bar, then sat down
next to her. How was this supposed to go? Should he spend time

on the preliminary flirting or did she expect him to get right to the business of seduction? "Can I buy you a drink?" he asked. A good start, but a bit of a cliché.

"Champagne," Darcy said.

She'd ordered champagne that night. So this was how she wanted it to play out—exactly the way it had five years ago. "Are you celebrating?"

Darcy laughed softly, as if pleased that he remembered the words he'd used the first time they'd met. "I don't know. I can't think of anything to celebrate."

"How about meeting me?" he asked. Geez, the line had sounded so slick five years ago, but now it was downright corny.

She bit her lower lip, amused. "Does that line actually work on women?"

"It used to," he replied. Kel turned to the bartender. "Can I have a bottle of your best champagne and two glasses?" He directed his attention back to Darcy, his gaze skimming her face. Two tiny worry lines marred her forehead and her hands were folded in front of her on the bar, her fingers so tense her knuckles were white.

When the bartender returned with the champagne, he poured them both a glass, then dropped the bottle into a silver bucket engraved with the Delaford logo.

"So, tell me, what are you doing sitting all alone in this place?"

"I'm not alone," Darcy said, raising her glass. The crystal rang softly as she touched her champagne flute to his.

Suddenly, Kel couldn't remember what came next. Had he asked her what she was doing in San Francisco? Or had they talked about their jobs? Damn, he'd replayed this so many times in his brain, but he'd always skipped over the incidental conversation and moved right to the interesting parts.

But then, it really didn't matter, did it? This little game they were playing was just a means to an end. "Would you like to get out of here?"

Darcy stood up and grabbed her glass and started toward the

door. Kel quickly signed his tab, then picked up the bottle of champagne and his glass in one hand.

"I'll take that as a yes," he muttered.

He caught up to her just outside the bar, then walked silently beside her through the lobby and to the elevator. Desire coursed through his veins as he waited for the doors to open. When they did, Kel spread his hand across the small of her back and steered her inside. The moment the elevator door closed, he turned to her.

"If you have any doubts, now's the time to tell me. Before I start pushing any buttons here."

Without looking away, Darcy reached over and pressed the button for the third floor. But Kel couldn't wait any longer. He slipped his arm around her waist and pulled her into a kiss, lingering over her mouth, his tongue tangling with hers.

The kiss sent a rush of warmth through his bloodstream and he felt himself growing hard. Darcy hooked her fingers in the waistband of his trousers and pulled his hips against hers, the heat of his erection pressed between. There was no doubt between them. She wanted him as much as he wanted her.

The elevator doors opened and Kel tightened his grip around her waist, pulling her along with him, his mouth still clinging to hers. They stumbled toward his suite, champagne spilling from her glass as they moved. When they reached his suite, Kel dug in his pocket for his keycard. He pressed Darcy back against the door, his chin resting on her shoulder as he clumsily slipped the card in the lock.

"Hell, I hate these things," he muttered, unable to get the card to work. He dropped the bottle of champagne on the carpet and it fizzed as it spilled.

With trembling fingers, Darcy snatched the card from his hand and turned around. He pressed up against the soft curve of her backside. God, he felt as if he were ready to explode. If he expected this night to be like their first, he'd have to summon at least a measure of self-control.

Finally, Darcy managed to get the door unlocked and they

both stumbled into the room, the last of the champagne splashing on the floor. Kel grabbed her glass and set it on the wet bar along with his, his face still buried in the hair at the nape of her neck, her backside pressed to his groin. He pushed her against the wall and drew her hair back, then kissed the skin just below her ear.

Her intoxicating scent filled his head and made it hard to think straight. But Kel's instincts drove him forward. What had happened five years ago didn't matter anymore. They were here, right now, and he wanted her beyond all rational thought.

He reached for the hem of her skirt and drew it up to her hips, then smoothed his hands along her thighs. Her legs were bare, the skin warm and silken.

Darcy sighed softly as he stroked her buttocks, his fingers tangling in the lacy scrap of her panties. But when his caress reached her belly, she pressed her buttocks against his erection in a silent invitation. They were both still fully dressed, but it felt as if she were naked in front of him.

He slipped his palms beneath the silk panties and delved between her legs, his fingers coming back damp with her need. Slowly, Kel explored and he felt her melting into him. He knew he could bring her to her peak with his fingers, but when she came, he wanted to look into her eyes.

Gently, he turned her around to face him. She leaned back against the wall and he delved deeper. Her eyes closed, Darcy arched back, but Kel withdrew and slipped his hand around her neck. "Look at me," he said.

She opened her eyes and he saw the passion swirling in their depths. Her lips parted and he kissed her, capturing her mouth as he had her sex. A tiny moan slipped from her throat and Kel knew that she was close. But then he felt her hand around his wrist, drawing him away.

She reached for his belt and began to work it open with clumsy fingers. His zipper was next and a heartbeat later, her fingers wrapped around him. Kel closed his eyes, enjoying the sensation of her touch. He'd fantasized about this so many times, wondering why all those years ago his response to her touch had been so intense. Even now, he couldn't explain it.

Kel kissed her again. "I need you to slow down," he whispered against her mouth. "I won't get a prize for finishing first." And there was no way he could continue on like this. He smoothed the back of his hand across her cheek. "We have time."

"I can't wait," Darcy said. She reached in her jacket pocket and withdrew a foil packet.

"You came prepared?" he asked.

"I wasn't sure when or where it would happen."

Her confession pleased him. "But you knew it would?"

She nodded, then slowly slid his trousers and boxers down over his hips. When she tore the condom package open, he held his breath, wincing as she sheathed him. They had to stop. Just for a minute or two. But Darcy was determined to have him and have him now. And all he really wanted to do was please her.

He'd thought about this for years, having her in his arms again, being able to touch her at will, to sink into her and stay there forever. With a low moan, Kel drew her legs up around his waist and pushed aside the silky barrier of her panties.

Kel closed his eyes, just the thought of what he was about to do bringing him closer to the edge. But for a moment he hesitated. How could he go back once he lost himself in her? Would it be everything it had been that night in San Francisco, the stuff of fantasies?

"Please," she murmured, her breath warm against his ear.

Kel slowly entered her, the feel of her heat around him sending a shockwave through his body. When he'd buried himself deep inside, he waited, trying to slow his pulse. How did Darcy do this to him, take away his self-control?

She shifted above him, her legs wrapped around his hips, and he couldn't stop himself. Kel began to move, carefully at first, just barely keeping his need in check. But as he drove into her again and again, he lost touch with reality. Every thought was focused on the sensation of being inside her, of losing control in her arms.

He wasn't sure how long they lasted. But when Darcy arched against him, holding her breath, Kel knew she was on the edge. He wanted to bring her back, but then she cried out, her body convulsing around him. Her orgasm went on and on until Kel couldn't hold back and he drove into her one last time. Then he collapsed against the wall, his face buried in the curve of her neck. They'd come to it so quickly, but the release seemed to last forever, the two of them shuddering and moaning their pleasure.

This was the way it had been, Kel thought as he inhaled her scent. And this was the way it was. Nothing had changed. If he'd thought he could put Darcy Scott out of his head for good, then he'd been mistaken. She'd found a way back in and this time, Kel suspected he might never recover.

3

DARCY STARED INTO her third cup of coffee as she sat at the restaurant table, patiently waiting for the caffeine to kick in. She hadn't slept more than a few hours last night, plagued with thoughts of Kel. Regret, confusion, frustration all swirled around in her head until she'd been forced to get out of bed and find something to calm her down. The half pound of truffles that she'd gobbled down at 4 a.m. hadn't helped matters at all. The moment the sun had risen, Darcy had conceded defeat and crawled into the shower.

She'd done the right thing, come and run, making her exit shortly after she'd pushed her skirt back down around her hips. Indulging in an entire night of pleasure wouldn't alter the facts. Even though the sex had been quick, it was still the best she'd had in five years.

With other men, Darcy had always been so careful, holding back, avoiding a complete surrender. She'd never really trusted Neil to completely possess her and that turned out to be a good thing. So why did she trust a stranger like Kel Martin? It didn't make sense.

With just a simple caress, he'd stripped away every fear and inhibition she'd ever had with men. Her brain had shut off and he'd set her body free to enjoy every wonderful sensation. Maybe that freedom came because she knew he was just passing through her life. He'd make love to her and then leave her. What was she really risking after all?

Darcy took a sip of her coffee. She felt as if she'd h

sexual lottery. A million-dollar orgasm with just one try. Now all she wanted to do was buy another ticket, and another and another, damn the odds and the risks.

She could still taste him in her mouth and feel him on her skin. If she closed her eyes she could recall the miracle of him moving inside of her. A tiny thrill raced through her and Darcy knew it wasn't the caffeine kicking in but adrenaline leftover from the previous night. It was over now, this little detour into passion. Her curiosity had been appeased and it was time to move on.

"You look like you've been dragged behind a bus." Amanda plopped into the chair across from Darcy. "Did you get any sleep last night?"

"A little," Darcy admitted sheepishly.

"I checked the register and I see that Mr. Baseball is still with us. Did you talk to him?" Amanda looked at Darcy again, taking in her sleepy gaze. "Wait…don't even go there. Oh, no, you didn't."

Darcy snatched up her napkin and dabbed at her mouth, hoping to hide the smile that wouldn't seem to go away. She winced, her lips tender and bruised. Was it that evident? Maybe she should have just scrawled a big red "O" on her forehead and been done with it. "I didn't mean to but I couldn't seem to help myself. At least I can finally stop counting. The dry spell is officially over."

"And now the typhoon season begins? You slept with a guest!" Amanda said. "Didn't we have a seminar on this?"

"We never really made it to the bed. We got as far as the wall. And technically, he's not a guest. He's an old friend who happens to be staying at The Delaford."

"Ah, you're friends now. I think you could come up with a much better activity to do with a friend. What about a nice walk or maybe a game of tennis?"

"All right, we're not friends, but we're very…closely ac—" Darcy groaned, then buried her face in her hands. "I can't talk about this."

"I don't care. I'm going to sit here until you tell me every detail," Amanda said, her arms crossed beneath her breasts.

"I expected it to be bad," Darcy began. "In truth, I wanted it to be bad so I'd finally forget about him. That's why I went along with the whole seduction, just to prove to myself that it couldn't possibly live up to the memory."

"And?"

"And once I realized it was going to be even better, I couldn't seem to make myself leave. We were…consumed. And now I'm going to spend the next five years thinking about last night, the same way I spent the past five years thinking about the first night we spent together. I feel like I've been sucked into a giant black hole of sexual frustration."

A thoughtful expression on her face, Amanda picked up the basket of pastries and chose a croissant. "Well, there is a way to pull yourself out. You could spend another night or two with Kel. Maybe the whole week." She bit the end off the croissant and chewed it slowly.

"How would that help?"

"Sooner or later, he'll fall off that sex god pedestal you've put him on and do something typically male."

"Like what?"

Amanda snatched up Darcy's glass of cranberry juice. "Do I need to be specific? Sweetie, in the end, they're all the same. They all walk around with your underwear on their head and think it's hilariously funny, they all leave their toenail clippings on the bathroom sink and expect you to pick them up, and they all ask you to have a threesome with the bimbo down the hall, hoping you'll be temporarily insane and agree. It's hard-wired into their hormones. If you're just patient, you'll see."

Darcy shook her head, wryly. "I thought when I found a man I wanted as much as I want Kel, I'd be in love. I'd have a grand romance and be swept off my feet by some sexually adventurous Prince Charming."

"We all want that, Darcy. But Prince Charming is usually dreadfully dull in bed. His naughty brother, the Duke of Debauchery, is the guy that's meant to make your toes curl. Some men are marriage material and others are just for fun. I think Kel Martin falls into the same category as carnival rides and bungee jumping. Fun, a little scary, but not meant for daily consumption."

"And that's exactly the way they think about us!" Darcy cried. "There are the girls you marry and the girls you just mess around with."

"At least you know where you stand with the Duke, right? It's just about the sex." Amanda sighed, gulped down Darcy's cranberry juice, then quickly stood up. "I'll just be going now. His highness is on his way over here."

Darcy twisted in her chair only to see Kel approaching. He was dressed casually in a soft blue Oxford shirt, khaki trousers and well-worn loafers. His hair was still damp from his morning shower and he hadn't bothered to shave, the stubble of his beard making him look slightly dangerous.

As Amanda hurried past him, she turned and looked at Darcy, fanning her face with her hand and mouthing the word "hot."

When Kel reached Darcy's table, he sat down in Amanda's chair, flipped over a coffee cup and filled it from the carafe. "Morning," he said cheerfully.

"Good morning," Darcy replied.

He stared at her as he sipped his coffee, studying her intently, the silence between them growing uncomfortable. Was he deliberately trying to make her uneasy or was he searching for something to say? She prayed he wouldn't want to discuss the previous night's activities. "You look beautiful this morning, Darcy," he finally said.

"Stop it," she said. He couldn't possibly be telling the truth. When she'd returned to her room, she'd tossed and turned for most of the night, then rushed through a shower before meeting with the staff at eight. Dark circles smudged the skin beneath her eyes and her hair had been haphazardly pulled back into a ponytail. Amanda was right, she looked like she'd been dragged behind a bus. "There's no need to turn on the charm this early in the morning."

"When I woke up, you weren't there," he said.

Darcy frowned. "You saw me leave."

"I didn't really like that part of the evening," he said.

"I thought that was our deal," she said.

He frowned. "We had a deal?"

"Like last time. It was just about sex, nothing else."

Kel stared at her for another long moment, then shook his head. "What the hell are you talking about?"

A sudden sick feeling settled into Darcy's stomach. Oh, God, had she been wrong? She'd just assumed he remembered their night together in San Francisco. Assumed they'd both silently acknowledged that this had all happened once before and it was about to happen again. That was what had given them permission to indulge. But maybe she'd been mistaken.

Darcy squirmed in her chair. "You know what I'm talking about."

He covered her hand with his. "Are you angry with me? I sure hope not, because I was thinking we might want to spend a little more time together."

Darcy gasped. This was exactly like a man! No matter how incredible the sex had been, it hadn't been enough for him. She yanked her hand away, rubbing the spot where he'd touched her.

"Do you golf?" he asked. "We could play today or we could take a drive. I hear there are some nice wineries west of here in Sonoma."

Darcy jumped to her feet and threw her napkin on the table. She'd had just about enough of this game he was playing. "You're telling me you don't remember that night in San Francisco? The bar of the Penrose, the bottle of champagne, the elevator ride? You were new in town, I just needed a drink to unwind and we ended up naked in your room."

A slow grin replaced his serious expression and Kel chuckled, then took another sip of his coffee. "I do remember that night, quite vividly."

"Then why did you pretend that you didn't?" Darcy demanded.

"Until you mentioned it, I wasn't sure *you* remembered that night, so don't act all insulted."

Darcy didn't know what to say. Her indignation slowly dissolved, replaced by the uneasy feeling that what they'd begun last night was not over—not by a long shot. She sat down in her chair. "And you recognized me yesterday at the candy shop?"

Kel nodded. "The minute I looked into your eyes. Why do you think I'm here, Darcy? I'm not really a spa kind of guy, although I've been thinking I could really use a nice seaweed wrap. And that salt scrub sounds like a good deal. 'It makes the skin glow with a youthful texture.'"

"It's called exfoliation," Darcy said. "And if you're not a spa kind of guy, then what are you? A sex kind of guy? What happened last night is not going to happen again."

He reached for her hand and distractedly twisted his fingers through hers. "Why not? I certainly enjoyed myself and so did you, unless you were…" He chuckled softly. "Were you faking it, Darcy?"

"No," she said, trying to ignore the way his thumb caressed the inside of her wrist.

"Then you enjoyed yourself as much as I did?"

She straightened, pulling her hand away and clutching it in her lap. "That depends upon how much you enjoyed yourself," she said.

"A lot," he said. "More than I thought possible in such a short amount of time. Why should we deny ourselves that kind of pleasure?"

"What are you suggesting? That we just carry on with each other until…you decide to leave?" The prospect should have sounded unthinkable, but in truth, Darcy found the idea strangely intriguing. A week of fabulous sex with a devastatingly handsome man, those incredible hands on her body, that mouth driving her wild in bed, and those beautiful blue eyes watching her as he buried himself deep inside her. What more could a girl ask for?

A shiver coursed through her body. Had she possessed just a bit more courage, she'd drag Kel to her office right now and seduce him all over again. But she'd do well to carefully consider all the consequences of his proposed interlude. "So we'd be together for as long as you're here and then we'd go back to our lives, no strings attached." Darcy twirled her spoon in her coffee as she contemplated the offer.

"Sounds good," he said. "With the understanding that we will take our time from now on."

"I'll think about it," she finally murmured.

"Ah, don't do that," Kel said, leaning back in his chair and shaking his head. "This should be a simple decision, Darcy. Either you want me or you don't. Don't think, just do."

"Who died and made you Yoda?" Darcy asked. "There are a lot of things to consider here."

"Like what?"

Darcy opened her mouth, prepared to list all her reasons for *not* sleeping with Kel again. But then she'd be forced to admit she might not be able to control her feelings for him. Yes, the time they'd spend together would be incredible, but she'd still be left to deal with residual effects once he'd gone.

And then there were the tricky morning-after conversations. *Oh, by the way, great orgasm last night. And that thing you did with your tongue, that was the best.* "I'd rate it 43 on a scale of one to ten," she muttered.

"What?" he asked, leaning forward and bracing his elbows on the table.

Darcy swallowed hard. "I'm sorry, I was just thinking out loud."

"Here's how I see it," Kel began. "We seem to have this attraction to each other. I haven't quite figured it out, but I'd sure like to. The problem is I can't be in the same room with you without wanting to tear your clothes off and kiss your naked body. So, I suggest we deal with that."

"You— You're thinking about that right now?" Darcy asked.

"I've pretty much been thinking about that 24 hours a day since I saw you at the candy shop," he admitted with a boyish grin.

And before that? Darcy wondered if he'd thought about her at all in the past five years. Had he stared at the ceiling, trying to sleep at night, with thoughts of her running through his brain? Had he caught the scent of her perfume in the air and remembered the way she'd kissed him, or seen her in a crowd and followed until he realized it wasn't her? Had he been obsessed with the memory of her?

"I have a job to do here," she said. "My father is coming in at the end of the week to do a walk-through and I have a million things to finish before then."

"But I bet not one of them is as much fun as I am," Kel said. He leaned over the table and caught her chin with his thumb, tipping her face up to his. His lips touched hers softly, his tongue barely grazing the crease in her lips.

God, why did his kiss have such a profound effect on her? She ought to be able to resist him if she wanted to. After all, she knew he'd spent years honing his talents on a string of other women. For Kel Martin, she was just one more in a long line of females to tumble.

So what was wrong with that? As long as she kept herself from becoming emotionally involved, Darcy could have a fabulous week with him. Ending each day in his arms, in his bed would be sheer decadence—something that even a fifty-pound box of chocolates could never match. And didn't she deserve a little pleasure in her life?

"I have to go to work," Darcy said. "I'll see you tonight and let you know what I've decided."

"I'll be waiting," Kel called as she walked away.

DARCY GLANCED over at the clock, then kicked back from the edge of the pool. Midnight. She'd spent the entire day thinking about Kel and nothing she did could distract her mind from what they'd shared the night before.

An afternoon business meeting in San Francisco had occupied her time but she'd barely been able to focus on the architect's plans for the new wing of the spa. Instead, she'd thought about what she'd be doing later that evening, running the possible sexual scenarios over and over in her head.

She'd expected to return by dinner, in plenty of time to discuss the terms of her decision with Kel. But a conference call with her father had delayed her for hours. Darcy had finally pulled into the parking garage at eleven, exhausted yet filled with a nervous anticipation.

A quick check of the computer brought up Kel's itinerary for the day. After breakfast, he'd played 18 holes of golf, then had two beers in the bar along with a late lunch. At four p.m., he'd enjoyed a deep-tissue massage with Cynda, then bought some toiletries at the hotel gift shop. He'd made two phone calls to his home phone in San Francisco and watched an action movie on pay-per-view before ordering room service—a steak and baked potato with apple pie for dessert. He'd also left three messages on her voice mail and a note at the front desk.

Darcy floated on her back and stared up at the ceiling of the pool house. The reflection from the underwater lights swirled in a soothing pattern above her and she tipped her head back and closed her eyes. Swimming always exhausted her. Whenever she found herself facing a sleepless night, when her mind was plagued with business worries, she'd come to the pool and swim laps until her head cleared and her body relaxed.

Resisting Kel Martin was what really worried her. The temptation to go to his room was almost overwhelming. She'd sat in her office for fifteen minutes considering her choices. Take a swim, try to sleep or sneak up to Kel's suite and see if they might be able to enjoy a repeat of yesterday's activities.

Darcy stroked to the far end of the pool where a huge glass wall overlooked the grounds. Outside, a full moon hung low over the horizon and a chilly winter wind buffeted the high pines. As she made a neat kick turn, her gaze caught sight of a figure strolling across the wide stone terrace outside. Probably one of the maintenance staff, she thought as she started another lap.

But when she returned to that end of the pool again, she saw Kel standing on the deck. He was dressed in an old T-shirt and a faded pair of jeans that hung low on his hips. His feet were bare and his hair tousled, as if he'd just crawled out of bed.

"The pool is closed," she said, grabbing onto the edge and tucking her knees to her chest.

He raked his hand through his hair. "I couldn't sleep. Too many things on my mind."

"How did you know where to find me?"

"The front desk clerk said you sometimes swim here late at night. I thought I'd give it a shot."

Darcy's hair was plastered to her forehead and she submerged once more and brushed it from her eyes. She watched as Kel's eyes drifted from her face to her chest.

"When you retire from baseball, you ought to consider a career as a private investigator," she said.

"Maybe so." He squatted in front of her, his elbows resting on his knees. "I need to find something to do with myself pretty quick." He shook his head, a rueful smile twisting his lips. "I'm pretty much done with baseball."

His words were so thoughtful, so direct, that Darcy felt as if she had been offered a glimpse of the real Kel Martin for the very first time. "How do you feel about that?"

He shrugged. "I'm not sure yet. You're the first person I've told. I was supposed to have surgery in the post-season and I just didn't do it."

"Why not?"

"Another shoulder operation, a year of rehab, all for a chance at another year or two at most. If the arm didn't come back, I'd probably bounce around the league. I was thinking, instead, maybe I should get a start on the rest of my life."

"Isn't baseball your life?"

Kel shook his head. "I thought so, but I know better now. I've had a good run. My arm has lasted longer than 95% of the guys in the league."

"Will you miss it?"

"It's not real—the money, the fame, the women. I knew it wasn't real from the start, but the past few years it was starting to feel…like normal life and that scared me."

"And what will you do now?"

"The things all guys do sooner or later. Marriage, a family." He chuckled softly. "But right now, I'm thinking about taking a swim."

He stood, then reached down for the hem of his T-shirt and tugged it over his head. Darcy couldn't help but stare. He really did have a beautiful body, lean yet muscular, his wide shoulders tapering to a narrow waist. Her gaze followed a light trail of hair that began at his collarbone and disappeared beneath the waistband of his jeans.

"It's not like people won't remember you," she said, searching for anything to distract her from a careful study of his crotch. "You—you pitched a no-hitter, a perfect game. People will remember that."

"I didn't realize you followed my career."

Darcy's smile faded as she pushed away from the edge of the pool, swimming to the middle. "You were all over the papers. It was kind of hard to miss."

"You followed my career," he repeated.

"What if I did?"

"I like that," he said. "I like knowing that you thought about me once or twice in the five years we were apart."

"More than once or twice," she admitted.

"Me, too," he said. "I thought about you quite a bit."

She watched him from the water as he unzipped his jeans and skimmed them down over his hips and knees. She'd expected boxers, but he hadn't bothered with underwear. "You—you didn't bring a suit," she stuttered, stating the obvious.

"I wasn't planning to swim," Kel said, standing naked in front of her. "I understand the whole theory of skinny-dipping is that everyone takes their clothes off."

Darcy shook her head. "Oh, no. I run this hotel. If someone walked in and found me in the pool, naked, with a naked man, the staff would never stop talking about it. If you come in, I'm getting out."

Kel stepped to the edge of the pool and dove neatly into the water, swimming to the center. He came up in front of her, grabbing her waist as he did. Darcy screamed and tried to kick away from him, but Kel held tight.

"I can't seem to get enough of you," he said, gently tugging down one strap of her tank suit and dropping a kiss on her shoulder. "Why is that?"

"You're seriously demented?"

He captured her mouth and plunged his tongue inside in a lightning-quick assault. "I think it's all the chocolate I've been eating," he said, his mouth now trailing up her neck to her ear. "Have you been eating chocolate? Because you taste delicious."

"I may have had a few pieces," she admitted.

He tugged the other strap down and her tank suit gaped in the front, exposing the tops of her breasts. Kel tugged a bit harder and the suit was suddenly around her waist. "That's much better," he said.

Darcy stared at him for a long moment. Why did she even bother fighting him? All her resolve just disappeared the moment he touched her. With a resigned smile, she skimmed the suit down over her hips, then kicked it off. "Satisfied?"

"Not yet, but I will be," he teased. "And so will you."

"What are you going to do with me?"

Kel yanked her naked body against his, his eyes fixed on hers. "I missed you today."

Darcy moaned softly, tipping her head to the side. "Why do you insist on torturing me?"

"Because you seem to enjoy it so much," Kel said. He drew back, then traced the shape of her lower lip with his finger. "You do enjoy it, don't you, Darcy?"

She hesitated for a moment as Kel waited for her answer. He needed to know she wanted him as much as he wanted her. But was she ready to admit that? He cupped her face in his hands and kissed her, his tongue invading her mouth as his fingers wove through her hair.

"Tell me you want me," he murmured against her lips. "I want to hear you say it."

"I want you," Darcy said, dragging her mouth across his. Her body conformed to his as he pulled her legs up around his waist, his erection brushing against her suggestively. They bobbed in the water, kissing and touching, Darcy marveling at the slippery feel of their naked bodies touching underwater.

"If we do this here, one of us will end up drowned," he said.

Darcy unwrapped her legs from his waist. "Then come with me," she murmured. She swam to the end of the pool and climbed the steps to the deck, turning to face him as she did, unfazed by her nakedness.

A stack of fluffy white towels, embroidered with a gold "D," sat in a nearby basket and Darcy grabbed one and wrapped it around her body. Then she turned back and watched as Kel followed her.

The sight of his shaft, hard and ready, sent a thrill racing through her. He was hers tonight, to enjoy for as long as she wished. Darcy picked up a towel and took it to him, slowly rubbing it over his damp skin and kissing the spots that she'd dried.

Kel closed his eyes, enjoying her little seduction, and for the first time, Darcy realized the power she held over him. Yes, he could seduce her, but she could just as easily seduce him. She slipped the towel around his neck and pulled him into another kiss, his desire pressing against her belly, hot and hard.

Darcy reached down and touched him, and Kel sucked in a sharp breath. Then, she stepped away from him and walked toward the spa. She could be a tease if she wanted to and Darcy wanted to return a little bit of the torment he'd lavished on her.

Each of the marble-lined steam showers were like small rooms, shower heads on three of the four walls with a low bench against one side. Darcy dropped her towel, then stepped inside and turned on the water, adjusting the temperature. A moment later, Kel joined her, grabbing her waist and pressing her back against the wall.

They stood under the rainfall of water, kissing, laughing, exploring each other's bodies slowly and deliberately. Darcy ran her fingers over the scar at his shoulder, then kissed it, as if that could somehow make it better.

"You are so beautiful," he murmured. Kel cupped her breast in his hand and then bent and gently sucked on her nipple.

"I'm too small on top."

He shook his head. His palms covered her breasts, his thumbs teasing at the hard peaks. "You're perfect exactly the way you are," he said. "See how we fit?" He straightened and pulled her against him, his hands firm on her hips. "As if we were made for each other."

"I'm sure there are other women in this world who fit," Darcy said, reaching around and placing her hands over his.

"Not like you," he murmured. "Not like you." He reached down and slipped his finger inside her. "See," he whispered. "Perfect."

Darcy held her breath as he slid in and out of her, teasing her closer to her release. But this wasn't going to be about her, at least not yet. She drew his hand away and wrapped it around her neck. "I think it's time I torture you for a change."

"Please do," he said, holding his hands up in mock surrender.

She pressed a kiss to his mouth, then trailed her lips lower and lower, down his chest to his belly, dropping kisses on his wet skin as she went. Then, kneeling in front of him, she slowly took him into her mouth. Kel groaned, furrowing his fingers through her wet hair in an attempt to control her.

The water seemed to heighten the experience, her palms sliding over his flat belly and narrow hips as she drew him in and out of her mouth, her fingertips exploring every hard angle and rippled muscle. As she brought him closer, with a hand to her head he urged her to slow her pace. But Darcy needed his surrender, wanted to feel it and taste it. Finally, with a frustrated growl, he bent down and drew her to her feet.

"We can't stay here," he said in a ragged voice. "We don't have a condom."

"We don't need one," Darcy replied.

He caught her gaze, confused. "Are you sure?"

"I'll take care of you," she said, her hand drifting back down over his abs to his belly.

"But I want to be inside you," he said.

"You will be. Just close your eyes."

He did as he was told and Darcy slowly began to stroke him. "How do I feel?" she murmured. "Tell me."

"Oh, God," Kel moaned. "I can't do this."

"You can," Darcy urged. "Just tell me."

He paused for a long moment. "You're warm…and wet. And so tight." He held his breath. "It's like I'm part of you. You're all around me…and it feels so…incredible." His voice drifted off as he surrendered to her touch. Darcy listened to the clues his body gave her, his quickened breathing, his tense grip on her shoulders.

"I want you to come with me," he murmured, reaching down to touch her between her legs. He drew his finger along the soft folds of her sex.

Darcy smiled and nuzzled his chest, slowing her pace so that she might catch up. It felt so good to touch him, to share her body with him, to enjoy his body without any fears or hesitation. With Kel, sex was so simple, just passion and lust and desire and nothing more. She didn't have to think about her past or about her future. For now, he was hers and she'd have him whenever she wanted.

They climaxed together, shuddering into each other's touch until they were both completely spent. Then Kel gently drew her back beneath the shower and washed them both. Darcy was so relaxed that she could barely stand and leaned on him lazily, her arms wrapped around his neck.

"Take me to bed," she said.

He wrapped her in one of the thick terrycloth robes that hung beside each steam shower, then grabbed one for himself. They walked back through the pool house, Kel grabbing up his clothes and retrieving his room key from the pocket of his jeans. Before they got to the lobby, he drew the hood of Darcy's robe up over her head to hide her from any curious staff members that they might encounter.

Darcy was too relaxed to worry about anything but crawling into Kel's bed and falling asleep in his arms. They rode up the elevator snuggled together, her nose buried in the soft dusting of hair on his chest. And when they reached his room, he helped her out of the robe, then tucked her into his bed.

They could have made love. Instead, they talked, lying in each other's arms and learning all the little details of childhood adventures and first loves and silly embarrassments. But with every detail that Kel gave her, she felt as if she knew it already.

She'd known him, in her heart, since the very first time they'd met. And everything that he told her now was simply confirmation of the man that she knew him to be—a man that she might not ever stop wanting.

4

"As YOU CAN see, the kitchen needs a bit of updating. New cabinets and appliances could do wonders. But the layout is good, nice and spacious."

"I don't do much cooking," Kel said as he strolled to the sink. He turned on the faucet to check the water pressure then turned it off. A window over the sink opened onto the view of Crystal Lake and the long lawn that led down to the water.

"Is there a pier down there?" he asked.

The real estate agent nodded. "There's also an old boat-house, original to the property. And there's a Victorian gazebo just beyond the trees that is just lovely."

Kel smiled. "Are the neighbors quiet?"

"Most of these homes have been in the families for years," she said. "The neighbors on both sides are retired. I suppose you're looking for a bit more action?"

Kel shook his head. He'd had enough action. If he decided to retire, he wanted a place where he could be himself, where people wouldn't constantly be staring or requesting autographs or asking him to recount their favorite moments in Giants baseball. And a place where he could have a boat and do a little fishing. He could have that here.

"I think I'll fit right in." He pointed out the window. "I'm just going to walk down to the lake. I'll be back in a few minutes."

"You have one hundred feet of frontage," she said. "There's also a sandy beach. And there's a nice little flagstone terrace they've built down there."

Kel stepped through the door and strolled across the wide cedar deck to the lawn. He hadn't expected to like the first place he saw, or even the second or third. In truth, Kel thought he'd have to look long and hard to find a house that pleased him.

Kel had never thrown money into real estate like many of his teammates had. Some of the guys had additional homes in Colorado and Florida and Arizona. Kel owned an old mansion in San Francisco's Pacific Heights neighborhood, a Mercedes, a pickup truck and a decent wardrobe of Italian suits and shoes. Beyond that, he'd spent his money on the typical toys: stereo equipment, televisions and computers.

Most of his teammates might call him frugal, but from the start of his career, Kel knew the precarious position he was in. A simple pitch could lead to a career-ending injury. In the blink of an eye it could be all over. His parents had always struggled to make a living, raising seven children on a high school teacher's salary. Kel wanted to be in a position to give them whatever they needed as they got older and, at the same time, have a comfortable future for himself.

When he reached the water, Kel walked out on the rickety dock. The lake was beautiful, calm and serene, the sun sparkling off the surface. A fisherman bobbed in a boat nearby, lazily casting his line and reeling it in. He waved at Kel and Kel returned the greeting.

"I could live here," he said, slowly turning and taking in the view. He could imagine his siblings coming to visit in the summer, the rambling house filled with his nieces and nephews, lazy days spent out on the water. West Blueberry Lane wouldn't make a bad address.

The agent was still waiting for him in the kitchen. She opened the door and he stepped back inside. "Well, what do you think?" she asked.

"How long has it been for sale?" Kel asked.

"Five weeks," she said. "The mechanicals need to be replaced along with the roof and that might be scaring people off.

I think it's priced a bit high. I think it might go soon. There's a woman in town that has been seriously considering putting in an offer. So if you're interested you should probably get an offer in before she does. And I know of a bank that will push your financing through quickly."

He nodded. If the agent knew who he was, she wasn't giving any indication. Financing really wasn't an issue, as long as Kel wanted the house. But this was a big decision. Buying a house in Austell meant that he was about to begin his life after baseball—and he'd begin that life living just a few miles from Darcy Scott.

"Let's put together an offer," Kel said. "Offer the asking price, no contingencies."

The agent gasped. "None? What about financing?"

He shook his head. "I can pay cash," Kel said. "I'm just going to walk through once more, if you don't mind."

Dumbstruck, the agent shook his hand and Kel walked back through the house to the living room. Maybe he was being too optimistic, but he was sure that he could find here the peace and quiet he'd always craved.

Kel wandered down the hall to the master bedroom. He tried to imagine it freshly painted and decorated, furnished with a comfortable bed. He could see the two them, snuggled in bed on a Sunday morning. He'd make breakfast for them and they'd spend the day reading the paper and making slow, sweet love. Kel paused and shook his head. Funny how the image automatically included Darcy. Since when had she become a permanent part of his future?

As he walked through the other bedrooms he thought about a family. He'd always known that marriage and kids wouldn't have been a smart choice as long as he was playing—not that over the years he'd ever found a woman he wanted to marry. His baseball career had occupied so much of his energy, he hadn't had a lot left over to share. But he had more time now, time to find the right person.

Kel headed to the front door and walked outside, taking one last look at the façade of the house. He could be happy here, with or without Darcy. But with her would be much better, he mused.

As he pulled out of the driveway, Kel glanced at the clock on the dashboard. Darcy had left his room this morning just after dawn. They'd spend the past three nights together in the same bed. Of course she'd be the first woman to come to mind when imagining his future here.

Kel turned the car towards The Delaford, then remembered his original reason for driving into town. "Damn," he muttered. Condoms. He usually carried an adequate supply of them, but he and Darcy had been going through at least three or four a day. By all rights, he should have been exhausted. But Kel felt like a guy at the top of his game. Life had never been better.

He'd seen a Price Mart store on the highway just outside of town and headed back to it. Kel parked the car in the busy lot, then reached into the backseat for a baseball cap. He pulled the brim low, hoping his sunglasses and the cap would obscure his identity. Had he been shopping for a toaster, he might not have been so concerned, but condoms were a different matter.

Soft music played in the background as Kel walked past the elderly man who greeted him at the door. He went directly to the pharmacy and searched the shelves, but eventually was forced to ask the pharmacist. The man gave him an odd look, as if he might recognize him, then pointed Kel to the correct aisle.

As Kel studied the selection, he found the absurdity of the situation amusing. It took him back to the days of his youth, sneaking around, trying to hide what he was doing with his high school girlfriend. Still, that wasn't far off. With Darcy, everything seemed so new and exciting. When she touched him, he felt exactly the way he had when he was seventeen and he'd first experienced a woman's body.

How long would that last between them? Would the thrill eventually wear off, or could he count on it to endure for a lifetime? Kel had never considered inviting a woman into his future, but he could imagine inviting Darcy.

He drew a deep breath, then reached out and grabbed his usual brand. And the last moment, he took an extra box, one that promised "increased pleasure" for his partner.

When he got to the checkout, he grabbed cash from his wallet, intending to rush through as quickly as possible. But a young mother with a cartload of disposable diapers stood in front of him, searching her purse for coupons. He glanced over at the adjoining checkout line, then groaned inwardly.

The woman standing in that lane worked at The Delaford. He recognized her from her occasional stints behind the front desk. Amanda, if he recalled correctly. Her gaze fell to the boxes he clutched in his hands, her eyebrow quirking up in amusement.

Kel turned away and dropped the boxes on the conveyor. He managed to make it through the checkout process without anyone else recognizing him, but Amanda was waiting for him once he'd collected his purchases.

"Big night planned?" she asked.

"How is that your business?"

"I'm Darcy's friend." She held out her hand. "Amanda Taylor. Don't bother introducing yourself. I've heard all about you."

"You have?" he said, shaking her hand.

"Would you like to grab some lunch, maybe have a little chat?"

Kel shrugged, then followed Amanda to the lunch counter located near the exit. She bought two hot dogs with the works, then handed him one, before settling at a small table in the corner of the café.

"Thanks," Kel said.

She nodded as she took a bite of the hot dog. "So, Mr. Baseball, what are your intentions regarding Darcy? I mean, I know you two plan to have as much sex as possible until you leave. She told me that. But beyond the sex, what are you thinking about?"

"You and Darcy talk about me?" Kel murmured.

"We're *best* friends. We discuss everything."

"And what does she say about me?" he asked. "How does *she* feel about what's happening?"

Amanda leveled him a look. "You want me to rate your performance in the bedroom?"

"No!" Kel said. "Well, not unless you feel qualified. I mean, if Darcy has made comments, I suppose it wouldn't hurt to know." He shook his head, cursing softly. "No, I don't want to know about my performance. But I would like to know how she feels about me."

Amanda leaned forward, bracing her arms on the table. "I'm not sure I should get involved."

"Hey, you're the one who invited me to lunch," he countered.

Amanda took another bite of her hot dog, studying him. "I don't think Darcy knows what she wants. And having wild, fantastic, mind-numbing sex every night isn't going to help her figure it out. Maybe you ought to give her a little space."

Mind-numbing? Were those her words or Darcy's, Kel wondered. "I suppose I could do that," he said.

After all, he'd already decided to buy the property on the lake. That meant their relationship wouldn't necessarily end in a few days. There'd be nothing to stop him from playing a quick round of golf at The Delaford now and then. And while he was there, he'd stop by and visit with Darcy. "But it's difficult to stay away from her," he added.

"Why is that?"

"Because I really enjoy being with her. And it's not just the sex, because if it were necessary, I could do without that, at least for a while. I just like talking to her and looking at her and holding her hand."

"You're not falling in love, are you?" Amanda asked.

"No!" Kel said. But as soon as he answered, he realized that wasn't entirely true. "I don't know. It's kind of difficult to tell since I've never felt this way before. I'm usually…in control."

Amanda sent him a wary look, then grabbed her shopping bag and stood. "I want you to know that if you hurt her, I'll break both of your arms. Not personally, but I know some guys who could. So watch yourself."

"I will," Kel said, certain that Darcy's friend didn't make empty threats.

"Somebody has to watch out for her," she muttered.

Kel nodded as he watched Amanda walk out of the store. Someday, maybe he'd get to be that person. But if he was going to fall in love, it certainly wouldn't happen after just a few days with a woman. Even he knew that it took a lot longer than that.

DARCY TURNED off her desk light and quickly tidied the files she'd been reviewing. She'd spent the entire day in her office, trying to keep her mind on work and failing miserably. Her father was due to arrive in a few days and she hadn't yet figured out how to broach the subject of her future with Scott Hotels and Resorts. In truth, all she'd been thinking about was her present.

The prospect of another evening with Kel brought a nervous flutter of anticipation to her stomach. When they were together, she felt so alive. She'd thought spending time with him would wash away the memories, but instead it had only created so many more. She'd come to crave his touch, the taste of his mouth, the feel of his skin against hers. When they were apart, Darcy found herself lapsing into wild fantasies about the erotic pleasures they might share next.

He had total control over her willpower, making her happily do whatever it took to please him. Yet his pleasure always seemed to be hers as well, and vice versa. When she looked into his eyes as he buried himself inside her, Darcy saw the surrender, the vulnerability, of a man who had carefully dismantled all barriers between them.

But there were also times when Darcy looked at him and wondered if she were perhaps coloring his reactions with *her* hopes instead of *his* realities. He seemed to genuinely care for her. They spent hours in each other's arms talking and teasing, learning all the intimate details that lovers needed to know. But in the end, he'd leave and all this would fade into the past.

A knock sounded on her office door and Darcy looked up, expecting to see Kel standing outside. Instead, Amanda strolled in, a dripping wet rag in her hand. "I thought you ought to see this," she said.

Darcy wrinkled her nose. "What is it?"

"It's your swimming suit. Jerry found it stuck in the water intake for the pool filter. Would you like to explain how it got there?"

"It must have fallen off when I was swimming the other night," Darcy said with a soft giggle. "When Kel and I were swimming."

Amanda sat down in one of Darcy's guest chairs, draping the wet suit over the arm of the other. "So I gather it's going well?"

Darcy drew a deep breath and let it out slowly. "That depends on how you define 'well.' The sex is fabulous, Kel has to be the most disarming man I've ever met, and I haven't had a good night's sleep since he arrived. When we're together, I can't seem to get enough of him."

"And how does he feel?" Amanda asked.

"I'm not supposed to care about that. I decided to embark on this little affair in order to get him out of my system."

"And how's that working for you?"

Darcy sighed deeply. "I can't stop thinking about him," she admitted. She opened her desk drawer and pulled out a new box of chocolates from Sinfully Sweet. "I had Olivia stop at Sinfully Sweet when she was in town yesterday. Try the chocolate-dipped caramels. They are absolutely to die for."

"So, if things are going so well," Amanda said, "why are you sitting here eating caramels?"

"He didn't call me today," Darcy said. "Yesterday he called me six times and today nothing. I think maybe it's over. He's bored and ready to move on."

"I ran into him today in town," Amanda offered. "He was stocking up on condoms, so I'm pretty sure it's not over."

"You saw Kel?"

She nodded. "I talked to him. I told him if he hurt you, I'd break his arms."

Darcy groaned. "No! That's not part of the deal. I can't get hurt because I'm not supposed to care about him, don't you see?"

"What I see is two people who are trying so hard not to care about each other that they can't see that they might be falling in love."

"No," Darcy said. "I won't let myself. It's as simple as that."

"Do you want this to end?"

Darcy plucked another caramel from the box and popped it in her mouth. "No. But it is getting in the way. I haven't done anything to prepare for my father's visit."

Though the distraction of having Kel around was enjoyable, she'd managed to forget everything that was really important to her. She'd worked so hard to build a career in hotel management and it was time for her to take the next step, to force her father to see her as his successor or to move on and find another job with one of his competitors.

If she'd learned anything in her life it was that she needed to be in control, that she needed to determine her own future. Darcy couldn't depend upon her father to know what was best for her, nor could she allow a husband or a fiancé or a boyfriend to alter her plans. She wasn't daddy's little girl anymore, so desperate to please and so starved for his attention.

"Maybe you should tell the guy how you really feel."

"I plan to. As soon as he arrives I'm going to tell Daddy—"

"Not your father. I was talking about Kel. And don't try to hand me the line that you don't know how you feel." Amanda stood up, grabbed a handful of chocolates from the box, then walked to the door. "Gosh, all this talk about sex has made me really horny. I need to find myself a man. I think I might have to talk Carlos into giving me a massage."

Darcy opened her mouth, ready to issue a stern warning about fraternization, but Amanda just wagged her finger and turned on her heel, leaving Darcy to her own sexual dilemmas.

Darcy reached for the phone and punched in Kel's room number, but then quickly hung up before it rang. If this was the end, then she wanted to hear it directly from him, face to face. She opened her desk drawer and grabbed the master keycard for the guest rooms and tucked it in her pocket.

The deal had been so simple at first. She had only wanted one taste of the forbidden fruit, just enough to satisfy her hunger. But then, she'd never expected to become addicted, to crave him so much that she couldn't control herself, to do anything for one more bite of the apple.

"I'm supposed to want more than this," Darcy murmured. She was twenty-eight years old. Her college roommates were all married and starting families of their own and here she was, contemplating yet another night of no-strings sex with an avowed playboy.

Closing her eyes, she sighed softly. She could go to her own room and try to fall asleep or she could have one last night with Kel. "Oh, what the hell," she muttered as she walked out of her office.

Darcy waved at Olivia as she walked through the lobby. "Take me off the board," she called.

When she reached Kel's door, she didn't bother knocking. She pushed the keycard into the lock and opened the door, then slipped inside. Kel was lying on the sofa, watching television, dressed only in a pair of sweatpants.

She let the door click shut behind her and at the sound, he sat up. "Darcy!" He scrambled to his feet and stared at her, his hand resting on his hip.

"You were expecting someone else?"

"Yes," Kel said. "Actually, I called down for a massage. They were sending someone up. Karl, I guess. I wanted him to work on my shoulder."

"I thought we'd see each other tonight," she said, "but I didn't hear from you."

"I was planning to call after the massage. I thought maybe you might like to have some time to yourself. You know, get a good night's sleep."

Darcy slowly crossed the room and picked up the phone next to the sofa. She punched in the number for the spa, then waited for the receptionist to pick up. "Hi, this is Darcy. I just wanted to let you know that Mr. Martin in the Bennington Suite would like to cancel his massage. He has other plans."

Darcy dropped the phone in the cradle, then shrugged out of her jacket, tossing it aside.

"We could both use some sleep," Kel suggested. "I've got a lot of things I need to think about and I can't really do that if you're distracting me."

Her fingers moved down to the buttons of her blouse, a tiny frown wrinkling her brow. "All right, if that's what you want. When we made this arrangement we didn't say we had to spend every night together." She pulled her blouse out of her skirt and dropped it off her shoulders, revealing a lacy black bra.

"Is that why we spend time together?" he asked, his gaze drifting to her breasts. "Because of our arrangement?"

She smiled and slowly approached. "I like our arrangement, don't you?"

Kel nodded his head. "Yeah, I like it a lot."

Darcy reached around for the zipper of her skirt as she walked into the bedroom of Kel's suite. "This should do," she said, standing next to the bed. "Why don't you take your clothes off and I'll give you that massage you wanted?" Slowly, she pushed her skirt over her hips and let it drop to the floor, allowing him a tempting view of her backside.

From behind, Kel slipped his arms around her waist and nuzzled her neck. "Leave the shoes on," he murmured.

Darcy turned in his arms and slipped her fingers beneath the waistband of his sweatpants, slowly pushing them down to the floor. As she straightened, Darcy made it a point to brush up against his shaft with her breasts.

"If I could have found a masseuse like you, I'm not sure I ever would have needed shoulder surgery," he said.

"Umm," Darcy said, pressing her palms against his chest and gently pushed him toward the bed. He tumbled backwards, taking her along with him. A tiny squeak escaped from her lips before his mouth captured hers. But Darcy scrambled to her knees and straddled his waist, pinning his hands above his head.

"You're not allowed to touch me," she said playfully. "If you touch me, I'm going to have to leave."

Kel left his hands above his head and she slowly ran her palms over his chest. His skin was warm, the muscles hard beneath her fingertips. "I think I need some lotion," she said. Darcy crawled off the bed and headed to the bathroom. She glanced at herself in the mirror and smiled. It was nice to know she could seduce him so easily.

When she returned, he was still lying on the bed, his hard shaft resting on his belly. Darcy skimmed her fingers along the ridge as she crawled back on top of him. "And how do you like your massage?"

"It doesn't really matter," he said with a sleepy grin. "As long as you're touching me it will have the intended result."

She continued to rub his chest, allowing her hands to drift down to his belly every now and then. Kel relaxed and closed his eyes and Darcy watched his expression shift between pure pleasure and breathless desire. She bent and kissed his nipple, circling it with her tongue. "Why didn't you call me today?"

"Amanda said you might need a break," he murmured.

"You talked to Amanda about me?"

"Uh-huh. I thought maybe absence would make the heart grow fonder." He opened his eyes. "I know. Stupid idea." Kel reached out and ran a finger along her shoulder to her hand. "I guess I'm going to have to make it up to you." His touch sent a tremor through her body. Kel took that as an invitation to touch her again and this time he ran his finger along her bottom lip.

"And how will you do that?" she asked.

He grabbed her waist and rolled her beneath him. "I'll find a way."

His mouth came down on hers in a sweet and gentle kiss. Their lovemaking had always had a desperate edge to it, but this was different. As Kel explored her body, he did it slowly and with exquisite tenderness, as if he were trying to memorize every detail.

Nestled between her legs, his arms braced on either side of her head, he studied her face. "What are you thinking?"

An odd feeling of melancholy settled into Darcy's heart as she realized their time together would end soon. What would she do without this warmth and comfort, this crazy, exhilarating excitement? She'd grown so accustomed to having him close that she couldn't imagine passing an entire day without seeing him or at least talking to him.

"I'm thinking I want you inside me," she said.

Kel reached over to the bedside table and retrieved a condom, then handed it to her. "I'm thinking that's what I want, too."

She slipped the condom over him and then sighed as he slowly entered her, a tiny bit at a time. Maybe Amanda was right, she mused. Maybe she should admit her feelings to Kel. What did she have to lose? If he shared those feelings, then there might be a future for them. But if he didn't, then at least she'd know where she stood.

Darcy pressed her lips to his ear. "What else do you want?" she whispered.

Kel moaned softly. "I want you," he said, pressing into her, his desire burning between them.

Darcy bit her bottom lip. "For how long?" she ventured.

"Forever," he said as he began to move. "Forever."

Drawing a deep breath, she swallowed her emotions and let her mind drift. There would never be another man like Kel. For the rest of her life, she'd remember exactly how this felt, the sweet sensation of his body against hers, the slow climb to her release and then the wonderful surrender.

"Forever," she whispered. If only that could be true.

In the end, as they lay wrapped in each other's arms, completely sated, Darcy wondered what Kel had meant. Would forever last until the end of the week? Or would it last their entire lives?

5

DARCY WOKE SLOWLY, her face buried in the soft down pillows, blocking the morning light that streamed through the windows. She reached over for Kel but found his half of the bed empty. Pushing up on her elbow, Darcy brushed her hair out of her eyes and glanced at the clock.

It was almost eight. Kel had a tee time for nine that he'd offered to cancel but Darcy had insisted that he go. A night of passion seemed to energize him but for Darcy it brought on a pleasant exhaustion. She yawned, then stretched her arms above her head.

"Two more nights," she murmured. Kel's one-week stay would be over the day after tomorrow. Her father was scheduled to arrive tomorrow and she knew whatever time she and Kel had left would be stolen moments between meetings.

Darcy sank back into the pillows and sighed. Just yesterday, she'd been so sure of what she had wanted: a career with her father's corporation, a house of her own on the lake, a future that she controlled. But lying here, after making love to Kel, all of that seemed so...dull. Right now all she really wanted was another night in bed with Mr. Baseball.

A quick rap sounded at the door and Darcy sat up, pulling the sheet around her naked body. Kel usually left the "Do Not Disturb" sign on the knob. She crawled out of bed, dragging the sheet with her, wondering if Kel had forgotten his key. But when she opened the door, she saw Amanda standing in the hall.

"Good, I found you. I figured you were probably here."

"What's wrong?" Darcy said.

"You need to get dressed. Your father's downstairs and he's looking for you."

Darcy gasped. "What?" She glanced around the room, frantically searching for her clothes. "When did he get here?"

"About ten minutes ago. He went to your office and then to your suite and he tried to page you, but you haven't been carrying your beeper lately. I managed to convince him to have a cup of coffee in the dining room and told him you were dealing with a little squirrel problem out on the golf course."

"Squirrels?"

"I was improvising and it was all I could think of. I bought you some time to go back to your room and change."

Darcy frantically gathered her clothes and began to tug them on. "Go back down to the dining room and tell him I'll join him there in fifteen minutes." She shoved her shoes on her feet and followed Amanda out the door.

"If you go down the service elevator to the lower level, you can cut past the gym to the east wing of the hotel without having to walk through the lobby," Amanda suggested.

It took Darcy exactly three minutes to make the trip to her suite, another seven to dress and fix her hair and two more to make it to the lobby. She arrived with two minutes to spare.

Darcy strode into the dining room and glanced around at the breakfast crowd. But she stopped her search the moment her eyes came to rest on her father. "Oh, no," she muttered. Sam Scott was having breakfast—with Kel Martin. She watched them for a long moment. Her father seemed comfortable, relaxed almost, if that was possible. He and Kel were laughing. Darcy couldn't imagine what they both would find humorous.

She smoothed her skirt, then walked across the room. "Hello, Daddy," she said, bending down to kiss his cheek. "Hello, Mr. Martin."

Kel tapped his finger on his cheek, a silent invitation for her to kiss him as well but Darcy sent him a murderous glare. The last thing she needed was Kel making friends with her father.

"I'm sorry I'm late, Daddy, but I got caught up with a problem out on the golf course."

Her father smiled at her, then indicated a chair across from him and right next to Kel. "That's all right, Darcy. Mr. Martin was keeping me company, telling me how much he's been enjoying his stay. He said you've been particularly attentive to his needs. That's exactly what I like to hear. A hands-on manager is the key to a successful hotel. Every detail must be attended to, don't you agree, Darcy?"

Darcy cleared her throat, trying to ignore the feel of Kel's thigh as it brushed up against hers. "Of course, Daddy. I think you'll find that our attention to guest service is always our number one priority. I have some figures on return visits that I know you'd like to see. Why don't we go to my office—"

"Not now," Sam said. "Kel has asked me to play a round of golf with him this morning. He's got a tee time at nine."

"But we're going to be busy today. I have so many things to go over with you. We have some very important items to discuss."

"That can wait," Sam said.

"Yes, that can wait," Kel said. "How often to I get to play golf with my best girl's dad?"

"Your what?" Darcy said, her voice rising to a slightly hysterical pitch.

"Kel told me you two have been spending some time together," Sam said. "I'm glad to hear it. It's about time you started thinking about your future."

"Kel and I are not dating and he is not my future," Darcy insisted. "We barely know each other." She sent Kel another look, then stomped on his foot beneath the table. What was he doing, dishing out silly stories to her father? "And about my future. I have some good news. I'm going to be buying a house."

"So, Kel, how have you enjoyed your stay so far?" Sam asked, ignoring Darcy's revelation.

"It's been great," Kel said. "As I said, Darcy has been very attentive. I have had one little problem though."

"You have more than one," Darcy muttered.

"Not a problem, a complaint," he corrected.

"You should take your complaints to guest services," Darcy said, pasting a smile on her face.

"I could call guest services, but I think you're better prepared to help me," Kel said. "You see, I'm having a problem with my shower."

"Maintenance will take care of that. I'll send them right up to your room."

"Maybe *you* might know how to fix the problem."

"Is it leaking?"

"Nope. That's not it."

"Hasn't it been cleaned properly?"

"It's quite clean. But every time I get in the shower I think, this is really huge. It's just too roomy for one person."

"You want me to get you a room with a smaller shower?"

"No, I don't think that's it. But I'm sure you'll figure out what's wrong and get it fixed."

"Funny," Sam said. "I never thought the showers were too big. Darcy, maybe you should look into that."

Darcy felt heat rising in her cheeks. She reached beneath the table and pinched Kel's thigh as hard as she could.

"Ow!" Kel cried.

Sam frowned. "What is it?"

"Cramp," Kel said. "I get them all the time when I don't sleep well."

"Is there something wrong with your bed?" Sam asked. "Darcy, maybe you ought to check on Kel's bed, too."

"There's nothing wrong with his bed," Darcy said. The words were out before she realized how they sounded. "Not that I know anything about his bed, personally. Just in general, all our beds are fine." Darcy stood, her legs bumping up against the table as she rose.

Her father reached out to steady his water goblet, sending her an impatient glare. "Aren't you going to order some breakfast?"

"I have a lot of work to do. I'll catch up with you later, Daddy. After your round of golf." She turned to Kel. "Could I talk to you for a moment? I just want to make sure I get your tee time right."

Darcy strode out of the restaurant into the lobby and waited for Kel to join her. When he did, she grabbed his hand and dragged him toward her office. "Exactly what do you think you're doing?"

"Having breakfast with your dad. He's a great guy. Quite a character. And what a businessman. He gave me some good tips on investing."

"That's not what I meant. You told him we're dating."

"Well, we are. Kind of. We could be if we didn't spend every waking moment in bed together."

"We are not going to date," Darcy said. "We had an agreement. This was only supposed to last a week. It's just sex, not a relationship."

His expression sobered. "Come on, Darcy, you know that's not true. It's not just about sex. Maybe it was in the beginning but not anymore."

"I'm not looking for a relationship, Kel," Darcy said. "Don't you see? That's why it's so good between us, because we aren't making plans for our future. We can just be who we are in the present."

"And what would change if we started making plans?"

"Everything," she said. "I want you to go back into the restaurant and tell my father you can't golf with him this morning. And I want you to tell him we aren't really dating and we're just friends."

"Are you sure about that, Darcy? What's your gripe with your dad?"

"What's going on between you and me is none of my father's business. And what goes on between me and my father is none of your business."

He shook his head. "You're wrong."

"If I'm going to have a relationship with a man, I want it to be my idea, not my father's. He's been running my life for as long as I can remember. I've never been good enough for him, no matter how hard I tried. He wants me to be just like my mother."

"And you don't want that?"

"Don't get me wrong. She's a lovely woman, but I'm not her. She was satisfied to live in a little corner of my father's life. She's never had anything of her own. I want to make something more out of my life, and that doesn't include marriage and a family."

"What's wrong with marriage and a family?" Kel asked.

"Nothing." She sighed. "I'm just warning you, don't get too close to my father. Before you know it, he'll have us married and producing a grandson every few years." She paused, trying to contain her frustration. "I'm good at my job. I'm really good and I deserve a shot to run this company someday. And I'm going to do whatever it takes to make him see that."

Darcy turned and walked toward her office. She hadn't worked so hard these past two years to let a man show up and come between her and her future. Kel Martin would walk out of her life in two more days and she would go on as she had before. But even as she said the words to herself, Darcy's conviction wavered. Somehow, she sensed that her life would never be the same again.

DARCY STOOD in the tee box of the second hole, staring out at the fairway. "I don't golf," she insisted. "I'm not any good at it and I would think that should be clear to you by now. It took me thirty-seven swings to get this far."

"Strokes," Kel corrected. He smiled to himself as he watched her struggle with the club. This may not be the relaxing afternoon he'd hoped he and Darcy would enjoy, but at least he'd achieved his goal. After all, he'd tricked Darcy into coming along with him.

Sam Scott had planned to join Kel, but at the last minute had to take a conference call. He'd insisted Darcy accompany Kel in his place and she'd immediately refused. Yet the moment Kel had tried to reschedule the round with her father, Darcy had magically agreed. It was obvious she didn't want him spending any more time with her father.

"I swear, you'll learn to love it," Kel reassured her. "Just keep your eye on the ball, keep your head down and swing. It's not that hard."

Darcy groaned. "I'm not athletic. I was always picked last for teams in school. I hate sports."

Though she'd laughed at her mistakes and generally been a trooper about the whole thing, it was clear Darcy hadn't had much sleep the night before, through no fault of his own. Her father had kept her busy for most of the day yesterday, then insisted that they all have dinner together. Kel had hoped they'd be able to sneak away to his room once Sam retired, but Darcy's father had other plans for his daughter. According to Darcy, they'd worked until three a.m.

Kel walked over to Darcy and stood behind her, wrapping his arms around her and covering her hands with his. It felt good to hold her. "Maybe you need to loosen up your hips," he said, his breath soft against her ear. "They seem a bit tight."

"How am I supposed to do that?" Darcy asked.

Kel checked her grip, then placed his palms on her waist. "You just shift slightly when your weight moves from one foot to the other."

She turned to him. "Can't we try something else? There are so many more interesting things to do than chase this stupid little ball around in the grass."

"Try one more hole," Kel suggested.

"Loosen my hips," she murmured. Darcy wriggled her backside, leaning into him and making direct contact with his groin. "Oh, there!" she said, feigning surprise. "That feels good. I think they're getting looser now." She wriggled again. "Oh, that feels good."

Kel clamped down on her waist. "Darcy, stop it."

This time she bent forward suggestively as she pressed her

backside into his crotch, her little golf skirt riding up. "I think I feel it now," she said playfully. "Is that better?"

Kel couldn't control his reaction. He looked down at the growing erection pressing against the front of his trousers. "You're right, this was a mistake."

Darcy turned and wrapped her arms around his neck, then brushed a kiss across his lips. "I'm glad you finally agree. How can golf possibly be any fun if we have to keep our clothes on?"

"We don't need to keep our clothes on," Kel said. He reached for his belt and began to unfasten it, but Darcy grabbed his arm.

"We're not playing nude golf. But if you come with me, we can get naked for all sorts of other reasons."

Kel pressed his forehead against hers and stared into her eyes. "We can't spend all our time in bed, Darcy. Don't you want something more than that? Something…normal?"

She sighed, turning away from him. "Why do we have to talk about this now? Can't we just enjoy ourselves? We only have one more day together. And with my father here, who knows how much time we'll have?"

"That's my point," Kel said. "I just thought we might be able to spend a nice morning together, doing something other than rolling around in my bed."

Darcy put her fingers at the corners of his mouth and forced him to smile. "There's no one I'd rather spend my time with. But we aren't a normal couple," she said. "We're just having fun here—that was the deal."

"You're right," Kel said, his voice curt. "I keep forgetting the deal."

"And you're angry now," Darcy countered. "I'm sorry. It seems, since my father arrived, all we've been doing is fighting."

"I consider it renegotiating," Kel said.

"I just don't understand what we have to fight about."

"What are you afraid of?" Kel asked.

"Nothing," Darcy replied. She walked back to the tee box and picked up her golf ball before strolling back to the cart.

Kel struggled to put his feelings into words, but that had never been one of his talents. A great curveball, a charming smile and a decent short game on the golf course, that's what he was good at. But he'd spent his adult life trying to avoid any emotional entanglements. And now that he'd gotten himself so tangled up in Darcy, he wasn't sure how to handle it.

Every instinct told him to hold her close and not let go. At first, it was all about the sexual fireworks between them. It felt so good to touch her, to have her touch him, to lose himself inside her. But with every minute they'd spent together, things inside him had begun to change.

Unfortunately, he'd managed to fall for a woman who had absolutely no feelings for him at all—at least none she'd admit to. She seemed perfectly happy to go on as they had, enjoying their time in bed then going back to her life as it was before he came to The Delaford.

Odd how the roles had been reversed. Usually he was the one who looked for a way out. Now, he was searching for a way in—into her heart and her soul, maybe even into her life. Perhaps signing the offer for the house on Crystal Lake hadn't been the best idea, but Kel had to believe that there was a chance for them.

"Why don't you take the cart back and I'll finish the round?" Kel suggested, unwilling to fight her any longer. "I could use the exercise."

She gave him a strange look. "Will I see you later?"

If he ever expected to get out of this mess without regrets, then he'd have to put some distance between him and Darcy, starting now. It would do him no good to hope that she wanted him for anything more than his talents in the bedroom.

"I don't know."

"I could always ride along with you," Darcy suggested, "and watch you golf. Maybe I could learn something."

He shrugged. At least she was willing to compromise. That was a step in the right direction. And for all that he wanted to regain some perspective, he still preferred to spend the day with her. "All right," he said.

She hopped in the cart, sitting behind the wheel, and watched as he teed off. "Wiggle those hips," Darcy shouted.

Kel hit a nice drive, straight down the middle and Darcy steered the cart over to him. But just as they prepared to drive down the fairway, Kel noticed another golf cart approaching at a fast speed. He recognized one of the bellmen from the hotel.

"Mr. Martin? Mr. Martin, I have an emergency phone call for you."

Darcy straightened. "An emergency?"

The bellman handed Kel a cellphone. "It's a Mr. Waverly."

Kel turned to Darcy. "My agent," he explained. "Every time he calls, it's some kind of emergency." He took the cellphone from the bellman and sent Darcy a reassuring look. "Don't worry. I'm sure it's nothing."

His agent's voice crackled over the fading connection. "Kel. Ben Waverly here. I've got some news."

"I'm on the golf course right now, Ben," Kel said into the phone. "Can this wait?"

"Kel, they want to trade you. To Atlanta. I just got a call from the front office. You need to fly out there for a meeting and a physical. They want to know what's going on with the shoulder before they sign on the dotted line. You're going to have to make a decision, Kel, and pretty quick."

"Let me get back to the hotel," Kel said. "I'll call you from there." He switched off the phone and handed it back to the bellman.

"Is everything all right?" Darcy asked.

"Not really," he murmured. He glanced around. "We should go back. I've got to take care of this and I can't do it from here."

"Tell me," Darcy murmured, her eyes filled with worry. "If something is wrong, I'd like to help."

Kel winced, then rubbed the back of his neck, trying to ease the tension that always came with a call from his agent. At least if he retired, he'd never have to deal with Ben Waverly again. "Would you? Come on, Darcy, that's not part of our deal," he said, his voice dripping with sarcasm. "I wouldn't want you to have to pretend that you cared."

"Why have you become so obsessed with our deal? This was supposed to be simple, wasn't it?"

"But it's not simple. It's gotten all messy and complicated, and now you want to cut and run."

"And you don't?" Darcy demanded.

"Maybe not." He pointed toward the clubhouse. "Drive."

She cut across the first fairway, glancing over at him as they bumped along. He kept his eyes fixed straight ahead, trying to contain his frustration. It would have been too perfect to meet the woman of his dreams just days before he retired. Maybe he was looking for something that wasn't there simply out of fear about the changes taking place in his life.

"That was my agent," he said. "I've been traded to Atlanta."

Darcy gasped. "Atlanta? But that's all the way across the country."

"Yeah, the last time I checked my map it was." He studied her expression and then drew a deep breath. The hell if she didn't care! For an instant, he saw it there in her eyes. She wasn't ready to give him up. "I was going to retire, but now I'm thinking I might be able to get a few more years out of the arm. They want to see me in a few days."

"You're going to go?"

Kel knew he shouldn't play with her emotions. But if this was the only way he could gauge her feelings, then he'd use it. "It's an option I should explore. If they don't want to put me into regular rotation, I might be able to get by without the surgery. It would probably mean a cut in my salary, but I'm all right with that."

"So you'll go to Atlanta?" Darcy asked.

"What do you think I should do?"

Darcy shook her head, forcing a smile. "What I think shouldn't matter."

"Yeah, I guess you're right. It doesn't make any difference what you think because you don't really care."

"That's not true," she murmured, her voice turning defensive. "I would miss you. I *will* miss you—when you leave here, and if you leave San Francisco. A lot of people will." Darcy pulled the cart to a stop in front of the clubhouse, then turned to him. "While you go take care of your business, I'm going to take care of mine. I've been waiting to talk to my father and I think now is the perfect time."

"Right," he said. "I do have some big decisions to make."

The only problem was Kel's heart was telling him to do one thing and his head was telling him to do the exact opposite. He wanted to believe he and Darcy had a future, but he knew she felt differently. And with just one night left together, Kel wasn't sure he'd have enough time to change her mind.

6

DARCY STOOD AT Kel's door, ready to knock. After their one-hole round of golf, they'd come back to the hotel and Kel had disappeared into his room to call his agent. Darcy had spent the next hour with her father, discussing a new corporate advertising campaign.

She still hadn't worked up the courage to issue her ultimatum, even though she'd decided exactly what to say. Darcy wanted a seat on the board immediately and a promise that she would be next in line for a vice presidency at corporate headquarters. And if Sam Scott didn't agree, then she was prepared to walk away. In addition, she'd decided she should tell him the truth about Kel—that their relationship had been over before it had ever started.

Things had been so easy between her and Kel over the past week. It had almost made her believe that they could sustain a real relationship. But since her father had arrived, things had begun to go bad. Maybe it was the impending end of their little "arrangement" that had set them both on edge, but they couldn't seem to be together without an argument arising.

She tipped her head back and sighed deeply. This was what she'd wanted, proof that the attraction they had was passing at best. Proof that she'd made the right decision to put her career first.

Tonight would be their last night together and she'd have to make it special. Tomorrow would be Valentine's Day and they'd say good-bye to each other for good. A sharp stab of regret pierced her heart and she pressed her hand to her chest. It would have been nice to have a Valentine for once. But Darcy knew better than to get caught up in silly romantic fantasies. Still, she did have feelings for Kel and, to her dismay, they were beginning to feel a lot more like love than lust.

Was she falling in love with him? Kel had touched her body like no other man had, but he'd also managed to touch her heart. He was sweet and funny and honest, all the qualities she wanted in a man. Yet she couldn't quite believe that he wanted her as much as she wanted him.

Darcy reached out and rapped on the door, then gathered her courage. Maybe it was time to risk her heart. What's the worse that could happen—he'd leave? He was already planning to do that.

The door swung open and Darcy looked up at Kel. He was dressed and toting his garment bag and a small duffel. "Darcy. I was just coming down to talk to you."

Her gaze darted back and forth between his face and the bags he carried. "You're packed?"

Kel nodded. "I've got to go home. There's just so much going on and I really can't think here. I've got calls to make and meetings to schedule."

Darcy swallowed hard and tried to control her emotions. Was this how it would end, in the hallway, he going one way and she going the other? "You're going to Atlanta then?"

"Yeah, I think I am."

She gnawed at her lip, trying to calm the whirlwind of thoughts in her head. "I—I just wanted to say a few things before you left."

He waited, but Darcy couldn't decide exactly how to begin. "Everything happened so fast between us," she said. "Sometimes I wonder if things could have been different if we…" Darcy let her voice trail off. It was silly to think of what might have been. "I had a wonderful time," she said. "And I'm glad we met that night in San Francisco, and that we met again in the candy shop."

He reached out and took her hand, drawing her into the room. His garment bag slipped to the floor and Kel pulled her into his arms and kissed her. He lingered over her mouth, his tongue teasing at the crease between her lips. When he pulled back, his gaze met hers. "Will you miss me?" he asked.

Darcy felt tears pressing against the corners of her eyes. She laughed softly, brushing a stray tear off her cheek. "Of course I will. Gosh, why am I crying? It's not like you're leaving for the moon. We might run into each other again someday."

"I'd like that," Kel said. "And maybe, just to make sure, I could call you and we could figure out a time and a place to meet."

Darcy laughed softly. "Wouldn't that be a date?"

"Yeah," Kel said with a slow grin. "I guess it would be."

"Well, I think that would be a sensible thing, just to make sure we don't accidentally miss each other."

Kel kissed her again, molding her mouth to his as his hands furrowed through her hair. "All right, that's the plan. Someday, I'll just give you a call."

"You'd better get going," Darcy said. She didn't want to weep in front of him and the emotion clogging her throat was making it difficult to talk.

"Will you walk down with me?"

Darcy shook her head. "No, I think I'm going to stay here. I wouldn't want to make a fool of myself in front of my staff. You never know what I might do to get you to stay a little longer. I have been known to tear off my clothes in your presence."

"All right then," Kel said. He brushed one last kiss on her lips, then opened the door. "See ya, Darcy."

"See ya, Kel," Darcy replied.

She watched as the door swung shut, then stood frozen in place for a long time, willing herself not to chase after him, to accept the fact that he had gone. When she was sure she wouldn't follow him, Darcy walked into the bedroom and flopped down on the bed.

They'd spent so much time in this spot, she mused. But without him, it was just an ordinary bed. Darcy grabbed his pillow and held it over her face, inhaling his scent. There would come a day when she wouldn't be able to recall this smell. "I'll just take this with me," she murmured. She sat up and hugged the pillow.

But no matter how hard she hugged, it didn't ease the ache in her heart. She'd miss the passion and the excitement, the wonderful anticipation she felt all day long while thinking about the evening ahead. But mostly she'd miss the quiet moments, when she curled into his body and listened to him breathe.

Darcy glanced around the room, searching for anything else Kel might have left behind. Her gaze stopped at a small item on the nightstand. She frowned as she recognized the incomplete chocolate heart, wrapped in blue foil, from Sinfully Sweet. "I guess he wasn't looking for romance after all," she murmured.

More chocolate was exactly what she needed now. "It's going to take a lot more than half a chocolate heart," she muttered.

She carefully unwrapped the heart. Inside, she found a small piece of paper. Darcy unfolded it and squinted to read the message. "*All you need is love.* Yeah right. Without a man, love is pretty much useless."

Darcy crawled off the bed, the heart and its little message clutched in her hand. She grabbed Kel's pillow before heading to the door. If she spent any more time in the room, she'd drive herself crazy. The sooner it was cleaned the better.

Before summoning the elevator, Darcy picked up the house phone that sat on the sofa table in the small lobby. Olivia answered at the front desk. "Hi, it's Darcy. Can you let housekeeping know that the Bennington Suite is empty? Have them send someone up to clean it as soon as possible." Darcy paused. "Has Mr. Martin left yet?"

"He just walked out a few seconds ago," Olivia replied. "I could probably catch him if you'd like. He may be waiting for the valet to bring his car around."

"No," Darcy said. "That's fine." She dropped the phone in the cradle, then pushed the elevator button.

When she reached the lobby, she went directly to her office, Kel's pillow still tucked beneath her arm. Olivia gave her an odd look as she passed, but Darcy kept her gaze fixed in front of her. So what if her whole staff was talking? A woman had a right to enjoy herself every now and then.

When she reached her office, she found Amanda sitting at her desk, her feet up on the edge. "I saw him leave," she said, sending Darcy a sympathetic smile. "Are you all right?"

"Of course," Darcy said, trying to sound cheerful. "I'm fine. I knew we only had a week and this works out perfectly. I didn't have time to think about what I was going to say or do. It was just a nice, quick good-bye. And now my life can get back on track."

"And that's it?" Amanda asked.

"Yeah." Darcy paused. "He's been traded to Atlanta so he'll be leaving San Francisco. But he said he might call me someday."

Amanda scoffed. "That's all he could manage?"

"This was just a physical thing between us, nothing more. Neither of us wanted any strings."

"Sell that story somewhere else 'cause I'm not buying it. I've watched you this past week and you've been so happy. When Kel is around, you just…glow. This guy is meant for you, Darcy, whether you're willing to admit it or not."

Darcy sat down in one of her guest chairs. "You really think so?" She placed the pillow on the chair next to her and at Amanda's inquiring frown, Darcy smiled sheepishly. "It smells like him," she admitted.

"I rest my case," Amanda said.

Darcy set Kel's chocolate on the desk and cracked it into smaller pieces, then handed a piece to Amanda. "All you need is love," she said. "That's what the message was inside. Do you think that's true?"

"Yes," Amanda said. "I do believe that." She placed a piece of the chocolate in her mouth. "All you do need is love. And great sex. And two bathrooms and separate vacations once a year. Also a dependable hairdresser, a good gynecologist, and a mother-in-law who lives at least a thousand miles away and—"

"Stop! I think you're missing the point."

"You know what my message said?" Amanda asked. "Nothing."

"It was blank?"

"No, it just had the word 'nothing' on it. I didn't find that particularly encouraging. Is that a question or an answer or just a mistake?"

"It must be a misprint."

"Or somewhere out there is a guy who has a matching 'something' message. I just need to search for a man who has a confused look on his face. What did yours say?"

"I don't know." Darcy stood and retrieved her purse from the top of her credenza. She rummaged through the contents, then finally dumped everything on top of her desk. "Here it is," she said, handing it to Amanda.

Amanda unwrapped it and pulled out the tiny piece of paper inside. "You want me to read it?"

Darcy nodded and watched as Amanda unfolded the message. Her friend gasped softly, her eyes going wide, then quickly refolded the message. "You don't want to see this."

"What does it say?"

Amanda's lower lip began to tremble as she stared at the message and her eyes flooded with tears. "It's silly and sentimental." She brushed a tear from her eye, then quickly stood.

"What?" Darcy said. What could the note possibly say that would bring such a reaction from Amanda?. "It doesn't say 'something,' does it?"

Amanda shook her head. "No. Kel Martin and I did not win a romantic dinner at The Delaford." She smiled ruefully. "It says—" Her voice wavered and she laughed softly, then handed Darcy the paper. "Go ahead. Read it."

"'All you need is love.' That's the same as—" Darcy stopped short. "Oh, my God."

"This is just so corny," Amanda said, tears streaming down

her face. "Don't mind me, this kind of thing turns me into a complete sap."

"It's a match," Darcy said, slowly standing. "What does that mean?"

"You win a romantic dinner for two at The Delaford!" Amanda cried.

"No, no," Darcy said. "That's not what it means." She stared at the two pieces of paper. Suddenly, it all felt so right, loving Kel, wanting a future with him. But how could that be? Two silly little pieces paper and she could see them growing old together. "This is ridiculous. This doesn't mean anything."

"It means what you want it to mean," Amanda said.

"And what do I want it to mean?" Darcy asked as she scooped up the contents of her purse and stuffed it all back inside.

Amanda reached out and grabbed her hand. "I think you know."

Darcy looked at her friend as tears filled Amanda's eyes again. Tears suddenly flooded her own eyes and a few moments later they were both crying. "I have to go," Darcy said.

"You have to go," Amanda replied.

"I have to talk to him." Darcy raced around the office gathering her things. "I have to find Kel and tell him how I feel."

"And how do you feel?" Amanda called as Darcy ran toward her office door.

"I'm in love," she said, laughing through her tears. "Am I crazy?" Darcy shrugged. "I am. But I don't care."

When she got to the front desk, she quickly punched up Kel's registration, then grabbed a pen and scribbled out his address and phone number.

"Darcy, where are we meeting? Do you have the budgets for me to review before we get started?"

Darcy glanced up to see her father approaching. Sam Scott had that impatient look on his face, one that usually ended in him giving her a stern lecture on proper business practices. "They're setting up in the Pacific Room," she said. "I'm not going to be able to make the meeting, but Amanda will get you a copy of the budget. She's in my office."

"Where are you going? You can't just leave me with this."

Darcy circled the counter and threw her arms around her father's neck. They never really hugged—her father wasn't a very demonstrative man—but Darcy couldn't contain herself. She felt as if she could fly. "Daddy, I want a seat on the board. And I want you to promise you'll make me a vice president within the next five years. And if you don't agree, I'm going to quit."

He opened his mouth to reply, but Darcy shook her head. "You know I'm good at this, Daddy, and you'd be a fool to let me go. And I know you're not a fool. You're not going to find anyone more loyal or devoted than I am. So I'd suggest you just nod your head and agree to give me what I want."

"You wouldn't quit," Sam said.

Darcy smiled. "Try me." She patted her father's cheek. "You think about it for a day or two. I have to go pack now."

"Where are you going?" Sam asked.

"San Francisco."

"When will you be back?"

"I don't know," Darcy said as she hurried to the elevator. "Tomorrow? Next week?" She pressed the button, and when the elevator doors didn't open, she pressed it again. Glancing at her watch, she calculated the time it would take to get into the city. Thank goodness, she'd have a ninety-minute ride to figure out what she was going to say to Kel.

This was crazy. She'd always thought love ought to be rational and deliberate and well-considered. That once she found it, it would follow a very precise calendar. But it wasn't that way at all. It completely messed up all her plans—and she really didn't care.

"Darcy?"

At first she thought she'd imagined his voice, that her excitement had gotten the better of her. But then, he spoke again. She froze, fighting back a whirl of emotion.

"Darcy, please look at me."

She slowly turned to find Kel standing a few feet away, his bags at his feet. Her heart skipped and her knees felt weak. He'd only been gone for fifteen minutes, but she'd already missed him so much.

"You came back," she murmured.

Kel nodded. "I couldn't leave. I got into town and I turned around. We're not finished yet, Darcy. I'm not sure what comes next, but there has to be something."

"There is," she agreed. "I know that now."

"Really?"

She reached into her jacket pocket and pulled out the tiny pieces of paper, then handed them to him.

"What're these?" he asked as he unfolded them.

"They're from the inside of our chocolate heart halves from Sinfully Sweet. Remember, she gave you a heart, too. They're a match."

He frowned. "So? What does that mean? We win a prize?"

"Don't you see?" Darcy cried. "This explains it all. We're supposed to be together. The fates are conspiring against us. Or in our favor. That's why I couldn't forget you after that night in San Francisco and why we ran into each other at the candy store. Do you realize all the different twists of fate it took for those events to happen? And now, look at this. We had matching messages. It's a sign."

"And now you believe we might have a future, because of some silly message inside a chocolate wrapper?"

"Yes," Darcy said. "It's fate." Why couldn't he understand? This made all the difference in the world. It was as if she suddenly had permission to feel the way she did. She couldn't control this, she just had to embrace it, and that freed her in a way that felt so good.

"You believe in fate, but you don't believe in me?" Kel cursed softly. "God, I feel like I'm going crazy here. Darcy, I came back here because I want to be with you. I'm in love with you. And it doesn't have anything to do with chocolate."

The sound of the words, the simple admission of his feelings, brought a fresh round of tears. He loved her. "I do believe in you. In us," Darcy finally said. "I was coming to tell you that. I was going to drive to San Francisco. And I've fallen in love with you too, Kel."

A slow grin softened his tense expression and his gaze filled with affection. "You've fallen in love with me?"

"Yes," Darcy said, slipping her arms around his waist.

He chuckled softly, then pulled her into a long, deep kiss. Warmth rushed through her bloodstream and her heart pounded. Darcy concentrated on the taste of him, trying to commit it to memory. It was only after he drew away, that she realized she'd never have to search for memories of him again. She'd only have to look into his eyes or touch his hand or listen to his voice. He would always be with her.

"I was hoping things might work out like this," Kel murmured, his breath tickling her ear.

"And why is that?" she asked as he kissed her neck.

"I bought a house out on Crystal Lake."

Darcy drew back, stunned by his admission. "When did you do this?"

"They accepted my offer yesterday. You'll love it. It's right on the water and it's this huge, rambling place with a boathouse and a Victorian gazebo and a terrace that overlooks the water. You'll love it."

Darcy stared at him. "West Blueberry Lane?" she asked.

"How did you know?"

It was another sign, not that she needed one more. "I will love it," she said. "But how are you going to live there if you have to move to Atlanta?"

"I'm not moving to Atlanta, Darcy. I'm ready to start the rest of my life and I'm going to do that here, with you. And I don't care what it takes—we'll prove to your father that you can run his hotels and love me at the same time."

"I gave him an ultimatum," Darcy said. "Either I'm going to have a seat on the board by tomorrow morning or I'm going to be out of a job." She toyed with a strand of his hair. "Maybe that wouldn't be such a bad thing. I could take some time off and spend every spare moment pleasing you."

Kel chuckled. "I know you, Darcy. You're not the type to spend your days looking after my needs. So maybe I ought to look after you. I can be in charge of the pleasing," he said. He glanced around the lobby. "So do you think my room is still available?"

Darcy looked over her shoulder to find Amanda, Olivia and her father watching them from the reception desk. "The maid is cleaning it now. But I have nice soft bed in my room with expensive French sheets that feel really good on naked skin."

Kel grabbed her hand and dragged her across the lobby. Darcy laughed as they began to run, as desperate as he was to have a moment alone with him. She'd never really considered herself a romantic. "Who would have thought that chocolate could have changed my mind about romance?" she said.

As Kel pulled her into his arms again and kissed her, Darcy made a mental note to order another box of chocolates from Sinfully Sweet.

"I think we should place a standing order for chocolate just to make sure this feeling never ends."

"This feeling will definitely never end," Darcy said softly, staring up into his gaze. "It lasted five years without us seeing each other. If we're together, it's bound to last a lifetime."

Epilogue

BROWN PAPER COVERED the plate-glass windows of Sinfully Sweet, softening the midday sunlight that usually streamed into the shop. Inside, the glass cases, usually filled with delectable chocolate treats, were empty.

Ellie Fairbanks stood behind the counter, packing a box of cash register tapes. She paused and took a long look around the shop. Boxes were stacked up against one wall and everything that could be packed was now tucked inside crumpled newspaper and foam peanuts. In an hour or two, the movers would arrive and haul everything out to their truck.

"I really loved this store," she murmured. "There are times that I think we should settle in one place and stay awhile."

Her husband came up behind her and slipped his arms around her waist, drawing her back against his body. Resting his chin on her shoulder, Marcus placed a soft kiss on her cheek. "You always get a bit sentimental when we close up shop. But you know that as soon as we find another location, you're going to get excited again."

Ellie turned around in his arms and stared up at Marcus's handsome face. As long as he was with her, it didn't matter where they lived or what they did. He was her home, her touchstone, her reason for living. "Maybe so."

"Until we settle on another location, I'll just have to keep you excited in other ways," Marcus murmured, his fingers furrowing through her hair. His lips covered hers in a deep and thorough kiss, and warm desire flooded Ellie's body, distracting her from her melancholy. There was still work to do to get ready for the movers, but right now all she could think about was her husband's touch.

"We did well here, didn't we?" she asked when he nuzzled his face into the curve of her neck. "It was worth all the hard work." She turned to the windows. The new owner had already scraped the gilt paint from the glass. It now displayed the new name of Sinfully Sweet. "Austell Confectionary." Ellie winced. "You think they could have come up with something…sexier."

"Well, as we both know, nothing could stop chocolate from being sexy."

"We went a long way toward proving our theories, didn't we?" Ellie said, picking up yesterday's edition of the *Austell Bugle*. "Daniel Montgomery and Carlie Pratt are engaged." She held the paper up to Marcus, folded to show an engagement portrait. "Don't they look happy?"

"Blissful," Marcus said. "But I'm not sure we should count them as a success story. I have a feeling you had something to do with them getting matching messages."

Ellie smiled winsomely. "Me?" she asked in mock innocence. "Perhaps. But anyone could see they were perfect for each other. And both *so* fond of chocolate. I just couldn't help myself."

"I saw them yesterday walking their puppies in the park. Cute dogs, but Daniel and Carlie had their hands full keeping them from tearing up the landscape. You should have seen the area around those trees by the fountain. Those puppies have dug so many holes they're giving the gophers a run for their money."

"Well, you can't discount my research methods when it comes to Rebecca Moore and Connor Bassett," Ellie said. "Not only did we prove that chocolate is a powerful aphrodisiac, but we also established that, in their case, opposites do attract."

Marcus chuckled. "And who would have guessed that chocolate-covered strawberries could have such a potent effect on a woman's sensuality?"

"Oh, I think Rebecca always had a sensual side," Ellie explained. "It just took the right man, and a bit of chocolate, to bring it out."

"Hmm," Marcus said. "As I recall we had our own little adventure with chocolate shortly after we met. Remember the hot fudge? I was still tasting chocolate on your body days later."

Even after twenty-seven years, the memory of that night still made Ellie blush. It was the first time she'd felt completely and passionately uninhibited. It was also the moment that she knew Marcus was the only man for her.

"And then there's Darcy Scott and Kel Martin," Ellie continued.

"Kel Martin? I remember when he stopped by the shop a few months ago. I didn't realize you'd given him a chocolate heart half."

"I couldn't resist," Ellie said. "But I certainly didn't expect it to work. When Darcy came in last week to place an order for The Delaford's signature chocolates, she informed me they were engaged. I couldn't believe it."

"Why didn't you tell me?" Marcus asked.

"I'm not sure we can count this one. It turns out they'd shared a one-night stand years ago, so they may have been preconditioned to sexual attraction."

"Did they eat our chocolate?" Marcus asked.

Ellie nodded. "They did indeed."

"Then I say we add them to our inventory of success stories."

Ellie slipped out of his embrace and picked up a basket from beneath the counter, the basket that had held the heart halves. "It was a good promotion. We should consider doing it again."

Marcus took the basket from her hand, ready to pack it in an open box, then stopped. "Look at this. There are two heart halves left."

Frowning, Ellie peered into the basket. She could have sworn the basket was empty when she'd tucked it beneath the counter. With a devilish smile, she withdrew the heart half wrapped in blue foil and held it out in the palm of her hand. "Would you care to see if we're a match, Mr. Fairbanks?"

Marcus took the heart and dropped it back in the basket. "I think I already know the answer to that," he said. "I knew it from the moment I first saw you."

Ellie slipped her arms around his waist again and drew him close, losing herself in the quiet strength of his embrace. "There will never be another Sinfully Sweet. But as long as you're with me, I think I'd be happy selling chocolate on the moon."

"The moon," Marcus said as if the idea were intriguing. "Now that would be a challenge. I wonder how the effect of an aphrodisiac would be altered by the reduced gravity on the moon."

Ellie tipped her head back and laughed. There was no end to her husband's curiosity. But then, she'd always considered that one of his sexiest qualities. Life with Marcus Fairbanks certainly wasn't boring. Loving him had always been an adventure—an adventure that would begin all over again in a new town, inside a new shop.

"Take me home, Marcus," Ellie said, slipping her hand into his and pulling him along to the front door, the basket looped over her arm.

"We don't have a home anymore," he said. "By now the movers have probably cleaned out the house."

"Then take me to a seedy no-tell motel," she said. "I have some needs that require your attention."

Marcus groaned as she pulled him toward the door. "Oh, Ellie, have you been eating our chocolates again?"

You always want what you don't have

Dinah and Dottie are two sisters who grew up in an imperfect world. Once old enough to make decisions for themselves, they went their separate ways—permanently. Until now. Will their reunion seventeen years later during a series of crises finally help them create a perfect life?

My Perfectly Imperfect Life

Jennifer Archer

HN34

Available March 2006
TheNextNovel.com

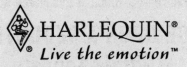

Now try chick lit…Blaze-style.

Coming in March, Jamie Sobrato brings you
the first story in a brand-new miniseries…

It's All About
Attitude

He's *so* not Prince Charming. But when
Nico Valetti sweeps her away in his white Ferrari,
Skye Ellison can't help thinking about long
hot kisses that wake up everything in her….

Read red-hot chick lit this March with

ONCE UPON A SEDUCTION
by *Jamie Sobrato*

HARLEQUIN

Blaze

**Follow the twists, turns
and red-hot romances in...**

THE WHITE STAR

ANGELS AND OUTLAWS by Lori Wilde,
Book #230, January 2006

HIDDEN GEMS by Carrie Alexander,
Book #236, February 2006

CAUGHT by Kristin Hardy,
Book #242, March 2006

INTO TEMPTATION by Jeanie London,
Book #248, April 2006

FULL CIRCLE by Shannon Hollis,
Book #254, May 2006

DESTINY'S HAND by Lori Wilde,
Book #260, June 2006

*This modern-day hunt is like no other...
Get your copy today!*

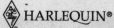